Praise for Barney Norris

Eventide

'Beautifully poetic . . . captures all the still,
sad music of humanity'
Guardian

'Wise and witty . . . [Norris] has an extraordinary grasp of the
way our limitless hopes clash with our finite possibilities'
The Times

'Barney Norris strikes gold again . . . Achingly familiar,
but sharp too . . . Norris has a talent for polishing the
ordinary, buffing it up with a damp cloth until it shines
and sings . . . brilliantly perceptive'
Time Out

Visitors

'Astonishingly accomplished . . . as this extraordinarily
mature piece demonstrates, Norris is a perceptive and
humane craftsman, who finds several layers of comedy in
everyday misunderstandings . . . He is a talent to watch.'
Evening Standard

'An absolute beauty, by turns funny, tender and desperately
sad . . . There is great richness and an almost poetic
resonance in the writing'
Telegraph

Five Rivers Met on a Wooded Plain

Barney Norris

Doubleday

LONDON • TORONTO • SYDNEY • AUCKLAND • JOHANNESBURG

TRANSWORLD PUBLISHERS
61–63 Uxbridge Road, London W5 5SA
www.transworldbooks.co.uk

Transworld is part of the Penguin Random House group of companies
whose addresses can be found at global.penguinrandomhouse.com

First published in Great Britain in 2016 by Doubleday
an imprint of Transworld Publishers

A CIP catalogue record for this book
is available from the British Library.

ISBNs 9780857523723 (hb)
9780857523730 (tpb)

Typeset in 11/15pt Giovanni Book by Falcon Oast Graphic Art Ltd.
Printed and bound by Clays Ltd, Bungay, Suffolk.

Penguin Random House is committed to a sustainable
future for our business, our readers and our planet. This book
is made from Forest Stewardship Council® certified paper.

1 3 5 7 9 10 8 6 4 2

For Charlie

We do not expect people to be deeply moved by what is not unusual. That element of tragedy which lies in the very fact of frequency has not yet wrought itself into the coarse emotion of mankind; and perhaps our frames could hardly bear much of it.

George Eliot, *Middlemarch*

The Burning Arrow
of the Spire

LONG BEFORE THE steep trickle of the Channel widened to make an island of England, before the first settlers arrived and started claiming the land around, laying down tree trunks to make pathways through marshes from ridgeway to mountain to hill, something unusual happened in the green south of Wiltshire. By a trick of the land, the rivers known today as the Wylye and the Ebble and the Nadder and the Bourne, which all ran through this landscape, all found their way into the Avon in the same stretch of flood-prone fields, pitched into one another by the sly gradients of the county lying in front of me this evening. Five rivers met on a wooded plain, and under the weight of that water, an extraordinary thing took place. The startled world, stirred by this confluence of riverways, started to sing bright notes into the blue air. A great chord rang out in the deep heart of England, and feeling welled up through the skin of the water like a shaft of light that breaks through cloud. The earth was awake and alive and amazed by every sensation it experienced.

Centuries passed, and people found this miracle in the green south of the island, this rare confluence of water giving voice to the song being sung by the world, either by accident as they passed through or drawn by the sound of it. However it happened, people undoubtedly came, and we know they heard the song. They kept trying to put it into words, to make a shape of it.

The first attempt was Woodhenge. You can still visit. You will find the remains of a wooden circle that someone built in the middle of a clearing, heeding the call, feeling the need to worship. The place is surrounded by trees and hills. There are stone circles intersecting with it. There is a tea room for visitors. The settlers moved on within a few thousand years, looking for some more permanent expression of the feeling in the landscape than wood could provide.

Stonehenge was what they made next, a few miles to the south. It was a miracle of Egyptian proportions. Great slabs of rock quarried deep in flint and rain of the Welsh hills and barged halfway over the country to stand opaque in the middle of nowhere, an Easter Island marooned on the soft green roll of a hill. People wonder what it was used for. The mystery must have been part of the point. The thing about stone is you don't get to the heart of it. It stares back into you, its secret intact and inviolable. The stone circle gave life to a million ley-line stories that still sprout from the soil around that place today. It created a whole world of imaginings, freedoms, rituals. But the stories and solstices that are part of the Stonehenge myth are only subordinate clauses of a greater phenomenon. They are only new phrases in the song that was born in the rivers, as it seeks and finds other outlets, pouring into new mediums, expressed now in story, behaving like a river pursuing a path of less resistance as it finds its way into the mouths of women and men.

The next iteration of the song in stone was a cathedral built in the middle of a hill fort. The men and women who worshipped at Stonehenge were long gone by the time Old Sarum was built a few miles to the south. Some other listener must have heard the rivers, understood there was life to be lived here and laid a foundation. Old Sarum, the first city constructed out of that impulse, was a garrison fort whose walls encircled a body of men, beds for them to sleep in, fires that kept them living and the cathedral at the heart of it. As had been the case before, it was the place of worship that best expressed the song in the air and the rhyming human desire to look up, imagine further, see the vastness of the world around and the ideas hidden in the landscape. It was around the cathedral and the sweep of its tower that this new society and its arguments were organised.

The first cathedral collapsed and was replaced by a second, built on the same spot from many of the same stones. But faith and the army don't mix well, and it wasn't long before the church fell out with the soldiers. Tensions rose, the cohabitation of the hill became insupportable, and it was decided the cathedral should relocate. And it is now that this process of stanza following stanza I have been describing reaches its climactic, capstone rhyme. This budding on the vine of flower after flower each successive spring, the growth of form after form like shapes in a coal fire as Woodhenge and Stonehenge and the Old Sarum cathedrals tried to mimic the music of the land around leads now to the apex of our story, as Salisbury Cathedral emerges from these myriad discarded drafts, the best expression of the land around finally soaring up into the air.

The minutes documenting the meeting where the decision

was made to relocate the cathedral are lost, but someone, recognising their absence as a fault in the historical record, has invented a story to stand in their place. The story goes that on the day it was decided the church would leave the hill, the bishop of the second cathedral on Old Sarum took a bow and arrow and stood looking over the land around. He announced he would fire into the landscape below, and wherever the arrow stuck would become the site for the new building. His problem, of course, was the same chauvinism that hobbles most men. When the bishop fired his arrow, by way of reminder that he was not, never had been, never would be in charge of the world beneath his feet, a white hart interceded between the blade and the ground, and the bishop watched, perhaps crestfallen, certainly amazed, as the arrow lodged in its haunches. The startled deer proceeded to run for three miles before expiring in the middle of the floodplain south of Old Sarum where those five rivers met.

Nowhere could have been harder to build on. Foundations could only be sunk eighteen inches. But the building work began all the same, and over the course of only five thousand years – the blink of an eye in geological terms – the song of the earth had coaxed the men who built their cover versions over the land fourteen miles south from Woodhenge, to Stonehenge, to Old Sarum, to the source of the music itself. It had reeled us in. And they say Christ was a fisher of men.

Salisbury Cathedral was built laboriously, lovingly. It lay on foundations that should never have held. A spire was added which ought to have fallen, and the pillars at the heart of the nave bowed and sang like a tree after rain, when the rain still falls from the canopy long after the sky has cleared.

Life welled up in the shadow of the building, a city that was named New Sarum, though it came eventually to be known as Salisbury. Events of historical importance blushed up in the streets, couples met and were married and grew old together, harvests were good or else failed, falcons nested on the spire, and the invention of the aeroplane meant there had to be a light bulb at the top, which someone sometimes had to climb up and change. House prices rose and kept rising and took flight, drink killed too many, and young men and women fell in love, and some of the sex was good and some was forgettable. The song went on. Five rivers ran together, and the earth sang in celebration at the top of its voice, a music hidden in the details of the everyday, in the footfalls of thousands of locals, the ringing of cash registers, the great soaring dream of the spire.

And the song sings on, finding a new path of less resistance to the sea and sky.

Salisbury Cathedral is the most beautiful building I have ever seen. I don't quite mean the look of the place. Buildings are not beautiful because of their shapes or patterns, the bricks or stones that make them. What are transfixing are the ideas and dreaming and longing they encase. They stand as memorials to the lives of the people who made them, who raised the money to raise the walls, who buried the men who fell from the scaffolding. What I see when I watch Salisbury Cathedral cutting the air is a diagram of prayer, the hope at the centre of my life expressed as the burning arrow of the spire shot into the sky, asking us to look up beyond the everyday, see the size and possibility and quietness of the landscape, and imagine something greater than we are. It asks us to stop walking and think. It demands we look outside ourselves.

I have stared at that spire every night for a year now, and I think it is the purest picture of the human heart I have seen. It seems to me from this vantage point that the city has been built as an illustration of the way all our ordinary acts, our cups of tea and walks to the postbox and phone bills and potato peelings, are shot through with a heartbreaking and extraordinary love. That there exists in all of us a song waiting to be sung which is as heart-stopping and vertiginous as the peak of the cathedral. That is the secret meaning of this quiet city, where the spire soars into the blue, where rivers and stories weave into one another, where lives intertwine.

The Other City

ONE WAY I bung a bit extra's the funerals. Cos there's always flowers at funerals, aren't there? In my trade you have a bit to do with dead people. Like you have a bit to do with brides and adulterers and all. It's about extremes, is selling flowers, that's why they're such bright colours. That's when people buy them – something banging, something shit. When I have a busy morning I know it's either been a car crash or it's Valentine's Day and no one's sent me a card again. I was never the one the nice boys fancied even when I was in school. But what's a girl to do? I carry on, that's always been my story.

I made myself a couple of friends straight off after I got my stall. You don't get anywhere without regulars. You have to have some steady trade keep you ticking. I did a bit of flower arranging in a couple of churches, charmed some grandmas, charmed some vicars. I shagged a couple of undertakers, and that's paid off and all. They say it's the ones you don't fuck stay loyal, but fucking them's a fair way of getting their attention, I'll tell you that for nothing.

So today I was doing this little old bloke's sending off into the sunset, or the ground. It was in St Martin's church, sweet little draughty place on the edge of the city with a lovely old rood screen they hid in the civil war. It's so funny how recent history can feel sometimes when you live in a place like this; you can stand and look at a thing people were hiding in the 1600s so it didn't get chopped up, and that was more or less the last important thing that happened in here. That might as well have been yesterday.

I think the vicar at St Martin's pulls the odd fast one. He'd sold this widow the works, had me doing lilies ring-a-rosy round the coffin, but no one came to the funeral. Just the family, poor little things feeling sad, though you could see in the photo they put on the coffin he'd been fit to bust a while before anything happened – wilted or withered or wrinkled or rotten, whatever the word. Dozen in all, dirty dozen snivelling in their dirty hankies. It's so fucking sad, an empty funeral. This vicar, he'd sold them an organist pumping out Chopin, and someone had shifted a fuck-off coffin the old girl looked like she couldn't afford – what are the best ones, are they oak maybe, mahogany? – and the old girl herself sitting there crying in her shit funeral outfit. Folk in Wiltshire don't half look backward sometimes.

I stayed for the service cos I like the music, it's dreamy, and the family smiled and didn't ask me who the fuck I was. People in England are that fucking scared, buttoned-up, stick up their arses, buried under everything, you can sit in a stranger's funeral and no one asks how you knew him.

I didn't go the burial or the wake, mind. It's not about taking the piss. I just like the words and the sweet dream music.

I chavved my pennies out of Rev's sweaty palm when it was over, his leering palm held out like I should lick it, like I'm a horse and he's feeding me carrots. Bowed and scraped cos you have to be grateful with the God squad. Smug cunts. They know you need them, know as well as you all the trade comes trailing after the bodies they bury, know you want them to call you and not some other slapper, never let you forget it. I'd like to shove it in his fucking face and see him eat it. But I need my regulars. I'd have a hard time making friends again now. Not many undertakers fancy a go once you're my side of sixty. It's all about sex with the vicars, too – they always want you, that's why they call you, that's the game. This is what I've learned. Sex is everything. There's sex in everything. Everything you do is sex, and you know for sure how it works when it stops fucking working. So I bow and scrape because I need the ones who don't see the real me when they meet me. I need the ones who remember what I looked like when I were young. Who are looking at me through memories, who still fancy me cos they like remembering their lives when they were young as well. I need those boys, cos I'd never make new friends now.

The old girl was standing in the churchyard like a dog without a master when I walked out the porch with my bags and my rucksack and my sadness over my shoulder. I thought she'd want to pass me by. I know what it looks like, a coffin in a grave, how far down it is, how fucking weird it is there's someone in there who was part of you. I wouldn't talk to anyone if I had someone to love and they went and died. But she seemed to think like the opposite, seemed to want the company. Cos she perked right fucking up when she saw me, like she was wagging her tail and trotting to sniff.

'Thank you for staying for the service,' she said, and she was looking at me like I might want to say some fucking thing back at her about how nice it was or where did she get her frock or what was she doing with her husband's money now he didn't need it. I didn't know what to say. I'd never really been thanked after a show before. Ignored, usually. Once or twice someone feeling pissed off if I hung around to listen to the organ when they carried the corpse out. No one's ever been glad about me at a funeral in my life.

'It was a lovely service,' I said.

'Do you think?'

'Yeah. It was lovely music. It was your husband?'

'Yes.'

Stupid question. I watched her want to burn up, want to wither up. Course it was her husband. People her age don't know no one except the one they're married to. That's why it's important to stay married if you can fool someone into marrying you. Cos your world ends around you all the time you're growing older.

'I'm sorry for your loss.'

She smiled, like she knew as well as I did what an empty fucking phrase is that one.

'Thank you. Are you going back to your stall?'

'Yeah. How do you know about my stall?'

'I've seen you in the market. You're in front of the Guildhall. I used to walk past you on my way to the library. I used to go to get him books.'

I thought it was so strong of her she could say that.

'Oh right.'

'And mine. But I never read as fast as he did.'

'Yeah?'

'He was always a better reader than I was. Have a good

afternoon, then.' She bowed her head like she was letting me pass, and I suppose she wanted me to fuck off, didn't she, so I said the same to her, have a good one or whatever, which wasn't big enough words either, and I walked on out through the gate to the road beyond and the shutdown pub and the bowlin' alley and the Laser Quest and the YMCA and the side way into town past the nightclub and the strip club and the dodgy Chinese and the cheap hotel. My Salisbury, the other city, the one you don't see from the cathedral. And I thought, I wish I had big enough words I could do something for her. I wish there was some fucking thing I could say. I wish I could get out the feelings I'm feeling and make a river of them and help her.

And then I thought I wish I had what she had. I wish I had something worth losing.

I was a wild child but he was wilder. First notch at thirteen – I lay down in a wood with this boy, this blond tousle-haired boy I met in the fields outside my house. I don't know why. I hardly knew him, didn't even fucking like him. We ran around for a few weeks – we were kissing, holding hands, I let him rummage around up my skirt and then he wanted me and I suppose I let him. When I were fifteen I'd slept with fifteen boys. After that, one set of notches grew faster than the other for a fair bit. Then in my forties the years overtook the boys again, and I'm once more like a girl these days, having had more hot dinners than lovers. There's second childhood for you. Long dry years stretching all around me for ever Amen.

I used to meet them at gigs and go with them into the shitters. Used to go with them in parks, end up on my hands and knees on the benches in Lizzie's and them disappointing behind me. Used to go with them at house parties, slip into bedrooms, slip into any empty room, more than one in a night if I fancied. I think I thought I loved it. Used to go with them in the shed at the bottom of the garden where we kept Dad's stuff if he ever wanted to come back and get it, if they were nice enough or canny enough to walk me home. Used to go with them all because it always seemed like what they wanted. But he wouldn't go with me first time.

We met at a disco in a scout hut in Harnham. Not a place you set out for expecting to meet the love of your life. I'd gone looking for lads, and there was a bar, and they let us bring vodka. Me and my ladies, me and my girls. I don't know any of them now. Wonder where they ended up, whether they're rich, whether they're happy. I fucking hope they're all as miserable as I am.

He was the tallest boy there, and I knew from the minute I walked in he'd picked me. Sometimes you can feel it, like gravity. Wherever I stood in the room I could tell where he was, which corner of the room and when he was listening to me. Like he was a plughole and sucking me into the middle of the world, cos I always thought the middle of the world was where he was after that evening.

And we made out in the car park and I put my hand on his cock and he took it away. So I undid his belt and I reached in and thought about blowing him there behind the scout hut against the Astra we were leaning on, but he said no, took my hand away, and I didn't understand it, felt embarrassed, felt ashamed like he didn't like me. And he said it wasn't like that, he just wanted to see me at the weekend, just thought we might get to know each other before we did anything else maybe.

I was seventeen years old. I fell in love for the first and only time, fell in love with the idea of just talking. Like he wanted to hear me, like he thought I might be interesting.

Even then, first night behind the scout hut, my hand on his cock down his trousers, he was playing the long game, reeling me in.

I'd never had a boyfriend before. What a funny word, that – seems cutesy and old world even when you're a kid. I still hear people using it today though, old people, scared to commit to any more of a real fucking life than they had when they were sixteen, scared to be anything more than provisional. Most of us are fucking suitcases buffeting our way through lost luggage, aren't we? That's the problem.

It was better, of course. Better than one-offs, I mean. The sex got better when you learned each other's secrets and you talked and you went on adventures. I didn't always believe him when he told me he loved me, but I always liked hearing it. Fucking massive feeling that. Like something in you's bursting if you love them back, like a massive fucking cardiac arrest.

He started fucking around pretty early. And I've had enough NHS counsellors tell me ever since he was a leech, he was a wanker, he picked me out cos he thought I was weak enough to keep in his pocket while he fucked around. Cos what it was was he didn't like shagging or nights out or pretty women, what he was addicted to was cheating on girls. Thrill of it, fun of it. Black ops. Fuck ops. He needed someone he was hurting before he could come, that was more or less the shape of it, the trouble with his dick. And I nod when they tell me, I nod when they explain me my life like it happened in a textbook. But they don't know shit all, really. They don't know anything. And if they were in my place they'd have forgiven him and all and gone on taking him back every fucking time he got caught with his cock in some stranger. Wasn't like there was anyone else in the world for me. Wasn't like I didn't need him just cos he fucked me over. I was in fucking love with him, wasn't I?

We had fights. I'd go back to my mum's, if we were talking, or I'd stay at a mate's house. He'd always find me, cos the other thing he got off on was having me forgive him. Got a hard-on crying to my shoulder, crying at my feet, crying down the phone in the middle of the night. And I'd always fucking melt in the end. I was like a fucking snowman round him.

That was the first two years. Then there were the good years, cos he stopped. He stopped for ages the minute he knew I was up the duff.

I went back to the stall and hung out there for the rest of the day, and it was just like most other days of my life – fucking quiet, fucking boring. Day after day after day after day nothing happens and it all feels so like waiting, but the thing is, the thing that scares you if you stop to think about it is, it's not waiting; there's nothing to wait for; you're not waiting for anything. It's just your life. Fuck me, it's awful when you stop to think. We're all in training for a race that won't happen. That's why I try not to think more than I fucking have to. Cos it's most of your life, the awfulness, so you put up and shut up and make your money and have your evenings and try to distract yourself and try to stay pissed enough or stoned enough to not stop and think. And most of the time that's enough to keep out the cold.

Night after night.

At the end of day I packed up and binned up and locked up

and went to the Hatchet and bought half a kilo off Dave. He stared at my tits the whole time we were talking, but I don't mind him. I'd put my push-up on so as to give him an eyeful. He's all right, is fucking Dave. I had a vodka and tonic and a vodka and tonic and a vodka and tonic and then we were out back having a jump in the ladies. No one ever uses the ladies shitters in the Hatchet. No fucking ordinary women ever drink there; they only keep them open for shagging or coke. And that was how my night ended, up against a cubicle wall again with lovely dirty Dave. Going back in the bar for another drink and thinking of the old girl standing in the graveyard for some reason, not able to stop thinking about that sad old fucker in her sad old outfit, shiny at the cuffs where she'd spent so many years rubbing her nervous fingers trying to make the arms long enough when they just weren't. Walking home alone to Coldharbour Lane at end of evening with the thought of her and half a kilo of weed in my bra, the swallow tattoo on my hand my only star to steer by.

What was she doing now? That was what I wanted to know. What do you do the first night after you bury your feller?

I got the booze sweats, every year as the pounds keep piling on and the bulk of my body drowns me a little further I sweat worse and worse when I drink. I lay on my back and I stared at the ceiling. And I thought of her lying the same way somewhere in Wiltshire, saw her face again and again as the room span. I forgot to close my curtains, and all the time I was awake and lying there I thought the cathedral might come over and get me, pull its legs out like they were roots and walk right over my ends to peek in the window. I hate the red eye of that spire. Staring into you like *Lord of the Rings*. It sings you to sleep when you let it into your head, when you start to wonder of an evening whether you really belong here. It's like nodding off to heavy fucking metal. So you think you deserve to live here? it says. You think you deserve to breathe the same air as me? You think you belong with my people, you're one of my people? You can fuck off if you think that.

Dealing's more like running a club than a business. I don't sell to anyone if I don't know them. I've got my regulars, and they're all I want to keep me ticking over. It's nice. You get sort of close to them over the years. Plenty kids I been selling to since they were fourteen or fifteen are thirty now. I watch their lives happen to them, clothes change, haircuts, shoes they walk in. They're my favourites, kids whose A Level results I remember better than they do. They all work in Londis or Costcutter or Co-op or Tesco now, but I remember how excited they used to get about turning into rock stars. Some of them get somewhere of course. A boy called Liam went and worked for the *Guardian*. I don't know whether he works there any more. Another boy called Andy joined the police. But most of them, I have to admit your average stoner's not an aspirational type.

The other trade comes from passers-through. Posh kids, grammar school boys. Rubberneckers thinking they learn something smoking. You pick them up by word of mouth, give your number out careful, and the strivers fuck off after a few years to London, cos they don't think there's life worth living in Salisbury. Smug cunts. But you take their money while they're knocking around. It's fair to say there's a fair bit of preying on the thick or the fuck-ups. You can't feel bad about it; you get used to it. You're the highlight of the week for them, and even if you're not doing them any good it's hard to feel guilty when they're that pleased to see you. I never sell from the stall, can't be mixing that up, so I deal in the evenings. Mornings I'm getting the flowers. And the texts roll in all day and I line up my trades. And I run my stall and I smoke my fags. And I meet them here and there in the evenings.

And it was on the night after I did the old lady's funeral I got busted. I was waiting outside the shitters in Vicky's for a sale and the cunt was late. There's a lesson for you: don't fuck around with timekeeping, never fucking wait if they won't turn up, cos you're out there with your arse in the air and your pockets stuffed and you never know what's gonna happen to you. Some cunt of a gavver, a pig like, he comes round the corner, grin on his face like he already knew he had me. Stopped and searched and I had an ounce in different baggies – that's the way you do it, buy in kilos, sell in ounces. And he carted me off, and I told him if I had a prick as big as he was I'd fuck his good day's work up his nose till it came out his eyeballs, and then I was in a cell and he'd locked me up, the fucking cunt that he was. And I sat on the little bench you get there and I wanted to cry, cos with my record and eight little baggies in my pocket I knew I was fucked, simple as. They'd roll it all out in front of me.

Smallsbury, they call it. Everyone knows everyone and everyone's business and everyone's treading on everyone's toes and of course if you sell long enough in a town that small you end up busted, and I was stupid, I suppose, for not thinking that when I still could have done summat about it. All the places I've been I've never known nowhere like this

29

place for showing you how petty people are and how they like to stick their nose in and have a fish around in the guts of you and find out how your life is and what you're doing with it. How stuffed their shirts, how up themselves, how self-regarding, how cliquey, how insecure, how vain, how careful looking after number one. Smallsbury's a club parades itself in front of you but you never join, and in the end if you keep on getting under their feet they fuck you up down some side alley.

I lived a lot of places in my wandering years. Chichester Putney Harlesden Holloway Shepherd's Bush Norwich Northampton Oxford Scarborough Aberystwyth Hull South Shields Ipswich Exeter Plymouth Watford Hereford Golders Green Andover Tooting Brixton Earlsfield Upavon Corsham Melksham Trowbridge Chippenham Devizes. Oh, my wandering days. I never found people anywhere with sticks fucked further up their arses than Smallsbury, though. But some reason or other I still ended up coming home. That's what people do. That's our lives. We don't pick em, we're born living them, and there is such a thing as home, you see.

My little one was born, my little boy, and for a long time I didn't give a fuck about anything else. Only how things might matter to him, what might happen for him if this or that changed or this or that happened. We rented a flat with my dole and his site work, and he got a job in a caff to top us up, and we didn't have anything, no money and nothing in the flat except what we scrounged off our parents. It must have been shaming for him, a job in a café – woman's work, really. And that's why I'll never hate him. Cos he did that for us, and it must have been a big fucking thing for a boy who wanted so much to act like a man. We went round the charity shops and got all our things for our baby – videos and toys and a cot and a mobile for over the bed and a pram, kind of thing. You get such a list together when you're having a baby, believe me. I've never been so happy before or since than when we filled that flat, and it felt so exciting cos we were acting like grown-ups but we weren't grown-ups, really.

When Rick was six months I started working some at the same caff as Jonno and leaving Rick with Mum. Every time I saw Mum she'd ask me when I was getting married, and somehow or other, I suppose it must have been me or Mum while she was pissed at some party, that got back to Jon and we started talking about it. How we'd like our little boy to have married parents, one surname, normal family, real life, you know the kind of thing. We had a colour TV by this time, we were proper strivers for a bit. And before we knew it we'd booked a slot at the registry office and a knees-up at the Red Lion, proper man and wife love story we were gonna be. Then Jonno got done for assault one Saturday night town centre, and we had to cancel the hotel and the guests and the registry office so sharp they all got pissed and kept their deposits.

That was a hard time. It was a bad fucking idea to work in the same fucking cafe as your feller, and I didn't miss that when he went inside – bawling each other out in front of strangers, smashing cups cos every minute of every day we were round each other – but it was worse than that having to move back in with my fucking mum to that horrible house I'd sworn I'd never go back to, and said as much to Mum when I left as well.

I kept my head down. Mum paid for everything and helped me with my Ricky. I wrote Jonno letters and I visited. I was always faithful. He didn't believe me, but I never went with any other *bloke. I had more important things to be thinking about than any-thing like that. But he was suspicious, I suppose, cos he knew if I'd ever gone away that's what he woulda fucking done in a heartbeat.*

My little boy. My Ricky. He was so perfect you couldn't ever describe it, not with a million words if you had time to write them. I was like some kind of fucking wolf when I thought about what my boy meant to me. I'd show my teeth, cos the muscles in my face went taut when I thought how much I loved him. Jonno missed his first steps, first word. I had to tell him so much he wasn't there for, and he cried in the visiting room to think of what was happening, and I tried to be kind but I was angry all the same because it was his fault, wasn't it, it was him had taken himself away from us.

Ricky's first word was still Dad, though.

When Jonno got out I thought we'd get back to starting our lives again, but it was all changed. He didn't want to get another flat straight off, said he hadn't the work or the money, needed to build himself up again, so we both stayed living in our parents' houses. There was no talk about marrying ever again. But I think if there had been he would have said it was kids' stuff. That was how he acted – like he wanted me to think scales had fallen from his eyes and he saw the world was harder than he used to believe it. I didn't buy it for a minute. I never thought he loved our little baby like I did, but I thought he'd got caught up in it all and I thought that was enough. But six months away and all that feeling died down. Six months away and the spell broke; he couldn't see what all the fuss was about, couldn't see why all his life had to be paying for the life of this little fucker he wasn't sure he loved very much. I don't think he was really up for love.

So I knew what was coming. I watched his eyes when he told me he was out with the lads this or that Saturday, and I knew what was going to happen. I looked after my baby and I fought with my mum, but I didn't think about moving out or asking him if we might live together again, cos the moment had passed. I could see it drifting away behind me like a station you've been through, like passing through Basingstoke on the way home from London and you see the lights fall away behind you as the train goes back into the dark. And I could tell what was waiting for me at the next stop.

Still, it was a shock when I did catch him at it. It was humiliating more than anything. He was shagging one of my mates from the caff.

They granted bail, course – couple of hundred quid of weed they were always going to bail me even if they lock me up later, and I walked out the station and got in Mum's car and we drove home. Mum looked after me like she always has. I don't know why I've always been so bad to her. If there's one thing I regret it's how old she is now and how long she's had to put up with me acting the fucktard, cos even if I apologised now, even if we kissed and made up, it wouldn't matter. She'd still have spent most of her life with me like a cloud over her shoulder, she'll always have had all that shit in her life even if she forgives it. That's why I've never tried to make up, I guess. No point, really. We drove without talking, and then she was in my ear while we were still in the hall, before we got in the kitchen, before we even stuck the kettle on.

'What were you thinking, love? What were you doing?'

'I'm sorry.'

'Don't apologise to me, Rita. It's your life, isn't it?'

And then Mum, she sat me down, stuck a cuppa under my nose, and she balled up the sleeves of her skanky blue cardigan in her fists and laid it all out for me. Spoke it all out, what I already knew but thought I'd hide in the back of my mind for a little while yet, all the news I didn't want on the radio – she sat me down and made me listen to it. What I'd done, who I'd turned into, what the fuck was going to happen to me now.

She told me I'd fucked it. For a few extra quid I'd given all my freedom, cos they were sure as hell gonna send me down. I didn't even need to do it. Paid my rent off the stall, didn't need the money. She told me I'd lose my stall if six months was what they gave me, even if it was only six months it was a sure thing there'd be fuck all to come back to. She asked me what I'd been thinking. How I could have risked all I had for no fucking reason. And I couldn't tell her. I'd always fucking done it, it was what I did, never thought of getting out I'd been doing it so fucking long. How do you put a stop to something so inside your life? How do you cut a bit of yourself off? As normal as breathing, dealing was, ever since my baby was born.

Then she talked to me about Rich. My boy, my baby boy. The man he turned into. And this was what I didn't want to have to stare at. This was what I wanted to leave alone. Cos there was no way he'd ever fucking talk to me again now. No way he'd ever let me see my granddaughter.

'Did you think about that?'

'No, I thought—'

'I don't think you thought at all.'

'I thought nothing was going to happen.'

'You were dealing – of course something was going to happen.'

'All those years and they never busted me.'

'Busted you for plenty else.'

'Yeah, but they never fucking busted me for this.'

She just shook her head. And I didn't argue, cos it's no defence, is it? Not once it's happened.

'You should have seen it coming,' Mum said, as if it were a train and I'd been playing on a line trying to flatten out pennies. 'You should have seen it coming.'

So I got in my car that evening and I drove to Southampton. Heart in my mouth and Spire FM playing on the radio till the signal gave out and I had to listen to Solent. *The spirit of Salisbury – one oh twooooooooo, Spire FM.* I've been listening to that jingle all my life, and I don't think they ever changed it. Play half the same songs and all. Spandau Ballet must be minted. Tonight the DJ was taking the piss out of me. They played all sad songs about love, and I don't know if I ever felt so lonely in my whole life as I did on that drive listening to Celine Dion and Tina Turner. Cos I haven't got no one, see. No hope any of the ones I miss are coming back to me again.

Rich lives off the Portswood Road. He's a teacher; they're all teachers or students round there. He was always a clever, lovely, lonely boy. He stopped talking to me so long ago I hardly knew how to get to his any more. When I parked up I already knew how it was going to go. But I had to go through with it. Sometimes the play writes itself. I'll walk up the same garden path with the same slope shoulders the day I get my diagnosis and the cancer starts eating me up. Some things just have to happen. When you know you're going away somewhere as far as the nick or the grave you try and see your kid.

Lucy came to the door, Lucy's his wife, and when she saw me she turned white like she'd seen a ghost. I tried to be nice, and she went to find Rich. I could hear a TV playing inside. I could hear a family evening. My granddaughter in there, growing up, and I'm missing all of it. Last time I saw her she wasn't even talking. She's a nice girl, Lucy. He did so well. She never got involved with us, me and Rich, knows it has to play itself out. I can tell she looks after him, and that's the main thing for me. Rich came to the door and stood in the doorway with his back to the light, and I knew he wasn't going to let me in whatever I said.

'Hi, Mum.'

'Hi, love, how are you?'

'I'm all right. Are you all right?'

'Not bad. What you been up to?'

He looked mad when I said that.

'Getting on with it, Mum. I've been getting on with it.'

'Have you seen your dad?'

'Not recently.'

'But you keep in touch?'

'A bit.'

'He all right?'

'He's the same. People don't change, do they, Mum?'

I knew I had to tell him now, cos he didn't want to make small talk, and he'd shut the door if I didn't get on with it. It was so sad knowing just what shape his face was going to make. It was so sad thinking I was going to disappoint him again.

'Listen, Rich, I needed to talk to you, cos I need to tell you I've gone and got myself in a bit of trouble. I don't want anything. I'm not asking for anything. I just thought you ought to know something's going to happen.'

He watched me. Careful like.

'Right. What is it?'

'I might have to go away for a little while.'

'What do you mean? Abroad?'

'Inside.'

He nodded. He'd known too, I guess, the scene we were playing, known it could only be one of a few things from the minute Lucy said I was at the door in the dark of the night and waiting for him.

'What for?'

'They think I've been dealing.'

'Have you?'

I couldn't look at him any more.

'Actually, yeah.'

He put his hand on the handle of the door.

'Right.'

'So I just thought we should see each other before I went away.'

And then he decided the scene was played out.

'Well, now we've seen each other. And now I have to go, Mum. I'm sorry you're in trouble, but you know I won't get involved with it any more, all right? I'm sorry you're in trouble.'

I would not cry. Whatever happened I would not cry.

'Thanks, Rich. I just wanted to see you. I'm sorry.'

'That's all right. You've seen me now. So I'm going to go back inside, all right?'

'All right,' I said. 'Good night.'

He closed the door on me. I could see through the window in the top of the door he was still standing in the doorway, so close, yellow light glowing out behind him from the light in the hall. And I remembered when he used to be scared of the kind of dark I was standing in now. And then I remembered the time he told me he was done, he wouldn't have anything to do with me any more. It is like a tattoo. I will never be rid of it. There below the surface of me – that memory for ever. And then I went back to my car and drove home, and didn't turn on the radio cos I didn't know a song that wouldn't hurt to listen to now.

It was the years we lived in Fordingbridge did for us I reckon. After Jonno went I was fucked right up. No clue what to do with myself and my feelings. The shouting and crying didn't stop when he left. Grief's not like a cancer, doesn't go when the operation's done and the darkness is out. It's a knife wound. Take out the blade and you still got the bleeding, wait long enough and it turns to a scar, but it's always with you the rest of your life. I was still bleeding pints for him those days, bleeding buckets. I started boozing. Pretty heavy on the drugs. Weed and speed and coke and whatever. Anything, anything, anything got me out my head so I didn't have to think about my life all day. I got straggly. I got starey-eyed. Youth went in about three months of damage, and I never did get it back. That's the thing about youth, you never do. Then realise it's the only beauty you were ever in love with, and you've chucked it out with everything else you thought you didn't want. While you were planning the parties.

Mum was panic stations. She was watching me killing myself, that was what she thought was happening. She was watching me forget about Rich, and she was ready to call social services. For my own good, she said. His good. So when I should have started loving him most, what I actually did was more or less abduct my own kid from my mum's house and run off to live with the gyppos in Fordingbridge.

If you don't know Fordingbridge you ought to give it a visit some time. Some of it's quite nice, if you like little towns in the middle of nowhere. There's a pub by the river with seats outside, and you can have your lunch there if you have any money. There's a bookshop. They'll order in anything they haven't got. You wouldn't think I'm a reader to look at me, but I read all the religious books. I know all about what everyone thinks is coming for us after the end. There are all quite nice shops either side of the bookshop on the main street too, and a Tesco and whatever, and there's a statue of Augustus John by the river cos he used to live there. I didn't know who Augustus John was the first time I saw it. He used to be a painter. He's dead now. He painted nice portraits, and I heard a story about him once I like. When Augustus John went over to Ireland he'd stay with a woman called Gregory, in a big house in the west of Ireland where she liked to put up dossers and poets on their uppers. And he was very athletic, Augustus John, and one day while he was dossing there he climbed a tree in the wood at the end of her garden, high as he could go, and carved something into the top of it. And he wouldn't tell anyone else what he'd carved, and people tried to climb and see, but they all got too scared before they got high enough and had to climb back down. He was brave, see, Augustus John, he was a proper Wiltshire brave and climbed trees better than the Irish. Then one day about a hundred years ago there was a big storm and the whole wood this tree was in blew down, and no one found the carving before the lot went up the chimneys of western Ireland, so this carving of Augustus John's was lost for ever. Except another dosser called Yeats wrote all poems about the wood that had vanished and wrote down the story about the secret carving in his diary, so we know it was there once, and now no one will ever know what it looked like. Though I reckon if he was anything like the Fordingbridge boys I knew, it was probably a carving of a great big cock and balls.

I didn't spend much time in arty Fordingbridge though, or even Tesco Fordingbridge. Cos the other thing about that town is there's a lot of travellers there, see. They live all round it in their caravans. I'd been seeing this pikey lad after Jonno left, lonely and wanting someone, and he was all right with me living in his caravan for a bit. So we moved in there, and then for a little while we were wilder than you've ever known anyone. The lads I ran with got away with murder. They used to rob anything, ram raid anything, and the police always knew all their names when they came round knocking, but they never found a thing. It was already sold or smoked or snorted.

It was hard to keep up with. The nappies and the rusks and the sleep and the mealtimes. I managed and I had my fun. I lived my life real simple for a little while, drank my vodka, ate my mushrooms. And my baby ran wild with the other wolfcubs.

The travellers are the real heart of Wiltshire. They've drunk deep and long from the rivers, and it's turned them loose and wild and free. They ride their horses round the country, and they know things the stuffed shirts hiding in their houses can't imagine, secret things we think are amazing but they live among all the time. The way you hear the sea when the wind's in the trees, like the whole world sings this one song you can make out if you listen. The way the world sings.

I couldn't handle it in the long run. I was only ever there for a holiday, really. I don't think there's fate or anything, that there's any belonging or anything permanent to us. I think we're visitors here and seeing the sights while we're at it, but all the same there are worlds you visit you know will never be yours. I suppose it's about what you get used to when you're growing up, when you're getting together a personality out of your odds and ends. I knew I was only there for a little while till I was ready to have another go at being alive and living in the real world. But I did see that wildness for a little while, and I was glad, because most never taste it.

What I had to give up to know what it felt like to make a fire every evening, listen to the kestrels, catch a glimpse of the panthers that roam the plain, was the love of my son. I didn't know it at the time, not for years afterwards. But when I look back I can see what happened. He was drinking shandies and smoking fags when he were eight year old, and once we left, after the five or six or seven years we spent in that life, he must have worked out how weird that was, must have been angry. And wanted to know why I didn't send him to school, why he couldn't have been normal, known the same things as everyone else. I taught him his spellings and his times tables, course, did my bit, but I know when I think of it now he missed out on a thing or two as well.

That's where the anger came. That and not having his dad around. When he was fifteen he went into this shell, didn't want anything to do with me. He found fucking books and that was it. Wanted a different hand to the one I'd dealt him. We were fighting from when he was sixteen. I told myself it was him growing up, but the fights went on and on and they got cold, got calculated. He went away to university, and I was so proud, but he didn't want to share it with me. He never really came back from Solent. Met his

41

Lucy, got his first job, just seemed to avoid answering the phone. I was so sad. Then one day I was pissed and I drove to see him, drove to have it out. He told me anything he ever done, anything he ever made of his life was in spite of me and the start I gave him, the poison I poured and poured and poured on his days. He was so cruel. But when I started to answer I caught a sight of my pissed-up face in the mirror in his hall, my bloated face, and I thought of the time he burned his hand on the hot plate, and the first time I saw him smoking, and the mornings I woke up not knowing a thing about the night before to find him looking at me, and I knew he was right. So he told me he didn't want me near his family, and I took it. Cos he was going to be a dad, and he wanted to be a dad you could be proud of, so I couldn't be in his life, he said, and I took it. Cos he was right. Everything I've ever done I've fucked right up.

I sat in my house the whole of that night thinking. When you're young you don't know what's going to happen to you. You do everything, try everything, cos you don't know what's going to be important. It's years before you work out what tune it is you're whistling. And it stands to reason if you live like that you'll let a thing or two slip past you. We all do it. We've all got someone it turns out we ought to have loved, a job we should have taken. My trouble is when I sit still, when I look at what's happened to me, I can see my real life, the life I should have been living, going on just under the surface of the world around me, and I can't get at it. It's like there's another me just under the skin, who I buried there, who'll never get out, who could have had such a fucking life but instead she's had to watch me have this one. Every day I'm haunted by my fuck-ups, ghost family, ghost house, ghost money, ghost happiness. That's a proper fucking gyppo curse, I tell you. To be able to see all the things might have happened if you'd only got it right.

About an hour before dawn I got up and went back to my car. I'd been on the gin all the time I was sitting in my chair, shouldn't have been thinking of driving really, but I was fine once I was going. You get in a sort of zone where everything's easy. Like your arms are doing your steering for you. I started north, and when I drove past Stonehenge the light was coming into the sky like air into a lung, colour into a movie. I'd have stopped and got out and gone to the stones cos the grass looked so pale singing in the wind, grey almost white, the hair on my head, but I couldn't stop now, cos I knew where I was going and if I did any thinking I'd realise I was mad.

I reckon what happened in Marlborough is some rich bloke bribed the train companies, back in the day when they were laying the lines, to keep a station out. Someone wanted to dodge all the mess and clutter that was going to come when us people started sloshing around, keep things individual, stop their place turning into every other place, cos it must have been clear enough from the start that what would happen if Londoners travelled everywhere was they'd want London things even in the middle of nowhere. So whoever the bloke was behind it, they made sure the train didn't stop in their town. There's a whole world of stories of blokes rich enough to get train stations built at the end of their gardens. I reckon someone round Marlborough way did the opposite. Shut it out, the modern world, the fleeting world, I don't want any part of it.

I don't blame him. Way I see it, all this shit we think is our lives, think is permanent, is only a moment we're living through. I mean what the fuck is plastic? What the fuck is plane travel? What the fuck is an iPad? In a hundred years people will look back at this time and see a bubble that blew up then burst. And all our human life we think is so big and important will just have been a brief little flowering that'll never come again. We'll look like mayflies when the music stops. And in my lifetime, or Rich's at least, I reckon we'll be driving horse and cart to market once again.

This is where my Jonno ended up. In a funny town in the barren heart of the Plain that saw all the shit we're gonna have to live through coming long before it started, the water shortages and food wars and migrations out of where the land burns up. He always liked to play the oracle. Place suits him in that way. Only trouble Jonno has is that Marlborough's way of turning its back on the nightmare fuck-up of the future was to freeze time in 1855 and live there for ever, and that was never Jonno's style. He wished he was a punk. Wanted to fuck everything. When he was mine he'd have laughed at everything you saw in Marlborough as wank and wanted to sweep it away. But this is where he's ended up, running an antique shop of all things, because that's the way life blows you. You don't really get to decide the direction if you're one of us who isn't born with money. Sometimes the wind changes and your face gets stuck.

It wasn't open when I got there of course, so I got a coffee and sat with it in my car in the silence and the morning, waiting. And the time passed ever so slowly, like it does when you sit and listen to it properly. I worried I was gonna fall asleep, but it was just worry for the sake of it really, cos I felt so wired with thinking I could hardly shut my eyes to blink. Jonno turned up at half eight, and I'd been worried I wouldn't recognise him but I knew him straight away, his walk, the way he held his head, it was my man. Of course it was. People don't change. I followed him into the shop, and he heard the bell and turned to see me, and he knew who I was and fucking all.

'Fuck me. Hello, Rita, what are you doing here?'

I didn't want to tell him yet, not when I felt like I had the power, like I had the surprise.

'Hello, Jonno. You all right?'

'Yeah, not bad.' He looked round him and I could tell what he was saying with that look was fuck you, course I'm all right. I got all this, haven't I? What you got? That's cos I know him, see, know what he's fucking like. 'You're up early.'

'I wanted to see you.' Too needy, I thought, too desperate, and already looking in his eyes I could feel I was losing the game.

'Oh, yeah? What about?'

'Our Rich.'

'Oh, yeah.'

'You know he doesn't talk to me.'

'He's said.'

'Talks to you though.'

'We keep in touch.'

'Harsh, isn't it?'

'Why?'

'I'd say you've done him more harm than I have in your time.'

He didn't say anything to that. I could see he was trying to keep very still, and I wondered if I was in danger now. 'I just wanted to know what you thought I could do? I just sort of feel like I want to know him again.'

Jonno was still, but he started to smile. He started to laugh in my face.

'It's a bit late for that, don't you think?'

'Why? Why's it too late?'

He turned away to put his keys by his till, and I wanted to pick something up and throw it, cos I don't want it, won't have it, all my life people turning away from me.

'Why the fuck is it too late?'

When he turned back there was that hardness in his eyes.

'Why don't you get it? You've been mad all your life, and he's right to keep you out of our granddaughter's life if all you can do with yourself is get arrested.'

'Who told you that?'

'Didn't you just get arrested?'

'Lot you care.'

'It's true, isn't it?'

Rich must have told him. He must have guessed I might turn up. He knows there's no one who loves me, no one who'll listen to me talk.

'Fuck off.'

'See what he's got? See what our boy's got? He's had to work so hard to have that, even that, just an ordinary life, from starting with a mum who was off her face every evening, who ignored him every evening.'

'Fuck you. Where were you then?'

'He's right, Rita. Not to see you. Anything else is asking for trouble.'

I screamed at him now, I couldn't help it, breathed in and screamed and broke the peace of the shop like it were a vase on one of his fucking shelves.

'You fucking dare say that to me?! When you been like you are with me?!'

He was across the room and his hands pinning me hard back to the door in a beat, slam up against the door, and it was like falling backwards into the past. I was twenty-one again and he owned me, he could do what he wanted with me, I was scared of him. If someone's had that hold on you once, it doesn't matter how strong they are thirty or forty years later, you're scared of them for ever.

'Listen to me.' His teeth were in my face, in my eyes, like a dog's. He was spitting, snapping, and I tried not to cry out or show any weakness, cos that's when they have you, the bastards, the bastards. 'You listen to what I'm saying. I haven't wanted anything to do with you for half my fucking life. Nor has your son, you get that? Cos you fuck us up. You fuck up. And I used to try and save you, but you fuck it all up.'

He kept shouting, but I didn't hear any more. I watched his jaws in my face, heard his noise, and I felt almost glad, because I hadn't been wrong about my Jonno being a cunt deep down; he was still the man he'd always been. When he let go of my cardigan I pulled it round me and walked out without saying anything else. Just like he'd always been. I was so stupid. I've got bad taste in people, always picked the wrong people; they wouldn't look after me. That's my trouble. I got back in my car and I wanted to cry, but I knew whatever happened I wouldn't, cos even if he never found out, I'd know, I'd know he made me cry. I'd know the satisfaction that would have given him.

What I have to weigh in the balance, the good thing that happened to me, was the flowers. It was a total accident I ended up with that. Not something I planned that went right, just luck, luck, luck. None of my plans ever came off right. When I was forty I needed a job. This was after I'd fucked up a lot. Been in trouble all my thirties. The difference between me and Jonno was always that I got caught and he didn't. I was staying in a tent, and I went to this nursery down the road and asked if they had work going. The boss was standing in the middle of a big room of raised beds, a big white tent to keep the heat in, surrounded by flowers I'd seen before though I didn't know what the fuck they were. He said, tell you what, let me try you on something. I'm gonna go away for ten minutes. See these? He pointed at the flowers, and I nodded, cos of course I could fucking see them, they were there right in front of me. He said, I want you to pot as many as you can by the time I get back. That all right? And he pointed again to a big stack of plant pots by the door so I knew what he was on about. He must have thought I was a total mong. I told him fair enough, so he went off for a cup of tea, and I got down to it. By the time he got back – twelve minutes later, I checked my watch – I'd potted seven of his flowers. I could see in his face he thought seven was proper brilliant. I think he'd been expecting one or two. He gave me a job there and then, and I felt so big, cos I'd never done anything brilliant before, never got a job because I had a talent. I felt so excited I might have found something I was actually good at. I asked him what kind of flowers I'd been potting, cos they'd be my favourite now they'd got me work, and he told me they weren't flowers at all, they were orchids, and delicate as anything, and it wasn't so much the number I'd potted that impressed him as the fact I hadn't fucked any of them up.

So I did that for a little while, worked for this gaffer outside Salisbury potting plants, and it were lovely. He never wanted to shag me or nothing, I just worked there cos I was good, and I got my drinking and smoking right down to nearly nothing, and then in the end I got a room of my own in Salisbury, and that was special to have that kind of life back that I'd fallen away from. I'd had bad luck with my living situation. Mum wasn't talking to me, no one else was putting me up, and I ended up on this farmer's land in a tent and borrowing his shower and his outside loo, which was cushty of him. I'd just walked up his drive crying one day after someone chucked me out of a car, and he'd fixed me up with a little plot of my own under a cedar hedge. Used to wake up to the lemon smell of the needles, it were lovely. But to get a proper room again with a window on the world and a door to keep it all out was magic. For that year I was happy. Then the nursery went bust. There was a fire, and my old boss hadn't had the proper insurance, and you can't come back from a fire without insurance. He got all us potters together and told us he wasn't going to be starting again, and I was so sad. He took me to one side afters and said, I heard the bloke runs that flower stall in Salisbury market square's looking to pack it in. Why don't you go and see if he'll hand his licence on to you when he does? You're good with flowers and you're good with people, it'd be good for you.

I cried again when he said that. No one ever told me I was good with anything before or after him. Makes me wonder where he is now, cos I barely saw him after that day. People come and go. I felt so proud I had new strength in me, and with that firing me up I *went into Salisbury to the flower stall, bought the bloke there a few drinks, and he said if I helped out for a month I could have the stall after he packed it in. So for a month I paid my rent dealing instead of making proper money, and helped on this stall learning the ropes. And then the old bloke retired and I was running a shop. And that was how I got my hands on the best thing in my life.*

So what I did was drive back home and fuck it up. When I say home I mean Salisbury, right – that's my heart, that's the fucking heart of me, ripped out and dropped in the middle of England. This is where anything worth telling anyone about ever happened to me.

I parked my car in the market square and didn't give a fuck about paying or displaying, cos it mattered fuck all now. The men in my life always wanted to hurt me, I can see that. I can tell that they wanted to own me. Fuck them, I was thinking. I owned my own life. I could hurt my own life without help from any smug cunt. It didn't matter what parking tickets anyone gave me, I was going to prison and losing my stall, and my mum and my son and the only bloke I ever thought I loved all think I'm a wanker and spat in my eye.

I went to the stall and I took out all the flowers I had and trampled them there in the street. Then I smashed my lovely little wooden stall to bits, little bits, tore up the piece of paper that used to be my trader's licence, cos none of it matters, it all ends anyway. I walked away before the police turned up, left my car behind me and walked back to my flat. In my flat I made a pile of everything, my photos and books and my memories, and I took it outside and I turned it all into fire.

And I turned on the taps in my flat and plugged the sink. I took a knife to the bed and the sofa, and a hammer to the telly, then went outside and I wanted to be clean, I thought I'd feel clean, but I felt so fucking dirty. Then the police turned up and saw what was happening, and I was back in that cell of myself with my solitude and nothing to interrupt it.

And for some fucking reason what I was thinking of was that weird old woman in the graveyard after she buried her husband, on her own and nothing to look forward to. For some reason what I did in the police cell was wonder what had happened to her.

Trial started. My lawyer was a bright spark, but I didn't listen to her cos none of it mattered now. I was going down and I'd taken it all with me, all my life fallen in on my head; I felt like fucking Samson. I wouldn't see my mum. Let it all fall away behind me, all disappear and the slate be blank. Let me get out of my life as if I were a snake and everything I've ever done just an old fucking skin. And I knew it was a stupid fucking wish, knew the slate's never blank, cos it all gets etched in, it all stays with you, your life is a blue tattoo. But I thought at least I could try to slash it into too many pieces for anyone to read what it said. I said nothing in court, argued nothing in court. Once I got inside I would fight and spit and turn my back imperious on everything. Maybe I'd even fuck all this and try to die, just get it all away from me for ever. My lawyer she pleaded with me to go in the box and explain myself, but I told her it was all bent, all crooked and broken anyway, the whole world gnarled up like a tree root, no point in me saying a word. I told her I couldn't see the point in my having been born, all the time the face of my son and Jonno's

51

spit in my face and my mum's disappointment hanging over me, and the way I'd let myself get old. I told her to fuck herself and that it was the rich like her born into everything had made sure I never had a chance of a decent life and how did she sleep at night. And all the time I thought about the old girl in the graveyard, envied her, wished I was her, thought everything might have been different if I'd only found someone to love me back.

You can imagine how I felt when the jury came back in and it turned out she'd got me off.

I didn't have anything any more. I mean, fucking nothing. I walked out the court feeling numb, because I'd got it so wrong. I'd ruined everything for no good reason. She found a weak point. She worked a technicality. And I should have been glad, but she made me feel a right idiot.

I went to Brown Street car park where my old moped's parked up. I leave it there, it's such a pile of shite, no one ever nicks it. I was feeling numb. I thought, I'll have a ride, that'll help. An hour or two with the wind in my hair then I'll feel a little cleaner and I'll work out what to do. I hardly use my moped any more. Till last year we were joined at the hip, but I'd get so cold in the winters, so I got the car, the banger. But I'd kept the tax up on my little scooter, I'd kept up the insurance, course I had. I loved it. I pulled the bike chain out through the wheel and jumped on, and the engine started first time and it felt good under me. I'd be rusty, been too long since I rode it last, but the machine was still working beautiful. I backed out of the little corner I kept it in, behind the cars against the far wall of the car park nearest the Arts Centre and the registry office, and headed off buzzing like a wasp in a tin into the evening. Just an hour in the open air. Just the wind in my hair. Then I'd work out what the fuck to do with my future.

A River Curling Like Smoke

1

THERE WAS ONCE a boy who didn't know how to speak out loud. It was as though his mouth had been sewn shut. He wanted to know how to open it, but he couldn't ask anyone what to do, because his words wouldn't come to him. Instead, he lived his whole life in silence.

In my world there isn't much talking. I'm sixteen now. I go to an all boys' school. Talking's not what you do. Life is about rugby and cricket and football. And life has just started to be about girls. The most exciting year you'll ever live, the old people tell you.

Talking isn't natural in my home either. Me and my mum and my dad never really went in for it. Boys in my class used to laugh at us, say we were people that time forgot, because we weren't like anyone ordinary. They said we were typical Salisbury – an oxbow family in an oxbow lake of a place. And it was probably true, we were probably old fashioned. I never cared about the Internet or knew how to download anything. I went for walks instead. And Dad must have looked strange at the school gate when he used to meet me, coming straight from his shop, when so many of the other parents were lawyers or still in the army. I've never played a computer game in my life, and I don't think my mum has ever sworn in hers. But that's what it's like when you live in a small place. All kinds of ways of being survive you might think would have vanished long ago, because people don't know they're weird if you don't tell them.

With Mum I always talk about school, because that's safe territory – she knows which questions to ask and I know most of the answers. With Dad it was football. I don't think either of us had ever been to a football match, but we kept up with the matches in the papers so there was always something to talk about. If it wasn't for football I don't know whether we'd have spoken to each other at all. So I found I'd started to sweat as I built up the courage to ask him the most embarrassing question I'd ever asked anyone.

'Dad?'

If the world sets its face against you, there are ways of fighting back. You can challenge whatever it is that's getting on top of you, do something about it. Or otherwise you can always get out of the world you're in and escape into another one. Make your own shape of it. Tell it like a story till it makes some sense. There's no problem you can't outrun for a little while, just till you're stronger, just till you're ready to face it down. You can be one of those boys who hides out in the middle of nowhere. But if you haven't learned that trick yet, there are worse things to do than grasp the nettle when a problem lies heavy on your heart.

'Dad?'

'Yes?'

'How did you know the first time you'd fallen in love?'

School had finished and I had come to see Dad in the shop instead of heading home. That was what I did when I had somewhere to be in town in the evening. I would pack some clothes into my rucksack in the morning then change in his stockroom before going on to whatever it was that kept me in the city. He would take my bag home when he locked up, always walking back over the water meadow footpath, past the Constable view of the cathedral in the day's last light, whistling away to himself. He was a good whistler, because he had had a good treble voice and been in the choir, so he understood about music, but he was never interested in whistling tunes other people had written. He whistled as a way of thinking, his song a melody exploring and wandering through the air while he took the same meandering route through the backstreets of his mind, over the waterways of the city.

I would come to see Dad and change in his spare room, and then if there was time he would make us a cup of tea before I went back out, and we would sit together in the quiet of the shop for a little while, cradling mugs in our hot hands, making small talk, sloughing off the day.

There was once a boy who drank tea with his dad at the end of every day and wanted to tell his father, every time he saw the steam rising up from his cup, that this moment, this scrap of time they shared, was the best thing in his life. But he could never find the words to do the job. It was as though his lips were sewn together.

*

59

I'm haunted by that. The way I was dumb and never told him how I felt about him. My life these days is like one of those long walks home after you've lost an argument, when you think of all the things you should have said in the heat of the moment. When you're confronted by the person you could have been, should have been, the witticisms that might have carried the day. These days I can't stop telling stories to myself, because I want to be eloquent next time something happens in my life. It's so strange when a song or a story can do that, put your own feelings into words as if you'd hidden them there yourself. I can't do that. It's only afterwards I can ever work out what I felt about anything. That's the curse. I can't speak in the present tense. That's what I wish I could change.

Grandad, Dad's dad, that is, had been a runner for a shoe factory before he joined the navy. His job had been to pick up leather from the train station in his village, where it arrived in consignments, and then to share it out to the men in his village who sewed the shoes together. Cobbling was slow to embrace industrialisation. I learned about it in the Northampton Shoe Museum when we went one time to visit where Dad grew up. Before the factories came, the men who had the skill to finish a shoe had workshops of their own at the bottoms of their gardens. They would get up and dress, drink their tea and head down to their sheds, go to work with their own tools on their own wooden benches. The arrival of mass production didn't change this straight away. The skilled men didn't want to centralise, didn't want to have to catch the bus, and because no one else had their talents they could get a lot of what they wanted, so the factory owners trying to mass produce shoes reached a compromise. They had the leather cut centrally and then sent out to these experts hidden in the villages around.

Grandad was the conduit for this delicate arrangement. He acted as an artery for his trade – an artery, not a dumb waiter. I've got that image right, because he only carried the leather one way. His job didn't extend to collecting the shoes once they were finished. The cobblers would gather up their aprons to make little bags for holding the shoes and run down the high streets to make the deliveries themselves instead. It said in the Northampton Shoe Museum that these cobblers had a peculiar, distinctive gait, which came of trying to run with a pair of boots tied up in an apron and hanging between your legs like massive balls. The Northampton Shoe Museum didn't say that last part; the testicles are my addition to the picture. The cobblers saved my grandad the journey because if they handed in the shoes themselves they got their hands on the money quicker and so could get faster into the pubs.

Dad bought his shoe shop when he finished in the army. The lease on the shop was for sale along with the business and the stock, so he had the lot. He talked about inheriting clients, saving hard work by taking over something that already existed. What mattered more to him, though, was going into his father's trade. I could tell it was important from the way he never mentioned it had happened. It stared him in the face that he was working in his dad's trade, but he never wondered aloud what Grandad would have made of things, and that was how I knew he cared. I'm always shy about the things I care about most as well, so I understood. I was pleased to realise I must have got my shyness from my dad; I love anything that makes me like him. I used to think Dad must be proud to have shifted his family a few rungs up the ladder of the trade he was in. Not a bad last line to a life, even if you never did anything else.

The shop was on Winchester Street next to the barber's. Dad mostly sold to people much older than him or to men in pinstripes, so the stock was old-fashioned and I suppose you could say straight-laced, if you were the punning type. It gave the room a sombre air. The shop was very light because of the big window in the front. There was a bell over the door, which rang out when someone came in. The walls were painted white, with a green bar running round them at waist height – it had been like that when Dad got the place, and every now and then he touched up the paintwork, but he had never changed the look of the room. The floor was a dulled red linoleum. The lino was shiny and slippery in places where weatherproofer had been sprayed on to new shoes without newspaper being laid down. I used to slide along those patches like they were windows into another world I could get through if I threw myself hard enough at them, launching at the floor where it shone in the light from the street and skidding across the room in my socks. Sometimes I used to fall over into the displays, and Dad would get angry.

There was a display of brogues and sensible flat shoes for women in the window, and hanging from the back of the white display shelf, so it was only visible from inside the shop, was a collection of shoe laces, boot laces, polish, weatherproofer, stain remover, chamois leather, brushes, insoles, all in varying shades from buck to black. The arcane curios and magical potions of the shoe shop world. There was a little cupboard room, where he kept all the new shoes in their boxes. Sometimes I would help him with a stocktake, rummaging round in there and trying not to knock over the kettle he kept on the elbow-height shelf with his plate for his lunch while he called out different styles and sizes, startling the dust on shoe boxes with my hands so it made lacing patterns and loops around me.

The back of the shop was its glory. Here, behind a wooden counter, Dad had a collection of machines for fixing shoes. Most of his customers were the kind of people who preferred repairing what they wore to replacing their old shoes with new ones, so Dad had learned the finer crafts of cobbling when he took over the business. This was where he spent most of his day, doing the same work his father had once helped others do, and this was where I found him the day I dropped in to visit, wanting to talk about love; a pair of goggles over his eyes, neck bent in loving concentration, running the leather of a shoe through one of his machines and the room rich with the thick smell of oil and leather and the sharp smell of metal parts heated up from moving. He looked up when he heard the bell go, smiled when he saw me, and welcomed me in.

'Dad?'

We were having tea over the counter at the back of the shop. I had lost his attention to a piece in the paper about Salisbury City. Steam from the teacups curled up to our faces in an intricate dance. He looked up and his eyes met mine. I thought my throat might have dried up and I wouldn't be able to speak, I felt so shy.

'Yes?'

'How did you know the first time you'd fallen in love?'

He smiled, as if I were about to tell a joke and he was gathering his laughter for the punchline.

There was once a boy who was embarrassed by everything.

'Why do you ask?'

'And once you knew, what did you do about it?'

He leaned into the conversation, and even as I hated him for the knowing smile he gave me, I loved the attention, loved suddenly being the only thing he was thinking about.

'Have you met a girl?'

I shook my head but couldn't keep looking directly at him. I carried on, this time speaking with a sinking feeling.

'What did you say to her? Did you plan it, or did it just happen by accident?' He laughed now, rocked back on his stool and away from me.

'I won't tell you a thing till you tell me why you're asking.'

'It's nothing.'

'Tell me then.'

'No, I mean it's literally nothing. I was just wondering.'

'Were you now?' He watched me, still smiling.

'Are you really not going to tell me?'

'Not if you don't tell me her name.'

'Whose name?'

'Very funny. Is she in the choir?'

'No.' I felt myself flushing red. I wished I hadn't asked. I had thought he might have wanted to tell me the story; I should have known he would have wanted me to tell mine first. 'I was just interested, that's all.'

'Course you were.' He took a sip of his tea. 'Where's your rehearsal tonight?'

'St Mark's.'

He nodded.

'Maybe you'll get to walk her home if you're lucky. That's a fair way out, isn't it? Do you know where she lives yet?'

'I was just interested!' I said.

He laughed and shook his head, turning back to his paper. I watched him for a moment.

'Are you really not going to tell me?' I said again.

He shrugged, grinned, but didn't look up.

There was once a starling who thought it could fly and touch the sun in the space of a single afternoon, if it only wanted to. One afternoon it decided to try. It broke away from its cloud of brothers and sisters and buzzed alone towards the great white heat in the distance, thinking it would be back before nightfall with a story to tell. But hours passed, and the sun was no closer. The starling felt sure something must have gone wrong, because after the first couple of days in flight it couldn't understand why the sun hadn't set yet. It wondered whether that was because it was getting closer to the thing it wanted, so it kept on flying. What the starling didn't know was that the world turned round, and that it was flying around the world, flying itself to death, never getting any closer to the sun in the sky.

Sophie. I knew I had to do something about her. I couldn't sleep for thinking of her, and everything falls apart when you can't sleep. You wake up later; you go to bed later because of how late you wake up; you pad round the house in the middle of the night looking for things to do that don't make any noise; you spend your time alone with your insecurity and arrogance and madness. Since I had first spoken to Sophie Lawrence I had gone to bed every night only to lie there for hours wondering whether I had gone mad. I could hear her voice in the room with me. I imagined the thrill of touching her neck, the softness of her face, what her hair might feel like in my hands. I imagined asking her out, holding her hand. I tried to imagine taking off her clothes.

This, for me, was unmapped territory. I'd never had a girl-friend. I'd never undressed anyone in my life. I didn't yet know there was a trick to bra straps, let alone what it might be. There was only one computer in the house, so the world of Internet porn was closed to me. You could hardly access it on the landing. I could never have bought anything from the sex shops on Fisherton Street. I had gone into one once and had to walk straight back out when I saw how bright and colourful the racks of DVDs were, blaring out from the walls. There was nothing secret or surreptitious about them. Sometimes boys brought magazines or playing cards with women on the back into school. Usually it was the unpopular boys trying to impress everyone else. They would pass them round under the desks, and after about half an hour someone would grass on them for a laugh. It was fun seeing those boys humiliated. Perhaps it made us feel more secure about our own positions in the pack to know there was someone below us. That was about the standard of humour in my classroom. It was a laugh watching a teacher go through the locker of a boy who had been caught with porn. They would gather the magazines or posters or pictures under their arm and take them to the staffroom. No one seriously imagined they ended up on the walls in there, but that was something to make a joke about as well. Otherwise we all had to go back to hitting each other with rulers or playing coin football or chucking Warhammer models around or talking about football or music or football to pass the time.

Sexual fantasy, then, was something I attempted with the stabilisers still on. I didn't have much of a repertoire to run through. I had gone to a sleepover in year nine and sat with half a dozen other boys in sleeping bags to watch a classic scenario, the plumber who comes to fix the pipes, on a DVD our host had nicked from his older brother. It had been too awkward for words, and we were all relieved when someone switched it off halfway through. I had liked the way the woman's breasts moved, but watching porn with six other boys is not the best time for detailed anatomical study. When I thought of Sophie I would try to think of the woman in the video, superimpose one head on the other body, but it wasn't much fun. Sophie wasn't like that. She was purer than that. If there's one thing all boys have in common it must be the way they think of girls as purer than boys are, too beautiful and good to be human, to be spoken to by the likes of them.

I walked to rehearsal through the Greencroft, past the Wyndham Arms and the firework shop, over the roundabout at the edge of town where fifteen years ago a boy from my school had been hit so hard by a car his head came off. St Mark's was at the top of the London road, a big church, good for concerts.

The joint schools concert happened every year. The boys' and girls' grammars got together to do a big choral piece. Last year had been Handel; this year we were doing the Fauré *Requiem*. In years seven, eight and nine the concert was mostly memorable for the challenge of getting to the end of the evening without fainting. You had to stand up in massed ranks for hours in a church overheated by the bodies pressed into it and shout your head off. Someone always had to sit down in the last movement. When I was in year eight the boy who had to sit down was me – a lightness had flooded through me, like standing up too quick, that swept my legs away, and I spent the last section with my head between my knees, hidden from the view of my concerned parents by the other singers around me.

From year ten onwards the concert was memorable because of the girls. It was practically the only time of year when I spent any time around them. The moment of socialisation, when the friendship groups that built up in classrooms began to move out of uniform and focus their lives on house parties, holidays, evenings knocking round parks or the bus station, sniffing glue or making snakebite, had passed me by. I told myself I didn't have a friendship group because I didn't live near anyone else in my class. It was easier for the boys in the villages. They came into school on Mondays with stories of time spent together in fields, making fires, smoking eighths, playing guitar. I was a bus journey away from anyone I liked, and because I had no group to hang out with I never found ways to meet girls. You couldn't just go up to them on your own. People mixed together easier in packs and groups and crowds. Friends would have girlfriends who introduced you to their friends. It was all closed off to me. That was what I told myself, anyway. I tried not to wonder whether it was really because I was too afraid to risk myself in anything as exposing and vulnerable as a conversation.

There was once a stalactite hiding in the dark of a huge crystal cave. The stalactite thought the floor of this cave, which glistened with magical rock formations, was the most beautiful thing it had ever seen, and all it wanted was to touch that ground. So it set out to do so. It knew getting there would take a very long time, thousands of years even, as the stalactite grew drip by drip ever longer, but it decided it didn't care how long it took. This was all it wanted. This was going to be worth it. And it is still there to this day, for all we know, down there in the dark, pouring incredibly slowly towards the thing it loves. And it is probably hardly any closer. But it hasn't changed its mind. It is still heading in the same direction.

The concert was magical because the choirs mingled before and after singing and during the break. The other tenors knew girls who lived near them, so if you stood in the right groups, you might be introduced to girls. I would try to stand in the right parts of the hall, convinced no one in the history of the world had found social interaction as difficult as I did, and wait.

As I walked to the rehearsal I tried to think of interesting facts I could share if I got to speak to Sophie. I was uncomfortably aware that I didn't know any. I wondered whether I ought to have bought a newspaper that morning and made sure I had a view on the major events of the day. Should we be in Afghanistan? Were we still in Afghanistan? I didn't give a toss, really, but perhaps she did. I wondered how you found that kind of thing out about people. In Scouts we used to wear badges signalling what we were good at and what we liked. The trick, I supposed, was to bring things up and then go quiet, let the other person talk till you knew their opinion, then agree with it in such a way that they talked some more and believed they were having a conversation with you. But such tactical masterstrokes felt much further down the line than I should be thinking of yet. What I tried to imagine as I walked to the church was a way of saying anything at all without coming across as a potential serial killer.

We had met at the previous rehearsal, standing next to one another in one of those awkward clots of strangers that form among kids while everyone tries not to look like a loser. I had tried to make conversation about the music we were there for. To my amazement, she had seemed to want to talk to me. Today she was already there when I walked in, laughing with three other girls by the music folders. I watched her for a moment. People reveal so much of themselves when they don't know anyone's watching. Unselfconscious, unaware of anyone else's eyes, the way a person stands or smiles or listens or tucks her hair behind her ear can show you a whole life that might be hidden during conversation under the glossing layers of what they want you to think they're like. We're only ourselves when we're alone, and silent. The rest is performance. When you're talking to another person you will usually find your life reduced, all your personality focused into the facet of yourself you think is appropriate for that conversation. Or, sometimes, contact with another person can make you more than yourself, make a new soul that hangs in the air between you. But you're never just yourself with someone else. So I love watching the way another person holds themselves when they are alone and thinking. Their actions and postures are windows into the vast and secret worlds below the surface of the day around me, the lives of others.

I knew at a glance she felt no insecurity around her friends, that they all liked her, but that she was never the first to speak up, never the leader. I knew her intelligence, which made her look like she was holding herself back, as if she was always thinking of something else, but could not be mistaken for lack of interest because of the way she watched the faces around her, diligent, inquisitive. I knew she was careful and methodical and tidy – I saw that in her hair and the way she stood. She was the kind of person who drank enough water and got enough sleep.

'Sam.'

I looked up, afraid I had been caught staring, and saw Adam Morris coming into the church, still in his uniform, shirt untucked. I sat next to Adam in rehearsals. He was in the year above me and good at music, and when I got lost in difficult passages of song I would follow his voice. I could never tell whether he knew I was doing it, but he was always kind, as if he was aware he looked after me in some way.

'Hello, mate. You all right?'

I shrugged, trying to be casual. 'Yeah, how are you?'

'Yeah.' He started to walk towards the music folders and I fell into step, pulled along in the wake of his conversation as he told me about an argument at the bus station. I tried not to look at Sophie again as we approached. It was because of Adam that we had been introduced. He caught the bus to school with one of her friends. I couldn't concentrate on what he was saying. He wasn't speaking for my benefit anyway, he just wanted to express his frustration at some boy in his year who was trying it on with his girlfriend, so all I had to do was nod and agree occasionally. My ear was caught by the liquid voice of a clarinet sounding an angular, elegant line of melody as we made our way to our seats. A cellist ran a bow quickly over the strings of their instrument. We sat and watched the petals of the band unfurl. It crossed my mind that Fauré would have got a thrill from this moment, realising that his idea might turn into so many minds and mouths and voices, so much hardware and time and talent and light reflecting from the brass and the woodwind and the strings before us, from the glasses of the lead violinist and the trombonist's watch, from Sophie Lawrence's hair as she turned her head and seemed to look, for just a moment, in my direction.

Mr Richardson, our music teacher, mounted the conductor's podium and shuffled through his score as if he had lost something between the leaves. The rehearsal began, and by surreptitious glances I established that Sophie was still in my line of sight where she sat among the sopranos, her eyes fixed always on Mr Richardson's baton, on his face when he spoke to correct us. I longed for that attention. I almost hated him for being able to stand there so easily, to be the centre of the room.

We limped through the music. It wasn't very good yet. There were too many of us to make keeping time together for very long a realistic goal at this stage, and I felt drowned every time the instruments swelled. But I knew all this from previous years; the rehearsals always took the same pattern. The slow dredging together of a performable version of whatever it was we were singing. There would be a sudden gear change as we reached the concert itself, when all the notes were sung and played in the order intended, when the presence of an audience made us all stand straight. I was used to the rhythm of these rehearsals. What was new was her.

When we spoke at the last rehearsal she told me she lived in town, near what we both still called the swimming pool park, though there hadn't been a pool there for years. They had knocked it down when they built the leisure centre on the other side of town. She told me she walked to school in the mornings and liked the Fauré. When I told her what my dad did she thought her father, an estate agent, might possibly buy his shoes in my dad's shop, although she couldn't be certain. She had said she would find out, and I wondered now whether she had gone home and asked, whether my name might have come up over a meal at her dining room table, as if I might live in the same world as her, as if I might intersect with a part of her life. I had learned all I could of her in the two minutes of breathless, agonised, halting conversation we had shared at the first rehearsal. Now I wanted to know everything else. Everything that had ever happened to her, every thought that had ever crossed her mind, every inch of her body.

At the start of the week I had been looking forward to this rehearsal. The idea of seeing her, hearing her voice, filled me up, and I began to dream impossibly of getting her on her own somehow, walking her home after rehearsal, even asking her out to do something at the weekend.

*

There was once a boy who wondered where you were supposed to take girls on dates, what you were supposed to do alone together with an afternoon or an evening to pass in one another's company. He could not understand how anyone could enjoy spending time with him.

What date could I possibly get through without her discovering how far below her I was, how little of her time I deserved to occupy? I had read somewhere that the cinema wasn't cool any more as a place to go on dates. You were supposed to spend a first date talking. I couldn't imagine having enough to talk about that might be interesting to her, and I wondered whether that wasn't exactly the point of having a first date at a cinema: you could sit in silence and get your nerves out of the way the first time, then try talking later.

The rehearsal trudged on towards the half-time break, and I realised with a sudden certainty that I couldn't do it, I couldn't talk to her. What would I say? How are you? Been busy? Do you remember who I am? We only met for a moment. Since we met at the last rehearsal I have thought of nothing but you, dreamed of nothing but kissing you, wanted nothing but to see you smile at something I say, wanted nothing but to hold your attention, even for a moment, and make you laugh, and I wondered whether you might like to go for a coffee some time?

And yet I had fallen in love with a girl named Sophie Lawrence. So that was it. I was lost. How could I not do something about it?

Mr Richardson dropped his baton and announced we

would stop for quarter of an hour, and I stood at once. I would go outside. I could loiter by the gravestones, pretend I was on my phone if anyone came near. The whole thing was so pathetic, I wanted to laugh at myself. It was ridiculous to make such a drama out of something no one else in the world would have noticed or known about at all. How can such huge things as feelings only exist in our heads? How is it that they never take form in the real world?

Adam put a hand lightly on my arm.

'You all right?'

'Yeah, just feel a bit – I'm just going outside.'

Adam nodded. It was nothing to him. He must have found me strange. He was doing me a favour, giving a younger boy the time of day when he didn't have to, offering me a way into the social world around me. It was nothing to him if I didn't want to take it.

I spent the break trailing round the side of the church and watching the cars on the roundabout, some with their lights on, that hour of the evening when it is neither light nor dark, and wondering what she was doing. Surely some other boy would start chatting her up? Even now she would be smiling and giving out her number. I could imagine the scene, one sweaty-palmed classmate of mine or another thumbing the digits into his phone then pranking her so she had his number too, going back to his seat with a smile on his face, feeling as if he had a fish on a line and was reeling her in. They would all know how to get what they wanted from her, they would know how to talk about sex, but none of them would love her like I did. I wondered whether the men who ended up living alone could be picked out from a very early age, if in fact our whole lives could be diagnosed in our childhoods, all the patterns established in school spooling out through adult-hood or old age.

The other little groups that had wandered outside headed back into the church, and I followed them back to my seat. Adam wasn't there, and I looked across to see him standing among the sopranos, holding forth slightly too loudly. He seemed to have no trouble talking to girls, but it crossed my mind watching him from this distance that he had the look of a bore at a grown-up party, like those uncles who think too much of themselves, and I wondered whether there was something too polite in the smiles of the girls listening to him.

Mr Richardson took to his stand again. I realised as the girls Adam had been talking to moved away that she had been there, standing with her back to me. As she turned to find her seat her eye caught mine, and my heart leapt as she held my gaze for a moment and smiled.

'Budge up.' Adam stood over me, hands on hips, mock-serious. I moved along one.

'Sorry.' I looked back at her. She had turned to face Mr Richardson again, but as I watched, her eyes flicked across to me again. I wondered whether I was imagining it or whether she blushed when she caught me looking.

'You fancy her, don't you?' Adam said.

'No.' I knew I was blushing.

'Why not? I do. I'd love to fuck her.' He looked at me, smiling. 'You don't like the rude words, do you?'

'I don't mind rude words.'

'I wonder what her cunt tastes like? Wouldn't you like

to strip her naked and pull her legs open and find out?'

'Erm. I dunno.'

Adam laughed then, and I didn't know what else to say. Every other boy I ever met seemed to know so much about girls. Why could I barely look at her? Why did I live my life so afraid?

After we finished, Adam made his way across the hall to the girls he would be catching the bus home with. He leaned into the conversation like a ship cresting a wave, and I followed as he tried to make a joke about Mr Richardson. I never liked laughing at Mr Richardson, and didn't laugh along, though everyone else did. I felt someone's shoulder against mine.

'He's a bit of a prick, isn't he?'

I looked around and she was standing right next to me, flesh and blood and breathing the same air I was. She was smiling, conspiratorial, head inclined towards Adam. 'Thinks he's brilliant.'

I didn't know what to say. I wondered what would happen if I was honest, and then the silence was stretching too long, so I tried it.

'I really like Mr Richardson,' I said.

She nodded. 'I go round his house sometimes. His daughter's in our year, but she doesn't do choir.'

'Why not?'

'I guess it's a bit like hanging out with your dad, isn't it?'

It must have been a trick in the way she stood, but she made me feel as if we had left the other group entirely, though we still stood in the middle of it; as if we were the only two people talking in all the world. I wanted to keep looking at her, but couldn't. I found myself looking down at my shoes, back up at her face, back down at her shoes, until I got a grip on myself and took to studying my hands.

'It's good music, isn't it?' I said.

'Yeah, I like it. You lot are better than us though; we've got a shit choir this year.'

'Do you think so?'

'We can't keep in time. It's Sam, isn't it?'

'Yeah. You're Sophie?'

Her smile seemed to say she knew very well I had remembered who she was, and I felt shy again. She must have been able to tell everything I was feeling, read me like my skin was water and the thoughts in my head so many fish swimming beneath it.

'Yeah. Where do you live?'

'Harnham.'

'Oh yeah? Tell you what, wanna walk home? I'm sort of on your way, aren't I? If you're not getting a lift. My parents don't let me walk home on my own.'

I shrugged, nodded, tried to look casual while my heart hammered in my chest.

'Yeah, OK.'

'Otherwise I'll end up spending half an hour at the bus station with this lot, and I just want to go home. You don't go to the bus station much, do you?' She said this like it was a good thing. The fact I was never invited to hang out at the bus station with everyone else, the epicentre of all social interaction, had always been a source of shame and humiliation to me. Now it seemed to have become the thing that made me worth talking to.

'I normally just walk home.'

I felt like my legs were going to give way. Some energy shot through my arms, my whole body, not a rush of blood but something else, some electricity pouring into every nerve ending. She was so brave. Was it really as easy as that? It felt like nothing had ever happened before. Or nothing that had ever felt half as alive as this.

She turned to her friends and announced she was leaving, and I watched to see whether some smile passed between them, but everyone reacted as if the two of us walking home together was perfectly normal. Perhaps we were the loners and it seemed logical we might get on. Adam raised an eyebrow when I waved goodbye to him, and I couldn't help smiling at the thought he might be impressed. Perhaps she was trying to get me away from everyone else. Perhaps I was going to have a story to tell tomorrow. But I already knew I would never tell anyone anything Sophie Lawrence said to me this evening. It was my adventure, my story to read to the end; it was secret. She was waiting for me in the door of the hall, and I hurried to catch up, smiling, sheepish.

'You good to go?' she said.

'Yeah.'

'Come on then.'

It was getting dark outside. The air was a deep blue and there were clouds coming out of the west and the sunset, but above us was only the sky and telegraph wires strung over the road like the streamers of air that get left behind in the wake of aeroplanes. She led me back a quicker way to town, through an underpass, past anonymous suburban houses you would never have suspected of containing whole lives if you didn't live in one yourself. The pavements were orange in the light of the streetlamps. It was cold enough for me to wish I had a jacket.

'I don't think we've met before really, have we?' she said.

'No. Except the other week.'

'Yeah. You're not in Adam's year though?'

'No, I'm in yours.'

'Are you doing music?'

We talked about composition; we talked about the fun of picking apart music we had never understood before, how you learned the language it was written in. We got to the swimming pool park very quickly, and I wanted the road to curl round and lead us away again, wanted to be lost with her, to walk with her for ever.

'I'm just up there, so I guess this is where I leave you,' Sophie said, smiling and slowing her pace.

I breathed deep. I might never get to walk with her again like this.

'OK. Listen, Sophie—'

'Yeah?'

'I was wondering whether you were around at the weekend? Whether you might fancy meeting up?' I knew before I had finished that it had gone badly. She seemed to flinch, to screw up her face as she thought ahead.

'I'm really sorry but I'm not free,' she said.

'Oh. OK.'

'Sorry. My grandma's ill and we're going to see her. I promised I'd see her this weekend.'

'OK.'

'Sorry. I'd like to.'

I wanted to say, there are two days in a weekend. What are

you doing with the other one? But that wasn't the point. It didn't even matter whether or not there actually was a grandma to give the story any substance. The point was that she was saying no.

'That's fine. Have a good evening then.' I started to turn away, wanting to get away from her as quickly as possible before she could see the shame in me, but she said my name and I stopped, looking over my shoulder.

'Sam.'

'Yeah?'

'Sorry. Maybe some other weekend.'

I wondered whether she meant it. I couldn't tell. I was too embarrassed to look very hard.

'OK.'

'See you soon then?' She stood looking at me, and I didn't know what she wanted.

'OK. Night.'

'Night.'

I turned again and walked away. When I looked back for a last time, she had vanished, gone inside to her parents and the warmth of dinner and the evening and sleep. I wondered whether I would be more or less able to sleep that night. I thought I knew the answer. I wondered about the shadows under my eyes. How deep could they get before my eyes caved in?

I had to walk another two miles home. I stuck to the narrow pavement of the ring road – that would save me going through the centre of the city and the darkness of the Greencroft. I didn't like walking through the Greencroft once the sun had gone off it. Boys from other schools hung about in little gangs by the basketball net or on the playground, and there was a bench where drinkers gathered like a murder of crows. They had been boys on swings scaring passers-by once as well, I supposed, and now, in their twenties or thirties, too old to participate in that game, they brought their cider or Super along to watch their successors enjoying themselves intimidating the choirboys. There was something sad about it, to see men returning to their childhood haunts, worse for wear. They didn't belong in those parks any more, but they hadn't found anywhere new to belong to either. Perhaps all adult life was an attempt to keep alight the fires that burned when you were young, when everything was possible and new, when a smile from Sophie Lawrence had the power to change the world.

The cars on the ring road flashed past, and when a lorry came I felt myself buffeted in the violence of its wake, the wind shaking me on my feet. Somewhere near the mouth of Winchester Street, where the road rose up on steep banks and reached roof level, I heard a voice below me. I looked down to see a woman with a dog.

'Excuse me? What are you doing?'

'I'm walking home.'

'You should come away from the road. Come down. You're going to die, my love.'

I know, I wanted to say.

2

THERE WAS ONCE a boy who had a story to tell but couldn't bring himself to tell it. So he distracted himself with other things, talking about love, talking about youth, talking about the surface of his life. But the story lay there all the same within him. And he knew he would not sleep again until he spoke it out. He knew there had to be an exorcism.

My father was my hero, and I loved his life as some people love their own life or success or adventure or the pursuit of women. While I was growing up I knew so little about him, and I hated that, felt it keenly as an absence. Few children enquire about the details of their parents' lives while they still live with them. It's once you fly the nest you stop to wonder where you came from. But my whole life, even while we lived together, was filled with wishing I knew more about my father and not knowing how to ask.

Dad wasn't the most approachable man in the world, but it was Mum who sealed my lips and kept me from starting conversations with him, from hearing about his life. All my life I've been afraid of my mother. There has never been any good reason. But when I look at her I see emotion buried, and the pressure under the skin of her has always scared me, the violence of it, the way it waits in the house for me every evening. I suspect my mum of depression; I suspect my mum of bipolarity; I suspect my mum of anaemia, which makes her short with the rest of the world because she gets so tired; I suspect my mum's character was formed by a great deficit of affection in her childhood, or at least by the perception of a lack of love, which she has never worked through, never confronted or resolved. What I know is that she has never been happy in her life, and so she guards Dad jealously as her territory, her treasure, the one good thing that happened to her. Our love for him always felt like a competition. Not one he was aware of, but a battle we fought between ourselves, a cold war we never admitted to, which meant I could never have asked Dad about his childhood or youth. It would have been conceding a position, giving Mum a chance to demonstrate how much more she knew about him than me. It would have made me vulnerable. An undisguised attempt to get closer to Dad might have brought retaliation in one form or another. Some love withheld down the line, some grounding for spurious reasons, some form of trouble me and Mum would both know could be traced back to my indiscretion but which she would conceal too well beneath some other anger for me to confront her about it. Above all else, Mum was an angry woman, though I do not know what wrong had ever been done to her.

Dad was everything I wanted to be from my first memory of him. That had been the time he saved my life. I was four years old and we had gone on holiday to Cornwall, to a farm outside the village of Delabole. I discovered later that Delabole had a story like anywhere else – King Arthur was supposed to have fought his last battle up the road at a hamlet called Slaughterbridge. At the time of the holiday, though, it was simply a paradise of cow parsley, strange lichen-licked rocks, open spaces I was unable to enjoy because I had earache. Mum fed me a disgusting banana medicine that made me want to retch, and Dad took me for walks. He showed me foxgloves, their softness when I put my finger inside the flowers, and glow-worms in the hedges at night, but all I really paid attention to was pain and how sorry I felt for myself.

On the last morning, feeling better, I walked out into the yard to explore and say goodbye to the farm. The mounting block and gate, the drain and the hay barn. I decided to climb the straw bales. I clambered in a sweat of concentration. If I got high enough, I thought I might be able to touch the roof, and then I hoped I could roll or slide back down again. The biscuit smell of straw in my nostrils and the sharpness of the stuff against my knees and stomach, I climbed. At the top, looking up at the roof girders instead of down at my footing, I fell down a gap between circular bales, into the heart of the straw stack. Panic came sharp as the heat at the bottom of that well of close darkness. My arms were trapped reaching upwards, frozen the way I had fallen, the gap so narrow I couldn't get them down by my sides. I thought I could hear rats, and there didn't seem to be enough of that dry burning air to fill my lungs. Between hacking coughs I breathed and screamed. I felt sure I was going to die, that I would suffocate, dehydrate, cause the whole thing to fall in on my head. I was too small to think sensibly, regulate my breathing, try to lever myself back out, wedge my knees against the bales and shimmy upwards. I thought my life was going to end in the dark and the heat. But I had been down there less than a minute when I felt a huge hand grip mine, an extraordinary strength lift me out of my prison, and found myself gathered into my father's shaking arms. That's my first memory of Dad. He had been watching me from the kitchen window while he drank a cup of tea, and seen me fall in. While I grew up I watched him. What he did with his days, how he responded to situations. I tried to learn to be like him.

A love for his father is always at the centre of the first years of a boy's life. So the summer Dad died was already a kind of ending before I even knew he was ill. The first time you find love for a person who isn't your flesh and blood begins a loosening of the earlier bonds you made in your life, as new colours come into the palette of your thinking, as you enter new orbits. What I had shared as a boy with my father was unspooling from the moment I saw Sophie Lawrence. The separation I experienced between myself and my parents the year I discovered love was starker than it is for other teenagers, as it ended with a line of words across a headstone. But it was only the scale of the thing that was different, not the feeling.

In the war for my father I have this much over Mum – I knew before she did that something was wrong. If a score was being kept of the fight for Dad, if there is a double-entry bookkeeper taking note somewhere of the love or closeness we shared with him, I know that will stand against my name as a badge of some kind. By being the first person to speak aloud the fears that had already been circling him for weeks when I first felt them, I was the one who started the whole thing careering downhill, began to turn the idea of sickness into a reality. If you can name a thing, then you own it. You can call it into being. Sometimes I think I killed him. It was after I spoke up that the testing started.

The Thursday after the rehearsal and my walk with Sophie Lawrence I walked back up the hill from school to find Dad already home. I liked Thursdays. Dad was usually out till six every day, and Mum worked later, so I got to spend a few hours with the house to myself. I didn't have to stay in my room; I could sit in the kitchen or the sitting room and listen to whatever radio station I liked. I could take long showers without Mum making any comment. But today when I tried the keys in the door I found it wasn't double locked, and when I stepped inside I heard retching in the downstairs toilet.

'Mum?' I could tell it was a man being sick, but it didn't cross my mind Dad might be home. All I could imagine was Mum throwing up or a burglar taken ill while lifting our TV.

'It's me.'

I heard Dad's voice and could hardly understand it. Who was minding the shop if he was here?

'Are you all right?'

'Fine.'

I heard him reach for the loo roll, tear a handful, wipe his mouth. He flushed the toilet and the tap ran for as long as it took, I supposed, to wash the taste away. Then I heard the bolt slide back and he stepped out of the toilet and into the hallway, grey and tired.

'Are you ill?'

'I just didn't feel very well.' He walked past me into the kitchen. 'Do you want a cup of tea?'

'Thanks.' I followed him and sat down at the table, head full of a cloud I couldn't put a name to. There was something wrong. I didn't know why it was so clear to me, but I knew his answers, his dismissals, were lies. Something made me want to keep asking him what was wrong. From the vantage point of memory it's hard to swat the idea that even then, at the first warning sign, I knew what was going to happen.

'Did you eat something funny?'

'I don't know.'

There were different kinds of not talking where Dad was concerned. There was an evasiveness that came from being distracted or bored; another that was something like shyness. There was the silence that came from what he thought it meant to be a man, from growing up around men who kept themselves to themselves and called that a virtue. There was also a silence that fell when he didn't want me to find something out, when he tried to conceal a present or holiday until the judicious moment, and it was something like that which I read in him now. Except the secret he was keeping was nothing like a holiday. He was feeling afraid. Diagnosing fear in your father is like watching the ground give way under you, like losing a map while you're out on a moor, like hearing your voice called by someone you're afraid of, like discovering your nightmares might be real, like becoming suddenly uncertain of everything. It is like the ending of the world. I watched him.

'How long have you been feeling ill?'

'I don't know.'

'Do you think you should see a doctor?'

'I don't know.'

I took the tea he offered, and we drank together for a little while with nothing to say to each other. Then he leaned forward. 'Don't tell Mum, will you? She'll only worry.'

I felt myself starting to panic. That was how wrong he thought things might be, that he wanted to keep it from her. All my life I had thought they shared everything. I muttered something in reply, said I had homework to be getting on with. I had to get out of the room. Homework is always a convenient phantom to call up when you want to be on your own. I said nothing to Mum, and Dad and I said no more to each other. But at dinner time and at the breakfast table I watched him, and I could see he was afraid.

It was another week before he picked up the phone and booked an appointment at the surgery on New Street. I lived for that week with a doubt that crept like bindweed. When the balance of possibility and probability finally tipped I wasn't with him. I was at school in an English lesson, reading James Joyce and talking about wanking in *Dubliners*. Dad went out of the shop to get a pint of milk. He doubled over outside the barber's shop, then found he couldn't stand up through the pain and the aching that shot through his body. Someone came out and helped him to a bench. He caught the bus home that evening, and when he got back fished out the number for the doctor.

There was once a boy who discovered he was going to die. The possibility of his death had never occurred to him during the first fifteen years of his life. It had never crossed his mind he might be mortal, let alone that it was in fact inevitable his life was going to end, as sure and natural as the fact of his birth or the fingers on his hands. There had been grandparents, a hamster, a dog, and he had once found the body of a cat in his front garden, suspecting the life had gone out of it and certain when he nudged it with his foot and found it seized up in rigor mortis. It had moved awkwardly over the lawn, the deportment of limbs and head stiff and unchanging as it slid away from him, a piece of a jigsaw pushed across a table. But he had never connected those endings with his own story. None of them had pressed home hard enough.

The diagnosis was so simple that the moment it happened was lost to the boy in the panic it caused. Probing his memory of the particular day when his youth had ended, the boy experienced a curious inability to focus his mind. When you stare at stars in the middle of the night you will sometimes find the one you look at directly will disappear from your vision; only the fires either side, in the periphery of what you see, remain in sight. This was the boy's experience of trying to remember the day he discovered he was going to die. From the corner of his eye it loomed large as the pole star, but when he tried to bring the events of that day to the front of his mind that clarity eluded him. The memory unravelled until all the boy could see was a slew of photo negatives overlaid one on top of the other so the individual images, which might have made sense on their own, started to look like schizophrenia, a thousand voices speaking all at once.

The result of that day was catastrophic. The boy went into something like shock. He couldn't sleep for weeks. It was as if he had fallen through ice into freezing water; his mind and his body seized up, shuddered and shattered by the car crash of this new and remorseless reality. He couldn't talk to anyone, couldn't find a way to express the profundity of what he had learned. Not least because he realised his discovery wasn't profound at all. It was as normal as the morning or the evening. And yet for the boy that knowledge felt like a valley carved through his skull – a sickness that had been in him since birth, only now discovered for the first time as it tore him apart.

Before it all happened I admit I didn't really know what cancer was. I had never known anyone diagnosed with it before, so I wasn't quite sure what was happening to him. I had heard it said that every man in the world died of prostate cancer eventually, if something else didn't get to him first. From that I had acquired the vague, uninterrogated idea that cancer was the way we were designed to die – the way nature stopped us from cluttering up the earth. Till it happened to Dad, I thought of it as the most natural end to a story. I knew it was the body eating itself, so I had a picture of my cells combusting, curling up like leaves in autumn, clotting till they looked like slugs, till my whole body was made from black puddings. But I also knew it could spring up across the body, place after place, so this picture was confused by the thought of tumours, which I imagined swelling like air bubbles in soap or cheese sauce or chocolate. I didn't know where cancers came from. Smokers got them, but they weren't a virus, airborne, infectious, carried by badgers or mosquitoes. They came from inside us. They were like ideas, which swell up in our bodies as well, are part of and not part of us simultaneously. So I thought of cancer in part as the worst idea it was possible to have. Or the idea that came to you when you had lived your life and were ready to die.

It's not like that. It's not normal. It's not natural. It's not easy and it's not like an idea.

There were once two ash trees standing in a clearing. One tree, older and broader in its trunk, began to die from the roots up. First its bark fell off. Then the leaves dried and fell from the lower branches. Then the branches fell to the leaf-strewn ground. Then the wood of the trunk began to soften and dry until it took on the consistency of Styrofoam and started to crack. Then one day the old tree fell with a great crash across the clearing. And the younger tree spread its leaves, which looked so much like the alveoli in a lung, across the blue air left behind by the ash that had fallen. It grew to fill the space, reaching up to the light of the sun.

They told me over breakfast. We always ate together in the mornings, tea and toast and marmalade for them, strawberry jam for me or chocolate spread or greengage jam if Mum had been feeling adventurous the year before. Dad usually had coffee, but not this morning. I came into the kitchen last, as I usually did. He was sitting at the table, staring at his hands. Mum was bustling with the tea cosy, and I wondered whether they were having a row, but I knew what was more likely to have happened. Dad had gone into the hospital for his tests a week before. We had been waiting to hear the results ever since.

'Morning,' I said.

'Morning.' Dad looked up and smiled, but his heart wasn't in it. I thought he looked pale, as if he might have been in pain. Pain is always worst in the morning, whatever the ailment. That's when the fur lies over the tongue and the head

aches and the back is stiff and the legs send shooting pains up
your spine as you swing or crawl your way out of the well of
yourself and the bed you've slept in.

The kitchen was Mum's territory. Some houses organise
themselves around the sitting room or the patio, the
conservatory if there is one, the children's room or the master
bedroom. It depends on the type of person who lives there.
Our house located its pulse in the kitchen. Here Mum kept
up a desperate lie by trying to make one room look perfect,
like the Waltons' kitchen, like a picture in a catalogue. This is
where she papered over the cracks and tried to persuade the
world her family was normal. There was an Aga and two of
the walls were all windows; the sideboards were made from
old school chemistry worktops. If you stuck your head into
the cupboards you could see graffiti on the undersides. There
were always flowers and candles on the table, and the walls
were blue but the room felt green and living because of the
garden pressing its eager face against the windows. Mum
brought the teapot to the table and poured out tea, the steam
rising into light of the morning, where it threaded through
the dust motes and disappeared, perhaps entwining invisibly
above our heads to make a single plume and buffet soft
against the skylights and the mirror on the back wall and
escape through the door into the hallway and the day.

'How did you sleep?' Mum asked.

'Yeah, fine.' I never slept well any more; I lay awake and
thought about Sophie till exhaustion knocked me out, but I
would never have told them that.

'I've had a bit of news just now,' Dad said. He breathed in
slowly, preparing himself. 'The hospital called, and they've

got the results of my tests. And I'm going to need to go in for a few days for a few more assessments and a few other things.' It was typical of Dad not to say out loud that they had told him he had cancer, that it had started in the lungs and already made its way into the lymphs. It was just like Dad not to be able to say chemotherapy out loud. Perhaps anyone would have been as evasive. It must be frightening to stare at your own death, to need to tell your son what was coming. I guessed what he meant. I couldn't have guessed how quickly it was going to happen.

'Right.'

'So I'll be shutting the shop for a bit. It's only a few days, so there's no point looking for cover.'

'OK.'

'I wondered if you'd mind looking in on it whenever you pass?'

'Of course. Have they said how long they want you in for?'

'Just a few days.'

I wanted to believe him. I drank my tea and we got through two rounds of toast. His appetite would fade in the weeks to come until we only made one round in the morning.

3

*T*HERE WAS ONCE *a boy whose father took his family on a last holiday before he went into hospital for a course of che-motherapy. The cancer hadn't been diagnosed till it was already well advanced, so the holiday had to be booked in a hurry because there was only one weekend when it could happen before treatment started. The boy's father booked the first house he found by the sea and drove his son and his wife there to spend three days together.*

The boy's father tried to be cheerful about what was happening, to say a weekend by the sea was just what he needed if he was going to be stuck in bed for a few weeks, but the boy thought it felt more like saying goodbye than charging anyone's batteries. When they arrived they went for a walk, but it couldn't be a long one because the boy's father said he felt tired. They had fish and chips looking over the sea and couldn't think of anything to talk about. The boy's mother started crying, and the boy and his father gave her a hug, but nobody felt any better. On the second day it rained, and they stayed inside reading and trying to play board games, but no one's heart was in it. On the Sunday they went on the same walk and looked out at the same views and the same flat line of the ocean, and wished they hadn't come.

Dad went into hospital. Mum went up to sit with him every evening. I was allowed to visit, but only for an hour a day. Mum said I had to keep doing my school work, that Dad would be home in a week or two. Dad didn't say much.

Odstock hospital is just along the road from us, within sight, give or take a few trees. I walked there every day after school. We'd have a cup of tea and I'd tell Dad what I'd done with the day. Then we'd try to do a crossword or an arrow-word, and when visiting hours finished I would leave to walk home. The lanes through the fields between the hospital and home were like walking through a secret no one else knew. The fields turned blue in the light of evening, and the bird-song was brilliant as a lightshow some dusks. The best walk was by the river at the bottom of the Odstock valley. The silver arrow of the river and the soft earth of the banks, the long, long grass and the puddles that never dried out, the lost tennis balls hiding in the fields and hedgerows where dogs hadn't been able to find them, the scurryings between the dock leaves and nettles that might have been blackbirds or might have been rats or mice.

The concert was on Thursday evening, and Mum and Dad didn't mention it, so I didn't remind them. I thought I might not go, pretend to be ill and hide at home, but I couldn't bear the thought of letting Mr Richardson down. After school on Thursday I walked to St Mark's, back past the swimming pool park, back over the roundabout, wanting something bad to have happened, wanting the concert to be cancelled.

The only consolation lay in the music. I didn't know the Fauré *Requiem* before we started rehearsals. My CD collection was the Stereophonics and Red Hot Chilli Peppers and Foo Fighters and Radiohead and Oasis and Blur and Bob Marley and Placebo and Elbow. The exciting thing about Requiems is that they're put together like the best concept album you've ever listened to. It's even better than Pink Floyd, really – they're all using the same words, so you can set one against the other, Mozart against Verdi, and see what they did with the same material, what shapes their brains made. I liked the Fauré best of all the Requiems I'd heard. The tunes were good. The baritone solo for the 'Libera Me' was great. I clung to this as compensation for the terrible fact that I was going to have to spend an evening in the same room as the girl I loved who didn't love me back.

Someone was standing by the entrance to the church, greeting people as they went inside but not following any of them in. I saw her from a distance – a girl in school uniform, leaning against one of the walls. When I had crossed the roundabout I knew it was her. Sophie and I had spoken a couple of times in the rehearsals since I had walked home with her, but it had been nothing more than saying hello. I had been too afraid of her to say anything more, I had just wanted to keep my distance. She moved away from the wall when she saw me and walked towards me, looking like she was feeling as awkward as I was.

'Hi,' she said.

'Hello.'

'You all right?'

'I'm all right.'

'Do you have to go in? I don't really want to talk to everyone in there yet.'

'No, we're not late, are we?'

She started walking away through the graves and round the west end of the church, and I followed her. She asked me how I'd been, and I didn't know what to say so I told her I was fine. She started to tell me about school, then seemed to tire of the subject, and stopped, and turned to face me.

'How are you getting home tonight? D'you wanna walk home together?'

'Yeah, all right.'

'Your parents aren't giving you a lift?'

'They can't come.'

'They all right?'

'Yeah.' I couldn't have told her anything else. That was the first thing I had discovered when I went into school on the morning after Dad went into hospital – it was impossible for me to formulate the words for what was happening. I hadn't told anyone anything about him.

'And I was gonna say, I'm free this Saturday in the afternoon, if you wanted to go for coffee or something.'

Why on earth would I want to go for coffee? I'd have to sit and think of things to say that weren't embarrassing for a whole hour. Coffee was worse than going for a walk. At least on a walk you saw different things that could start conversations. With coffee you were just sitting in the same place, desperately trying to impress a stranger with nothing but the cobwebbed contents of your head.

'Yeah, coffee would be great. I'm free Saturday.'

She smiled, and I knew that even if it went terribly wrong,

coffee with her would be the happiest thing that ever happened to me, if only she would keep smiling like that.

'Great. And let's walk home after this.'

'Aren't your parents coming?'

'Yeah, but they always slink off with the car. They think I'll spend hours talking to people. So I get left behind. I think they want me to make new friends.' She grinned, as if this was hilarious. 'We should go in, shouldn't we?' Around us the graveyard was emptying as the other singers heard some call from inside, the orchestra clearing its throat or the rap of the baton against the music stand.

I didn't know what I had done to make things better. It couldn't have been as bad as I thought. I sat down next to Adam and grinned at him. He smiled but said nothing. As the concert began, the lights were turned up on the stage for the first time. I could feel the heat on my face, and because the orchestra opened an ocean of space between us and the audience I found I was singing into the dark. We sang some spirituals. Sophie's school sang John Rutter. I watched her, brilliant under the lights. In the interval we didn't talk, but I thought I caught her eye once as she looked across towards me from where she stood with her friends. I couldn't tell exactly where she was looking; the light was behind her. She didn't go over to talk to her family. I supposed the embarrassment of talking to your mum in front of people in your class was as sharp for her as it was for me. But all the same I thought of Mum and Dad and what might be happening to them at that moment.

In the second half we all processed back on together. The Fauré started with the band, and I was swept along with it. If

I timed the look right, in a bar when the boy in front of me moved his head out of the way, I could watch her singing. At the end everyone clapped and it was hard not to feel that they really had enjoyed it, that they hadn't just given up an evening out of duty to hear their children sing. I looked over at Sophie again, but she didn't look back. She went over to her parents. I watched them from a distance, a couple in their forties, maybe they were fifty, well-dressed, kind-looking, civilised-looking people. They smiled. They hugged her. You could see they loved her. They made for the exit, smiling, encouraging her to stay on, go into town, have a drink if she could get served anywhere, have fun. I lowered my head and pretended to be putting my music away when she turned towards the place where we had all dumped our bags. Looking, I realised, for me.

'That was good, wasn't it?' she said. Her eyes were shining and I wanted to reach out and hold her, be part of the happiness visible in her. 'Do you need to hang around, or—'

'No, I'm good to go.'

I walked past the whole audience of parents and schoolchildren and out of the church with my head held high and my heart bursting, because even though no one noticed us going, even though we weren't really the centre of attention at all, I felt like nothing else in the world was as important as we were for as long as it took us to walk out of that church together in front of everyone.

This time I walked her to her front gate. She stopped, leaned on the post and said, 'This is me. So shall we go for coffee on Saturday?'

'Yeah, that'd be cool.'

She looked at me, and I had the strangest feeling that what she was waiting for now was a kiss. It couldn't be possible. She couldn't mean it. She was just being nice to me, she was just wonderful; she didn't fancy me, she couldn't.

'What's your number then?' she said. 'So we can work out where to meet.'

'Oh yeah.' I gave her my number and she pranked my phone so I had hers.

'Right. I'd better get home then,' I said.

'Are your parents home?'

'Why?'

'They couldn't come to the concert, so I thought they might be out.'

'Oh. Yeah. They'll be home by now.'

'I was going to say you could come in for a cup of tea if you fancied it.'

If I hadn't known better, I would have thought she was asking me into her house. But it couldn't have happened.

'I'd better get home, really. Thanks though.'

She shrugged, put her hand on the latch of the gate, and I wanted to hold her.

'That's all right. See you at the weekend then?'

'All right.'

'OK.'

'Night then.'

'Night.' I turned and walked back down the road the way I had come, headed for the swimming pool park and the two miles home. Such well-worn miles, but they both seemed new, box-fresh this evening. I heard her open and close the gate, heard her key in the lock of her front door, her parents' voices rising to meet her, 'Bravo' ringing down the street behind me. Nothing has ever been more perfect than that walk home, remembering what had just happened, hoping for no more than that, not even dreaming any more of a kiss or the woman in the porn film with the plumber. All that mattered was the feeling that carried me home.

Mum was still out when I got back. I hated nights like that, because it meant Dad hadn't been feeling well. Mum turned her mobile off on the ward, like you were supposed to, so I couldn't call her, and it was eleven o'clock, far too late to go over. He must have felt very ill for her still to be out. Perhaps she would stay at the hospital all night.

I got out my phone and there was a text from Sophie. *Thanks for walking me home. X.* I read it five, six times. I had her phone number. I could never have imagined in my wildest dreams that someone like that would ever let me have their phone number. I typed a reply. *Pleasure. See you at the weekend hopefully. Xx.* The second kiss was agony. I made myself a sandwich then checked my phone again. There was another text from her. *Definitely. X x x.* I sat down on my bed but didn't undress. I knew I wouldn't sleep if I tried now, there was no chance for hours yet. I looked down at my shoes and wished I had the money to buy new ones. I would have to work out what to wear on Saturday. Whenever I talked to her I felt as if there was another conversation, real speech, contained in the looks between us. A tension in the air that felt like ours and no one else's, where things were actually being said, not small talk. I was never quite able to hear it, couldn't quite make out the words. But I knew they were there all the same.

*

There was once a boy who was afraid of everything. Other people could walk quite calmly down the street as if nothing was happening, but to this boy the whole world seemed like a pit of jaws longing to snap shut round him. It was his curse to be born with an overactive imagination, and he saw the potential disaster in all things. Shops could topple forwards and crush him; wiring could burst into flames; a bath might be filled too full to the brim and become too heavy for the floorboards and crash down on to his head. This was to say nothing of asteroids or lightning or sharks. Because of his terror at the possibility of anything happening to him at any moment, the boy couldn't live or enjoy himself at all. He stayed at home, ate as little as he could because food was full of dangers, and only touched things passed to him by people he trusted. He never saw anyone in case they decided they wanted to kill him or infected him with illnesses they didn't know they had.

The boy's mother and father told each other they were half the problem. If they weren't around he would have to find his own food and leave his room; by dribs and drabs he would have to live. One night, making as little noise as possible, they packed a suitcase and left. They would live for a time in another country. They hoped when they came home they would have cured their son.

The boy realised at once what had happened when no one came to feed him the next morning. With no one to help him get what he needed, he was going to have to overcome his fear of the world.

Dressing in clothes without buttons or zips, so nothing could stab him, he walked up to the door of his bedroom, took a deep breath and opened it. When nothing happened, when the world didn't end, he stepped out on to the landing. He made himself walk round the house, waiting for something to lash out and scald him. He went into the bathroom and practised turning on taps. He began to experiment with the shower head, starting back every time the water flowed. Taking his whole heart into his mouth, he took off his clothes and stood in the bathtub while the shower ran ice-cold down his back. Still the world did not end. He went downstairs to the kitchen and opened the fridge. He took out a piece of cheese and ate it. He took out a bottle of milk and drank. He began to believe he could do this. He could learn to live. He opened all the drawers in the kitchen, picked up a carving knife. The urge to drive it into his eyes did not overwhelm him. The boy put the knife back down, crossed the room, opened a window and breathed in the air. Then he found the spare keys, unlocked the front door and went outside. He walked out of the garden gate, hobbled shaking and sobbing over the road and into the fields beyond, hardly able to believe what he was capable of if he forced himself.

The boy lived at the very edge of Salisbury, in a place that had once been a village in its own right but had long ago been swallowed up as the city grew. Immediately around his house was a new estate, but a path still ran through those houses to a playing field and an undulating view of slope fields beyond, old holloways and drovers' paths you might have been able to walk back in time along till you got to a year before the city was even thought of, sloe hedges and a river curling like smoke at the bottom of the deepest dip in the fields. This had been the boy's playground when he was very young. Here, he had seen a buzzard startled up out of the hedgerows, skylarks bursting bright and sudden as their song from the cover of grasses and crops, and he had visited the gypsies' horses that were always tethered there, cropping the grass into UFO circles prescribed by the length of their securing chain. It was to these the boy now made his way; if he could look one in the eye, perhaps even step into the circle of short grass where it could reach him, then he would have become braver than he could remember being in the longest time, since he was very young, since he was new and not afraid of anything.

He found one at the very top of the first field he entered past the playground, an old mare puffing and blowing in the heat of the day and lapping at a bucket of water someone had left her. The boy forced himself not to run away. Even in the teeth of his fear he remembered something, an echo of an older time. He watched the old nag's face as it slobbered at the water and remembered that horses were beautiful. The mare looked up from her drink, saw him, went as still as the boy was. The boy stepped forward, and nothing happened. He stepped forward again, into the circle of short grass where the horse could reach him, and waited. He stepped forward one more time and patted the horse on the nose.

Suddenly he could do anything. He could feel the change happening inside him. It was as if the pillow he was resting his head on had been turned to face the other way up and he had discovered a new coolness around him. Everything was different. All the time he had been hiding from the dangers of the world, life had only seemed dangerous because of what he was thinking, not what was actually around him. All he had ever needed to do was change the way he thought. His first emotion was grief. He had thrown great shovels of his youth away for no reason. He had never made a friend. He lived off memories ten years old and had no more recent life to speak or think of.

He would make up for lost time, for years when he had experienced nothing. He would put himself in the way of every danger he could imagine. He wheeled away from the horse and looked around him for something to risk.

*

I looked at my phone again. I went out into the hall and took my coat from its peg by the front door. Looking behind me once, checking I had a key, I opened the front door and stepped out into the night.

The strangest feeling in the world is knowing your dad might be dying, or that there is a war, or that a bomb has gone off somewhere, and still being distracted by hunger or shopping or homework or who you fancy. I don't know how I ever thought of anything other than Dad in those last weeks we had together, but I would spend whole hours not thinking of him every day.

It was colder, and a night wind had brought cloud cover overhead, hiding the stars. The moon was visible as a pale blush to the clouds. I did my coat up and put my hands in my pockets. Down the hill into town, past the cathedral lit by floodlights, along Exeter Street past the Guildhall up Endless Street then right till I came to the swimming pool park, till I came to her house. I walked down the street till I got back to where I had left her. I looked at the upstairs window and wondered what the hell I was doing. I picked up a handful of gravel from the square of front garden of the house next door and threw it at what I guessed from the fairy lights round the frame must be her window. The stones rattled briefly like rain, and as I stood waiting a fine rain began to fall. After a couple of seconds a light went on in her room, pouring out in a yellow glow through the curtains. I pulled the collar of my coat up round my neck and watched as the curtains opened, tentative, light of the room silhouetting Sophie above me. She saw me, leaned forward, opened the window.

4

THERE WAS ONCE *a boy who got everything he wanted. In the arms of a girl he loved, he found perfect happiness. They went on expeditions into the New Forest, caught a bus to North Gorley and vanished into a landscape buried in gorse till she said she was hungry. They laid out a picnic blanket. He took out Oranginas in their fig-like bottles and they sat down with their legs crossed, facing each other. She took from her purse a packet of baccy, Rizla papers and a bag of hash, and rolled, cupping her hands to her face so he heard rather than saw the flame's flaring. He pretended he'd done it before, but she guessed and laughed when he coughed. She took the spliff back off him.*

'Come here.' She filled her lungs and put her mouth to his, opening his lips with the tip of her tongue and breathing in. They had sex for the first time there on the bank among the rabbit warrens. He doubted he lasted a minute. But for as long as his mouth was on her breasts, as she pulled his jeans clear of his heels, not speaking, not quite stoned enough to lose all self-consciousness, as long as he held the white instep of her foot and her nails scored him, touching, loving, they felt as though they had invented something.

They went to the cathedral, doing the tour for the first time, seeing the view and the thirteenth-century graffiti, the builders' names carved into the wall. She took a disposable camera and they snapped each other all the way round, leaning out over parapets, smiling shyly, standing in the tower, sitting in the cloisters. Hardly any of the pictures came out once the film was developed. But there was one of the boy sitting in the cloisters she said was nice. She kept it in her purse and gave him a picture of her eating an ice cream on holiday by the sea. He put it in his wallet and looked at it in lessons. He carried the thought of her and the image of her every-where. If that had been all of his life, if that could have been the only thing in his life, he would have been perfectly happy.

But none of it matters when your dad starts losing his hair; none of it matters when you come home and find your dad back from the hospital and sitting at the table in the kitchen again, waiting to tell you bad news, again. He wished he could tell her the truth. But something always stopped him from saying the awful words out loud. So he kept it from her, and the silence ate him up.

There was once a boy who fell in love with a balloon. He chased it through the streets of Salisbury, over the hills, over mountains and through rainclouds and out across the sea. He chased it through France, Spain, Portugal, all the way down the coast of Africa, up the Zambezi, through the dark woodland of the Congo. He chased it through the townships of Pretoria, across the field of a rugby international, eyes fixed all the time on a red balloon that hovered in the sky, never wavering. He chased it through shoals of killer whales and packs of penguins. He chased it to Antarctica. When the balloon got to the South Pole it finally gave up, stopped and waited. The boy staggered to meet it. When the boy held the balloon, put his arms around it at long last, it popped.

I went to see her after school. We walked round the back of her school, to the water meadows beyond the new leisure centre, into a wide field with a river running through it, and I laid her down and I kissed her and she wrapped her legs around me. I walked home in the evening, smiling, tired, a strength in my arms and legs that was like love coursing through me. He was sitting at the table and Mum was upstairs in their bedroom. Mum was crying. I heard her later when I went up the stairs.

'Sam, they've seen how I've responded to the first course of chemo and they've decided not to go through another. It hasn't actually done very much to slow the rate of – it hasn't actually done very much. So I'm back now, and that's good, and the good news is my hair will start to grow back! But the cancer's not going to go away, Sam. Do you understand what that means?' He couldn't say it. I couldn't say it either. I went to my room, and me and Mum and Dad sat in our different cocoons in the house and cried, and none of us thought to get us together so we could all cry in the same room.

The lease on the shop was put up for sale, and until someone bought it the shop was boarded up. I couldn't believe it had become as black and white as a phone call to an estate agent, a situation explained to a bank manager, the nails hammered in. Dad came home, and there was a lot of new medicine in the bathroom, painkillers mostly, nothing to cure him. Even at the start it had already been too late for that. I should have been there every day. I should have spent every evening sitting with him. But I had discovered Sophie

Lawrence, and night after night I left him and Mum alone at the top of the hill and went into town with her instead, went to her house, went to the movies.

I knew she wasn't serious about me. I knew it was a passing thing, something I had made happen, something she would grow out of. So I had to drink up every second of her time while I could, I had to be near her. I didn't let myself think about what was happening at home. I didn't tell her about Dad. We never went up the hill to mine; hers was easier. I told white lies, said he was under the weather, said it might be pneumonia. I couldn't let anything interrupt this moment while she was mad enough to want to spend her time with me.

When I did go home we always ate guilt and silence for dinner: guilt because I hadn't been there enough, silence because I didn't know how to ask Dad how he was, what was happening to him, how he felt. I didn't know how many more times I would see him. And a grief none of us knew how to speak out loud hung in the air, following us from room to room like cloud cover, like a fire that was choking us all. We watched TV in the same room. We ate at the same time, at the same table. We washed up the same plates and cups and cutlery. We were never together. Dad would ask about Sophie. He tried to be happy, to tease me. I suppose he must have thought at least it was something to have lived long enough to see his son have his first girlfriend. But his heart wasn't in it. We could still talk about football. That was safe ground, the neutral territory we had always migrated to when we had been in need of a conversation. Men can always talk about football and avoid baring anything, exposing wounds or bones or terrors to each other. You could dodge any issue with Southampton FC. It wasn't real speech, real sharing, just the batting of a ball of words from one mouth to another, but it kept out the silence. So we stuck to football and didn't make eye contact while we spoke. Then one afternoon I came home and Dad was in the sitting room and Mum was still out.

'Sam?'

I put my bag down in the hall and stood in the sitting room doorway. He was reading a paper, glasses on the end of his nose. This was all he could do now he had stopped working. He got too tired going for walks. He paced round the house instead, read, slept, passed the days. It seemed so unfair that there might be so few hours left to him and the very thing which was making them rare, making them precious, should also ensure he had so little energy he couldn't do anything, ended up bored for the last hundred days of his life.

'All right?' I said.

He shrugged.

'Yeah. You?'

'I'm all right.'

'Come and sit down for a second.'

'Everything all right?' I said.

'Yeah. I just wanted to talk to you about your mum.'

'Oh. Right.'

'You're going to have to look after her. Next year, for as long as you're around. You understand that?'

'Yeah.'

'You're going to have to be good for her and not be any trouble, because I'm causing her trouble enough.'

'You're not causing trouble, Dad.'

'In a way I am.'

I looked at my hands balled up in my lap and tried not to cry.

'You're not causing trouble.'

Dad stood, awkwardly, slowly, the strain showing in his face.

'D'you want a cup of tea?'

'All right. Thanks.'

'I'm going to have to go back into hospital quite soon, Sam. Understand? And you have to be good to your mother.'

I nodded. I had to close my eyes.

'Yeah.'

He went into the kitchen, and I should have run after him and held him, but I didn't. I sat and blinked back tears in the sitting room armchair on the carpet I shouldn't have been walking on in my shoes, until the flood receded, until I could bury myself and my feelings again. Then I went into the kitchen.

Sophie was the only thing that stopped me from screaming. Seeing her, being with her, that dulled the feeling, helped me almost forget for an hour or two. I went into town after school the next day, wanting to be away from Dad, from the sorrow in the house, and knocked at her door. If only he had told me what would happen to him. If only he had said out loud what he must have known.

It was her dad who answered. He smiled when he saw me but stood in the doorway so I couldn't see past.

If Dad had only told me how he was feeling I wouldn't have gone there in the first place. I would have stayed home and done anything, if only something had been possible. I wouldn't have left his side.

'Hello, Sam.'

'Hi. Is Sophie in?'

'She is, but she's a bit preoccupied this evening. She's got a bit on her hands. On her mind. Would you be able to call her tomorrow maybe?' His hand didn't leave the doorframe. He was going to shut me out, leave me out in the street with my solitude and my madness, and I didn't understand, didn't want to leave. I wanted to see her. Why would she shut me out tonight?

If only Dad had told me.

'Is she all right?'

'She's fine; it's just work. Sorry, Sam.'

I felt like I was going to cry. Mr Lawrence seemed to notice, seemed to want to step forward in concern, to reach out a hand – 'Are you all right?'

'Yeah, fine.'

'Are you sure?'

'Yeah, I'm fine.'

I walked away, getting as far as the swimming pool park, then sat on a bench and texted her. *You ok? X* I waited. The streets of Salisbury fell away before me, sloping down into the river basin, into the floodplain and the cathedral at the heart of it, jutting like a plug from the navel of the city. Ten minutes passed and my phone vibrated. *So sorry. I had a boyfriend last year who went away to uni. He's come back and I'm explaining to him about you. Don't worry. X.*

I got up and walked into town.

I didn't know it then, but I had already missed my last

chance at time with him. I would never see him in the house again. I would miss the moment the ambulance took him away.

Getting served in Salisbury is easy. There are almost as many pubs as people. That's what happens when you've got half the army training up the road. I went to the Chough in the Market Square, asked for a lager and didn't get asked for ID. I sat in the corner and drank it. I had another. I went outside to call her. The woman who ran the flower stall opposite the Cross Keys was having a fag, leaning against the brick of the building and watching the cars slide past.

'You all right?' she said. 'Look pigsick.'

'I'm all right.' I called Sophie but she didn't pick up.

'You old enough to be drinking?' the flower woman said.

'Yeah.'

'You're about fifteen, aren't you?'

'No.'

'It doesn't help,' she said. 'It really doesn't.'

Her flower stall was nowhere to be seen, and I wanted to ask her what happened to it, but she looked sad, so I kept quiet. I went back inside and got another beer. I had ten quid left in my wallet. I went into Tesco and bought a bottle of vodka, and an old bloke with watery eyes didn't ID me at the till. His hands were shaking, and I thought, I never want to get old. I went outside again and looked around for somewhere to drink. I went into the park behind Tesco. I called her again but she didn't pick up.

He and I would never go into town together again. What if everyone in the world was as sad as I was and only some of us showed it? What if the whole world was sorry it was living?

He would never drive me anywhere ever again.

I called again. She didn't answer. I started to cry because my dad was dying and I couldn't swallow the vodka without a mixer. A text came. *Can't talk now. Don't worry. Talk later. X*

I got up and started walking.

I walked to Dad's shop and peered through a bit of window that hadn't been properly covered over. I could see my own eyes squinting back in the glass and hated them, their small-ness, their paleness. I felt like everyone coming in or out of the Anchor & Hope on the other side of the road would see me for what I was, wretched and clueless, someone to pity or bully or ignore. At the junction of Winchester Street and Brown Street I saw the lamps of a car coming towards me. I watched as it approached the corner. The engine noise rose and drowned out the night. That was why I didn't hear the bike. At the very last moment before the car swung right, a rider on a moped came out of Brown Street into the path of the bigger vehicle, a bluebottle humming dumbly forward, going half the speed of the monster that gnawed into it there outside McDonald's in the place where the two roads met. The moped was flattened and the rider, head looking ridiculously oversized in her helmet, was flung across the ground in my direction. The car went into a skid, into the front of the second-hand store ten feet along the road. The night was torn open by the huge sound of the shop window shattering. I heard the thump of the moped rider hitting a bollard and looked over to see her curled unnaturally round the iron pole as if she were protecting it. The moped was caught under the bonnet of the car and had been dragged into the antique shop. There was noise behind me, the door of the Anchor & Hope flung open, light and voices and people pouring out to see what had happened. I walked up to the rider. She wasn't moving. I could see her hands were curled into balls, feet tucked up under her. She had curled up like paper in a fire as she flew through the air. I reached for my mobile, but then a man walked past me and crouched down in front of the body, already talking on his phone, asking for an ambulance.

'She's not moving.'

I watched him. He seemed calm, certain of how he should face the situation. I envied his confidence, the ease with which he leaned forward to put a hand on her shoulder, the octave his voice dropped when he said into the telephone, 'She's not conscious. I don't want to move her.' I watched other men rush past me to the car, grown men who knew what to do.

I was frozen by the memory of an accident I had seen when I was seven years old. Mum had been walking me to school and we saw a woman walk in front of a lorry. I don't know whether she knew what she was doing. There was a half-scream cut short as the lorry ploughed into her. She went under like a piece of paper going into a printer. Mum covered my eyes and pulled me away, and we took no part in getting an ambulance out to clear up what I suppose must have been the scattered phrases of her. Mum dragged me the rest of the way to school, and I spent the day trying not to think about what had happened. I expected us to talk that evening, but when I got home nothing was said. I never found out whether Dad had been told what I saw.

That had been years ago, a tragedy happening almost too fast for me to take in. But now as I watched a crowd gather round the body of the moped rider it felt like someone was reaching into my stomach and wrenching at what they found. I was lost in the feeling of trying to look back while Mum pulled me away. Standing on the street with the vodka inside me I felt as weak and confused as I had been then, as helpless.

The mind is like a floodplain. The slightest rainfall can leave it awash with old stories that seep into your newer terrors and swell them, drown you under long-forgotten feelings as your life rushes back over you. From the market square I saw the flashing lights of an ambulance approaching. I started to walk. I knew they'd want to talk to everyone who saw the accident, and I didn't want to talk to anyone. I walked away from the poor broken body, the mangled snub nose of the car in the shop front, through Brown Street car park and along Endless Street. I walked out of town, over the ring road, through Vicky Park past the rugby pitches until I could see Old Sarum against the horizon. I didn't know where I was going. I just knew I didn't want to be near the accident and I couldn't go home to Dad. If only I had, one last time.

I kept walking till I got to the Harvester at the foot of Old Sarum. The hill fort was visible as a denser darkness blotting the night around. I started down into the trench that circled the fort. The banks were thick with nettles that stung my hands, but I kept going, feet sliding on the earth below the overgrown grass, moving so I wouldn't have to stop and think. I got to the bottom of the trough and walked out from under the yew trees, looking up at the next slope. The inner defences were much steeper. I waited a moment to catch my breath. I started to climb again.

On an ordinary day I would have stopped before I got to the top. It was too steep to be safe. Halfway up I thought I was going to fall. I grabbed handfuls of grass and held on, dragging myself up when my body started to tire, till I reached the lip of the settlement. It was ringed by a waist-high fence. I would have to stand up at the top of the whole steep slope, lungs red with breathing, and swing my leg over the wire, so that for a moment I would be pirouetting eighty feet in the air, clear night opening around to catch me and wrap me in an infinity of broken backs and splintered necks and lying in ditches till morning came and a Japanese tourist found me and a paramedic pronounced me dead. I performed the manoeuvre without disaster and levered myself into Old Sarum.

Old Sarum is a ruin now, but the foundations remain and the moon lights them up pale and shining and flinty after dark. From where I stood I could see the placement of the buildings laid out like a map, like an idea expressed in stone. The cellars and underground stores were still sunk deep into the ground, and here and there the blue light of the moon on grass fell away into pools of deep darkness that marked their position. These were all ringed with stones, the last resting places of a thousand lives that had been lived here and forgotten long ago. I thought I would walk around them. I thought I would look down into the cellar spaces that survived. I thought I would wait somewhere absolutely quiet till my heart stopped beating so hard. From one side of Old Sarum there was a view of the city, all orange lights mapping out the streets and the warm glow of hall lights falling into the street through house windows, and above and beyond it all the spire of the cathedral lit up and rising serenely into the night to greet Orion's belt and the stars around it. On the other side, Old Sarum looked out over farmland. Quiet land. Arable fields ploughed and left for weeks on end for life to gather and grow there and be harvested again. This view, in the middle of the night, was nothing more than a stretch of wheat or grass that faded away into the absolute darkness of the night and the far distance of the west of England. No streetlights, no houses, only the dark for miles. I wanted to stop for a little while, loiter with the ruins and stare into that.

I hadn't walked ten feet when I knew there was someone else there. There was a light on in the gift-shop Portakabin by the entrance. I could make out the dim sound of a radio playing. I looked around. I couldn't explain why I had climbed up here, but the moonlight on the stones of the old grain stores and cathedral was beautiful, and I felt sad I wouldn't get to explore it, as I realised it must be a security guard. There was no point in hiding. If there was a guard it was better to go to him than let him catch me. I walked towards the sound of talk radio, that seemed to be coming not from the Portakabin but a car parked next to it. When I was ten feet away the car exploded into sound and fury, and I saw through the rear windscreen the teeth and hackles and rage of an Alsatian. The driver's door was flung open and a boy bundled out who didn't look much more than five years older than me. He looked me up and down. Watching his fear I felt myself begin to calm, eyeing the dog that beat its muzzle on the window but feeling safer now, because the guard was a boy as surprised as I was.

'What are you doing here?' he said.

'I was lost. Sorry.'

'You were lost?'

'I was walking and I didn't know where I was.'

'Are you on your own?'

'Yeah.'

He relaxed visibly.

'You're not supposed to be up here. How did you get in?'

'I climbed.'

'Wasn't it steep?' He shook his head as if in admiration. 'You're lucky you timed it right; I was going to let the dog out in five.'

I looked again at the car's rear window. The boy seemed to decide to be lenient with me. 'I'll have to escort you off, all right? Down to the main road. Will you know where you are from there?'

'Yeah, I think so.'

'And don't come up here again, all right, because he bites.'

'Right.'

'This way.' He gestured past him to the site's main gates, closed off and spiked at the top so you couldn't get over them. I walked past him, and he fell into step next to me.

'So do you sit up here every night then?'

'Yeah.'

'Where are you from?'

'Salisbury.'

'Oh yeah.'

'I've been away. I just moved back. I'm Liam.'

'Sam.' It seemed amazing to me that all the time my life had been going on, there had been a bloke sitting up here nights, oblivious to me or anything else happening, just sitting here waiting for moments like this one and listening to the radio.

'Do you get a lot of people coming in?' I asked.

'I've never had it before actually. You gave me a fright.' We could see the Harvester from the gate. He bent down to work a padlock, then swung one of the gates half open.

'So don't come back up here, yeah?'

'OK. Thanks.'

'No worries. Just don't climb in again.'

I turned and left him to his private kingdom. Once I was back on the road I looked around and wondered what I was going to do.

I would walk in her direction, back to the swimming pool park. Not to talk to her. Just to be near where she was.

Mr Lawrence answered the door. I could see in his face how I looked.

'Sam? Are you all right? You ought to come in.'

'I won't come in.'

'You ought to.'

'I can't, I don't want to annoy . . .'

I couldn't get any further. I couldn't say her name because it was too sad. She didn't want me. I could tell. I could smell it in the air. She didn't want me any more; someone better had won her back. And I had never told her about my dad, and now there was no one I could share it with. I started to cry.

'Come on, Sam. Come and sit down,' he said.

He led me into his sitting room and helped me down on to the sofa. I wanted to talk to him and tell him I wasn't coming in, I didn't want to come in, but there was another noise in the room that was too distracting, a deep moan like someone had something terribly wrong with them, like someone was in terrible pain. It took me a moment to realise I was sobbing, deep sobs getting the bends as they came up for air.

Sophie came down the stairs. She looked at me from the doorway. I couldn't speak. She watched while Mr Lawrence pushed me back into the sofa, laid my head on a cushion while the world ended around me.

'Sam?' she said.

'Yeah.'

'Are you all right?'

'He's very drunk,' Mr Lawrence said. 'We should get him home.'

'Shouldn't we let him sleep it off here?' she said.

'I won't come in,' I said.

She sat down. She put her palm on my forehead. I wanted to hold her but I couldn't move.

'You are in, Sam.'

The whole world was ending around me, and as I passed out I tried to imagine myself driving away from it all in a car with my dad, getting out of the place we were in, getting to the seaside, taking our shoes off, drowning our feet in the water.

There was once a boy who was trapped in a car going somewhere he was afraid of. It was very dark outside the vehicle; he couldn't see anything, except sometimes bright lights flashed by. When that happened he heard people shouting, but he couldn't see where they were. It looked very cold on the other side of the glass, but inside the car it was too hot. The boy started to sweat; he couldn't help it.

He wasn't driving the car. It sped through the night alone, and the boy couldn't get out of the passenger seat. He didn't know exactly where he was being taken. All he knew was that he couldn't slow or alter his progress, and he was heading somewhere bad. By the light of the headlamps he counted osiers on either side of the road – twelve, thirteen, fourteen, like a scoreboard until he felt sick. One side was in leaf, the other had been cut right back. They looked like thigh bones sticking out of the ground. He had the feeling that as soon as he passed each tree it didn't exist any more, but he couldn't turn his head to check. The car sped through a pack of horses weaving in between each other right across the road, shoaling like fish, like clouds, running fast, not getting anywhere. The car went right through them and the horses were all around but somehow none of them went under the wheels. As soon as he had passed them the boy was sure the horses didn't exist any more. The car took off and started to head up into absolute night. The boy wondered what you flew too close to when there was no sun in the sky.

And that was where I woke the next morning to find half a dozen missed calls on my phone and a text from Mum telling me Dad had gone back into hospital and asking where on earth I was. I could hear Sophie and her parents in the kitchen. I thought about going to see them or writing a note, but then I realised it didn't matter. None of them would talk to me again now. I had been so stupid. My head hurt so much and I wanted to throw up. I tiptoed out of the sitting room, let myself out of the house and walked into town. I knew I ought to go to the hospital. I knew he was lying there; I didn't know for how much longer. All I could think about was Sophie: her face as I passed out, her kind face, her lips I would never kiss again because I had been so stupid, the way I had lost her. I played her back like a film reel.

I couldn't go up to the hospital and didn't feel ready to climb the hill for home. I headed for the close and the great impassive sight of the cathedral gliding through sky and history while my life raced by under it, a pebble beneath the wet belly of a river, hardly rippling its hide. And my head split open with each step, and I wanted to take it in my hands and crush till yolk spilled out and the shell was pressed between the flesh of my fists. Entering the close from the High Street and stopping to stare when the spire reels into view, the picture is enough to break your neck as you crane to gulp it. What you see is more than the day around you. Other lives lurk under the thin skin of the world. Your own, of course. Almost visible to you are the other times you've looked up at that view. Where you stood, who you stood with, what you were feeling. But in the shadow of a very great monument you get to feel you're treading water in the wash of other people's afternoons as well. As if a mirror might hold some trace of the last person who looked in it, a ghost who looked back into you.

That's how it is with a thing like grief as well. It lies oil-slick over everything you do. It will pour out through the gaps in the most ordinary afternoons.

I didn't look left or right as I crossed the little road to reach the grass and was secretly pleased when I wasn't mown down by a verger or lay clerk on a bicycle, as if I had taken on the Green Cross Code and won. I passed the statue of the Walking

Madonna. Some misty winter nights walking home she had a way of looming out of the whiteness as you passed that was almost like movement. She might have seen so much in this place if they had only carved her eyes a little better. People walking towards their God, kids making out and smoking and eating pizzas and sniffing glue on the benches at the edges of the close. The trees were bowing low after the rain to weep and console the grass beneath them.

I wanted to cry and I couldn't. I wanted to be sick and I couldn't throw up. If the world turns its face against you, there are ways of fighting back. Or if you don't have the strength for that, you can hide somewhere for a little while.

I went into the cathedral. I walked past the donation kiosk, nodding to the woman sitting behind it, because you don't have to pay, they only want you to think it's compulsory, and went into the tree-high hull, roots of the roof darning together above my poor head. There were rows of empty chairs. I sat down near the back, not looking at anything. This was killing time. I had no reason to be here. I would just sit still for as long as I could bear and then I would go home. The place meant nothing, except it gave me access to memories of other times spent here, processing or watching prize days or singing in the choir. Nothing happy or unhappy, just days in my life. The mind slides back and forth, imagining tomorrow, free-associating endlessly from memory to memory because each day always seems to suggest another you have already lived, to pull you further back into the past. Of course the past is denser and pulls us more closely into its orbit. The present is only ever one day long. The past grows richer and subtler each day as it snakes behind you all the way back to the source and centre of your life.

'Excuse me?'

I wiped my eyes and looked up to see a woman dressed as my mother peering down at me. She had a green sash over one shoulder, so I knew she was a tour guide. They were sad people. Talking to them, you got the impression they volunteered not quite out of love for this place or anything it meant but because it was better than sticking your head in the oven or going back through the *Radio Times* once more just in case you'd missed something worth reading. They seemed to live alone. Their children were the sort who forgot to visit. She would have seen me come in without paying. She would have come over to give me a piece of her mind. There was something kinder, more solicitous in her face than that story, but I knew what she wanted to say.

'Yes?'

'Would you like an order of service?'

'What?'

'An order of service. We're about to start.' She held a piece of paper out towards me. I looked down at her small soft hands, the nails unpainted, took the paper and thanked her. She walked away without a second glance at my bloodshot eyes or the hair hanging lank across my face. I watched her all the way to the chancel, where she disappeared from view. The service sheet had a logo on the front I didn't recognise – I never came to church for the religion, so I never really looked at the handouts. The organ started playing, and I looked up to see there was a man in the pulpit. Thirty or forty people sitting further forward had stood up, presumably at the chaplain's or vicar's or bishop's suggestion. Habit and the strength in my legs took me over. I found myself standing in turn, like a Mexican wave washing round the empty section of a stadium. I leafed through the hymn book just fast enough to have time to look back up and wonder what I was doing when the organist got through the introduction and we started to sing.

> *Dear Lord and Father of mankind*
> *Forgive our foolish ways*
> *Reclothe us in our rightful mind*
> *In purer lives thy service find*
> *In deeper reverence praise*
> *In deeper reverence praise.*

The miracle of a ritual. I felt my shoulders begin to ease. I thought to myself, I don't want to believe in this. But when you run a story through your neural pathways like a line of beads through your hands, it stands to reason you unblock them, and your own life flows through afterwards, rushing out of the oxbow lakes of the plans you didn't see through to their conclusion, the phrases that wouldn't come till long after it was too late to use them. A hymn, nothing more than a tune and a string of words someone had invented, was somehow making things feel better.

> *Drop thy still dews of quietness*
> *Till all our strivings cease*
> *Take from our souls the strain and stress*
> *And let our ordered lives confess*
> *The beauty of thy peace*
> *The beauty of thy peace.*

Prayer and faith didn't need to be hated really, even if they weren't mine. They were just a route people took to a place where they could be safe and think and listen. Sometimes the church seemed like a cruel runner's-up prize, a compensation for people who couldn't be happy in their own lives. Better luck next time, sort of thing. A way to fill a gap, keep people quiet. But as I sang, the picture changed. It was so clear once you were in flight that the church, like any other ritual, was nothing but a ladder to help you reach the high fruit of a feeling. And then to kick away and soar.

Breathe through the heats of our desire
Thy coolness and thy balm
Let sense be dumb, let flesh retire
Speak through the earthquake, wind and fire
O still small voice of calm
O still small voice of calm.

I wished I was holding her now, that she was with me. I wished he wasn't lying now in the bed in the hospital, rationing each breath like sweets or painkillers till he came to the last.

I didn't go up for the bread and wafer or the blessing on my head. I listened, dried my eyes, sang again when the appropriate moments came round like choruses. The rhythm of that ritual was a song in itself, just as day and night or anything you choose to name looks like verse and chorus in a certain slant of light. When the service ended I stood up and left. There was a lightness in me that was like wanting to tell someone something extraordinary, wanting to speak out loud and affirm in the sound of my voice the fact that I was alive and asking questions, but my head still beat a rhythm like the sobbing of someone who has been crying a long time. I walked down to the far end of the close, towards Harnham, my village at the edge of the city, past a cricket pitch where the England team were supposed to have once played a match some time between the wars, past yew trees, through a black-bird's song, listening to the crunch of gravel till I passed through St Anne's Gate and out of sight of the cathedral.

All this happened in what seems like the long ago now. I turned sixteen just the other day, a hard birthday to celebrate when your dad's not there, because of course it's hard to know what it means to become a man when he's no longer around to show you. So I had my cake with Mum, I went to school, and after school I thought about what I had learned in the last year. All I could say I knew any more about was the past. But I thought if I could meet my younger self, sit down over a Diet Coke with the boy I was, knowing what I do about what was about to happen to his life, I would tell him to go to bed early so he never lost any of the last days of his childhood to lying around. I would tell him every day he didn't keep a diary was a library he was burning, because already there is an island of small things whose coordinates are lost to me, whose forms were too intricate and delicate to survive the transit of the passage of time in the mind alone. I might have so much more life to live when I will have to rely on nothing but the outlines of memories of that year for my sustenance, days I can only see as the imprint of a body in a bed, not the body itself. I should have taken photographs.

I would tell him his life doesn't start when he leaves school; he's already in it. It has been passing since the day he was born, and everything he puts off, chooses not to do or say because he is hoarding experience for his real, adult life isn't a thing safeguarded but a treasure risked. The world is full of things put off for the wrong reasons, which can suddenly become impossible without any warning. They hang in the air like ghosts, their mouths and eyes sewn up for ever. They will never be able to speak, but if it was you who put them there, you will always be forced to see them.

I would tell him that doors have a way of closing.

I would tell him the things he does with his days aren't his real life. School and going into town and TV and team sport are only the surface he should dig beneath, because his real life runs deeper than that. It is his family, his heart, births, marriages, deaths, friendships, other people. I would tell him the world is other people, and everything he doesn't share with someone else is an event that never really took place. I would tell him it's life and the living and the meander of a conversation that holds all the meaning in the world.

I would point out which of his friends were going to drop him, who was going to laugh when they heard the news. I would tell him to keep doing his homework, because the worst of all is that whatever happens, unless it's your own life that finishes, the world is going to keep revolving, and there will be no choice but to keep on moving through your life as day follows remorseless day. You will be whisked away from the scene of the accident before you have time to really look, your exams will come round and there will be new decisions, though all you will want is to stop and stare at the world on fire. You won't be allowed. The world doesn't just lie around waiting for anyone. It moves on. I would tell him if everything starts to spin out of his control at a pace he can't take, he should try to tell it like a story, make a shape of experience he can control, find a way to understand it, make a moral out of random experience and live by that.

I would tell him to love as if he might never get the chance to love again. Because a day never dawns when it is impossible that the person you love most in the world is about to die. Your dad can die at a moment's notice, and so it is important, while you're in the world, that you remember to love.

I got to the house and walked down the little path through the vegetable patch, and while I was fumbling for my key Mum opened the door. We looked at each other for the moment, then she slapped me hard in the face.

'Do you know how worried I've been? Where have you been? Where have you been?' She turned and strode back into the house, and I followed her, raising my hand to my face.

'Is Dad OK?'

She didn't speak for a moment but held the back of a chair by the kitchen table, staring hard at the apple trees in the garden.

'I've just come back to pick up some things for him and then I'm going straight back.'

'Is he OK though?'

'I'll be there for the rest of the day and the rest of the evening, so you'll need to sort your own supper.'

'Can I come with you?'

She turned to face me, and there were tears in her eyes,

but drowning them out was an anger that made me afraid.

'I think I'd rather you stayed here.'

'What?'

'I don't want you at the hospital while you're in that state. Why don't you sort yourself out, and then we'll speak later and see whether you can come? I don't think your dad needs to see you like this.' She walked past me, heading upstairs to their bedroom. She would be finding him clothes; she would be finding him a toothbrush. I stood very still in the hall till she came back downstairs. 'Have some paracetamol and a glass of water and get an hour's sleep,' she said. 'I have to go.'

'I can't come with you?'

'No. Not till you've sobered up. All right?' Then she walked out of the house and left me alone in the silence of the hallway and the morning. And beyond that all the silences of Wiltshire and Hampshire. I sat down at the kitchen table, not knowing what to do. I took out my phone, and there was a text from Sophie waiting for me. *What happened to you?* It didn't matter what she did and didn't know any more. I sent her a message that read, *My dad's dying.* I hoped she might call, but nothing happened.

Half an hour later I was sitting in the kitchen with my head in my hands when I heard the doorbell. She was standing on the front step in her school uniform, out of breath. For a moment neither of us said anything.

'What do you mean your dad's dying?' she said.

I thought I might as well tell her everything.

'All the time we've been seeing each other, I've been telling you he's been ill, but I haven't been telling you everything. He's got cancer. He had chemo for a while but stopped because it wasn't working. Last night he had to go into the hospital. Mum's with him now, but she won't let me go and see him.'

She came into the house, and in the hallway, as she shut the door behind her, she took me in her arms and held me, my face against her shoulder, my arms around her. We stayed like that for a long time. Then she led me into the kitchen and we sat down on the sofa by the Aga.

'I didn't know,' she said. 'I'm so sorry. I didn't know.'

'I could never find a time to tell you. I didn't want to scare you off.'

'You wouldn't have scared me off.'

'I thought I was never going to keep you very long. I didn't want to waste our time feeling sad.'

She flicked her hair from her eyes as if she was angry.

'It wouldn't have been wasted.'

'No.' I nodded. 'I know.' Then I couldn't say anything for a little while, because I couldn't bear that I'd got it wrong, all my life I'd got everything wrong.

'Why don't you have a shower and then we'll go to the hospital?' she said.

'Don't you need to go to school?'

'It doesn't matter. Go on, have a shower. I'll wait down here.'

I nodded. I wanted to go. After Mum had left I had felt I wouldn't be able to, I was too afraid of making her angry, but Sophie saying it made it seem normal. I would go, and I would see him, and things would be OK. I stopped in the door of the kitchen and turned back to face her.

'Did you sort things out with your ex?'

'Let's talk about that another time.' She smiled, but I could see it was just for show.

'OK. I'll be back in a minute.'

I walked upstairs to the bathroom. I turned on the shower and tried to wash myself away in the heat and steam of the water. When I came back downstairs ten minutes later she was already standing, ready to go. We went out of the house and walked along the main roads to the hospital. I wouldn't show her the secret ways through the fields. I couldn't think of anything to say to her any more, and she let me walk in silence. I suppose she assumed I was thinking about my dad, but I wasn't. I wish I had been now. What I was thinking about was her, and how unfair it seemed that things had a way of happening all at once, so you could never give any of them the attention they needed, the attention they deserved, and ended up getting them all wrong.

We got to the hospital. I thought about telling her to go home, telling her I didn't want her to be there when I saw him, because I knew it was over between us, but I realised I couldn't. I needed her for just a little longer. I couldn't face my mum without someone else next to me. I needed her for just another hour. We walked into the hospital, not knowing that Dad had died thirty minutes earlier.

As Close to the Stars as Possible

MARTIN HUGHES: I understand you've been examined by a paramedic at the scene, is that correct?

George Street: Yes that's right.

MH: Very good. I'm going to leave you alone for a moment, I just need to collect my notes, OK?

GS: That's quite all right.

MH: Would you like a glass of water?

GS: No, I'm quite all right, thank you.

MH: OK. If you do begin to feel unwell at any point during the interview, just let me know and we can get you some medical support, OK?

GS: That's very kind, thank you.

MH: Concussion can take a little while to kick in, so if you suddenly find yourself becoming tired, just say.

One thing a death will do is make you reflect on how many different kinds of love there are to be experienced in the world. Because in the way you remember a person who has died, you discover a lot about the relationship you had with them in life. Or perhaps it would be better to say that certain things you have always thought to be true are finally proven. Only today, I have had confirmed my suspicion that it is possible to be hurt far more deeply and completely than I was when my mother or my father died, for example. In that, I think, there is a lesson about the variation that exists from love to love in a life, and the kind of love I have lost today.

The police car got us to the station at about quarter past nine. The driver stopped by the front entrance and another policeman helped me out. I was led to an interview room, past the front desk, through the locked door, into a cubicle on the left, and now I have been left alone, and I wish they hadn't done that, I wish there was someone else here to be with me and stop me thinking.

I don't mean I feel today like I've learned that I didn't love my parents. But when they died, Dad first and Mum eight years later, although I felt the loss keenly, although on each occasion I felt bereft, I was able to place their deaths among the natural order of things, to understand those disappearances as events that were always going to happen at some point. Because the rational part of me recognised that death is an event in life, and most people are required to live through the deaths of their parents. When my father died I remember the strange feeling that from that day forward I was taking his place in the world. I never had a child to follow after me. So perhaps no one will ever take up my role.

I felt I was taking my father's place not only because I was going to take over the farm, and live to a very great extent from that day forward the same life he had known, but also because I realised that everything he had ever thought or stood for or taught me could only remain in the world now if I carried it forward with me through the days remaining. I had, in some way, assimilated his life into mine.

The picture came to me of human lives as waves, lapping

in succession at an indifferent shore. His had fallen back and been consumed by the wave coming after, which was my own, and now it was my turn to roil forward up the sand towards the strandline. So the sadness of his death was complicated by the idea that the family of which he and I had been instances in a long stream of being flowing back into the darkness of history was moving forward with his death, was flowing into me. It felt almost as if I had become more alive because he had died. Or that I had a responsibility to be so, now I was the head of the family.

And, as it has transpired, the footnote of the family as well, because I suppose there will be no one at my funeral now who bears our name.

There are sirens that cry out here, as if the whole building were another police car, a great police ship in which all troubles sail. I suppose the building must never sleep, there must never be a moment when someone's sorrow isn't starting up these wailing sirens. A light flashes in this room when the calling starts, so bright, it hurts the back of my skull. I don't want to look at it, but I can't take my eyes from it. Because I think it is calling for me, this light that is flashing. I think it wants to tell me my old life is over, now I have taken another life, now her life is over as well. In the flash of the orange light above the door I see her face quiet on the pillow, and the curled-up body of the woman thrown from the motorcycle, against the bollard, against the kerb.

When my mother died the mood was very different. I believed she had been waiting for death for a long time, that we had all known since Dad died that death was really the only thing left to happen for her now. What grieved me most

139

on the morning I found her was that my link with the world of my childhood was washed almost completely away, the only foothold remaining in that time from there on being whatever had lodged in my own memory, now no other witnesses were living.

Now I am old I wish the young man I used to be had worried less about the past and lived more heedlessly in the present. I suppose I did as much living as I could. But I burn to tell men and women who are still young now how quickly it is going to get behind them, how fiercely they ought to love it while they can.

MH: Sorry about that. You sure you don't want a cup of tea or anything?

GS: No, thank you though.

The police officer has come back into the room at last. He does not look happy to be here. He didn't look at me as he walked in, so I don't look at him; I look at my hands instead. I suppose I feel ashamed, ashamed and afraid. I suppose they all feel sorry for me. The old are a regular subject for sympathy. People like me have nothing to look forward to, and everyone young is afraid of that time creeping up on them some time soon. So when they think they see it in someone else, it's nice to pity the condition. It makes you feel like it is not yet yours, makes you feel safe and distant from the loneliness that comes at the end of life. So much of sympathy seems to me to be about making yourself feel better. There is very little real empathy in the world, I think.

Today is a very different experience to the days when my

parents died. There is an even chance in a marriage, I suppose, that you will have to live through the death of your partner. That is a gamble I suppose you sign up for when you walk to the altar. But even if I did sign up for this, I still feel like someone must have betrayed me. As if I have been misled. No one ever warned me it was possible for something like this to happen to me without it killing me, so that I might have to live through it and deal with a feeling like this one. What I am learning now is that the love I shared with Valerie was of a very different nature to anything else I have known in my life. Because she was not a part of my life. She was not something I have lost. She was the reason I did everything. I can barely comprehend what that is going to mean for me now she is gone.

GS: Actually, would it be possible for me to have a glass of water?

MH: Of course. I'll be a moment. Do you want anything else?

GS: No, thank you.

I remember the first death that really touched my life, the tragic ending of my childhood friend Ned Bassett, who was killed at thirty when he overturned his tractor on to himself. I think of it still, every time I pass the spot, all these years later. He worked with me on the farm, and it was me who found him when he got so late coming back that I started to worry and set out to see whether anything had happened to him. Today I am reminded of Ned because I feel again the injustice I felt on the day of his death. Not that Valerie has died young. But a slow death, a painful death, feels to me like an act of cruelty, and Valerie deserved anything but that. I suppose when you love someone there are no good deaths, no endings you would wish on them; you would only wish them life. But there is something evil about cancer. It seems so very, very wrong for life to burn itself up like that.

And yet all of this is complicated because in amongst the anger and the awful sorrow at what has happened I can't help feel a relief that she is no longer suffering. And a strange and wonderful gratitude for her life, and the fact I got to share it, which is not lessened by any anger but does a great deal to make all the anger I have seem pitiful and small next to all that came before it. A whole human being's life.

And beyond that there is another thought lying in wait for me, a melancholy I do not feel able to engage with now – the thought that this was not just the death of my wife but the end of a line, the end of my family. How enormous that idea seems to me today, though I have been ignoring it for years. When I die it will be as if none of us ever existed, as if none of the days of our lives ever took place.

MH: Here we are. Right then, shall we begin?
GS: Yes.
MH: Could you state your full name and address for me, please.
GS: George William Street, Manor Farm, Martin.
MH: Thank you. Now taking your time, and in your own words, could you tell me what happened to you this evening?

*

142

It is on the downland surrounding the village of Martin at the mouth of Cranborne Chase that our story has really played out, and I can't tell how I feel about its coming to an end here in the city of Salisbury, ten miles to the north of our home. At first sight it seems like a tragedy for our endings to be uprooted like this and take place out of the context of everything that has come before, all the little triumphs we have shared. It seems to steal something away. But no river ends in the place where it started. And perhaps it is a kindness that the memory of this day will never cast its shadow too closely over our home. Perhaps it is right that a death takes place away from where the life was lived. And perhaps we haven't been too brutally torn from our moorings by coming here. Being a farmer in Martin, there's not much call to visit Salisbury more than every once or twice in a month for the market day, but it is still the brightest star in the constellation of settlements here where the green south of Wiltshire flows into Dorset and Hampshire.

The place where we made our life is a fairly brief interlude of cultivated land between the wildness of the New Forest to the south and the wildness of Salisbury Plain to the north. There can't be forty miles between the ending of one and the beginning of the other, and in the sweep of land between them there is Salisbury and then a tapestry of farmland as rich and giving as any land in England.

The farmed stretch of Wiltshire is a highly organised, modern model of agricultural work, the twentieth century having imposed an efficiency on us all that led to startling changes in the way crops were grown compared to the way things were done round here a hundred years ago. My farm, which is about two hundred acres, I suppose now constitutes something of a historical document in itself, being so much smaller and more piecemeal than the big industrial outfits that surround me. But even I am not a mixed farm any more, growing one crop in one field and something else in the next. That tradition is very long gone. All my acres are given over to cattle. Even I have adopted the most efficient model I possibly can, in order to keep hold of some version of the way of life I grew up with and not have to sell up and move into the city.

GS: Well, I don't know where to start. Where do I start?
MH: Perhaps you could tell me where you were driving to?
GS: What do you mean?
MH: What was your intended destination when the accident occurred? Where were you going?
GS: Well, I don't know. I don't know, do I? I suppose I was going home. I couldn't think of anywhere else to go. I didn't want to go home.
MH: To Manor Farm, that's your place of residence, yes?

Place of residence is, perhaps, a more appropriate phrase to use than saying home, because I can't be sure whether we're ever at home anywhere, whether we ever belong anywhere. The more deeply you inhabit a landscape, the clearer it becomes that that landscape does not in turn feel deeply inhabited by you. I walk round my farm, and I can see layers and layers of memories on every corner, whole lives that have been lived there. But after I die, no archaeologist will ever be able to reveal those pictures that are visible to me. The world

144

holds no trace of what happens in it unless we carve it in with violence or concrete. The whole of life as I have experienced it lives only in me, in my head, and the world itself is indifferent. What I think of as everything there is in the world, is no more than a reflection on the surface of the river. And the river will still be flowing when there are other faces reflected in it, and it will tell them nothing of what passed there before.

MH: Mr Street?
GS: Yes?
MH: Are you feeling OK?

I take hold with both hands of the rim of the plastic bucket chair I am sitting in and try to turn my thoughts to the room I am in, not my history. I have let the silence drift on too long. I suppose I have been trying not to think about what has happened. Perhaps I am in shock. I clasp my hands together so they don't shake, and stare down at them. Perhaps if I keep things small, keep the world focused on as tiny a thing as the light from the striplight falling on my hands, I will be able to wrestle back some control.

GS: Well, I'm having trouble knowing what to tell you, you see.
MH: Why don't you just tell me what you remember?

I can hardly keep from smiling then. I know that's awful, but I can't help hearing how stupid he sounds. What does that mean, what I remember? Does he want my whole life spooled out in front of him? He's going to have to ask smaller questions than that if he's going to get what he wants. Who am I, after all, to say where one thing stops flowing into another?

MH: Mr Street, I need you to tell me what happened.

The room we are sitting in is like a cubicle on a building site somehow. Not that I know very much about building sites, but I've been on them. A window in the door but no external windows, nothing on the walls, a striplight overhead, nothing here really but the table and two chairs, me and him, and of course the mirror window beside us, the famous mirror window you read about in every detective story. In all my years I've never been into this room before, or a room like it, but I've pictured it often enough, The Interrogation Room, reading my detective stories. Nonsense, she used to call them, though she always meant it kindly. Quite distinctly I hear her voice, and it frightens me, ringing out without an echo in this harshly lit room.

Are you reading more of your nonsense?

Even if I am imagining it, the sound of her voice in this room changes all the air around me, affects me as if it was as real as a stroke, as a heart attack. I am transported back to the first time I heard her speak. It was 1963, a dance in a scout hut on the edge of Salisbury. The ripples of the sixties had barely lapped at the banks of the city then. We have never been a forward-thinking county, but we knew about Elvis and Chuck Berry and the like, and all us young men wore our hair Brylcreemed back from our foreheads.

GS: I'm sorry. I'm just – let me try and tell you then. My home is a farm, I'm a farmer, I live at Martin in Dorset, just over the border into Dorset, do you know it?

MH: Yes, I know the area.

GS: Well, that's where I live. I've always lived there. I was going there when I set off. I was going home. I was tired, you see, and I'd stayed out as long as I could. And I hadn't been driving for ever so long, five minutes, I don't know. I hadn't got anywhere at all, really. I'd been parked up by Sainsbury's for a little while. I just parked there for a few hours and went for a walk. I was just wandering. I stopped to have a cup of tea in Reeve's, I just didn't want to go home yet, you see?

MH: OK.

GS: Are you married, officer?

MH: No.

GS: Do you have someone you love?

MH: What is—

GS: I lost my wife this morning, you see. That was why I didn't want to go home. And I liked walking round Salisbury because she came from here; it was here that I found her.

So it goes like this. I'm twenty-one – God, what I wouldn't give to be twenty-one again, to have it all in front of me again. I've come with my mates, the other hands on the farm; we head out together into Salisbury at the end of the week to let our hair down, to see and to be seen. We like to go to dances, spend our money on drinks for ourselves and the beautiful girls you can meet at a dance. Not every Friday night, because there isn't a dance to go to every week, but at least once a month we'll all get into our best shirts and our smart jackets, slick back our hair, then jump into Ned's car and ride into town. Ned was the only one of us to have a car back then; apart from these outings there was never much call for any of us to leave Martin, so cars didn't seem much of a priority. It felt at the time like the most perfect happiness that was possible in the world to be driven into town in Ned's car with the thought of a beer on your lips, a girl on your knee, your feet flying over the cheap lino of a community hall to the music of the touring bands or the local bands trying to pretend they'd spent the whole week opening for the Beatles on tour. They were pale enough imitations, but us lads were all jealous of them because the girls seemed to think they were immortal. No one in the world ever wielded more power than a boy who knew how to play guitar at a dance on a Friday night.

When I look back it's harder to feel it as purely, of course. I can't help but notice that even though I was the youngest of the bunch, I always got to sit in the front of the car. All the time I spent with my friends on and off the farm we always knew I was different, marked out from the rest of them for another kind of life than their round of work days and evenings and weekends. I was going to own the farm once my father died. One day I would be the boss of them all, so it was never me who crammed into the back seat.

My dear departed friends. I have outlived them all now, Ned and David and John. And there's another inequality, because perhaps it was the work I paid them to do that meant they died so young? The drudge of harvest and winter and morning after morning.

I am trying to keep the image of her away from me, trying not to look at the light, but it keeps rushing up on me no matter what memory I hide in.

Burrow deeper. Get away. Keep it away for as long as you can.

We were good with the girls, the young men of the village of Martin. We liked to imagine we had a reputation, that whenever we walked into a dance, all heads would turn. I think in the end it's confidence gets you everywhere at parties like the ones we used to go to, so the glorious thing was that it didn't really matter how good looking we actually were, our prophecies ended up being self-fulfilling. Most weeks there'd be at least one of us missing by the time Ned came to drive us home. The lucky deserter would have to get the bus home the next day, or hitch a lift if we'd gone out on a Saturday night and he woke up in a girl's bed on a Sunday morning when there were no buses running. On the nights it was Ned who didn't come back, John was allowed to drive the car. He drank more than Ned, and I was always privately terrified of these journeys, though of course I tried to act relaxed while they were happening.

Although I was the baby of the group, my luck was usually as good as anyone's, and I saw as much of the Saturday-morning bus as the others. A good shame, that one. Sometimes the men who drove past you would shake their heads and smile when they clocked your last night's clothes and the rings round your eyes, as though they had played that game too, long ago.

Golden, burning days indeed.

I knew she was different the moment we met. I'm sure that

would seem strange and old hat to other people if I said it aloud. It was a Saturday dance in an old prefab in Harnham, and the band was good, and I liked the mood in the air the minute I walked through the door. I saw her straight away. She was standing with three or four other girls by the make-shift bar, smoking a cigarette, and I suppose we must have made a bit of an entrance because all those girls stopped talking and looked at us boys looking back at them.

I only saw her, not the other girls standing around her. She had the most extraordinary eyes the colour of amber, and that sweep of auburn hair I loved so much for the rest of her life, and I remember she wore a blue scarf with some kind of pattern to it. I imagine it must have been floral, but the picture won't come clear and that scarf of course is long vanished; I haven't seen it in years and years. Whatever its pattern may have been, I remember it sort of showed off her eyes and the shape of her face very well.

Of course, you didn't go straight up to a girl at a dance. So I held her look for a moment, then left her alone for half an hour. Then, with a couple of drinks inside me, when the room was packed and everyone dancing, I went up to the girl who would become my wife and asked her what her name was, and she told me her name was Valerie. I asked her if she wanted to dance, and she came out on to the floor with me, the two of us walking hand in hand. She was a better dancer than I was, but I suppose I must have been good enough, because I didn't take my eyes off her and she didn't take hers from me. When we were hot and out of breath I asked if she wanted to go for a walk, and she said she did. I kissed her then, once we were outside and alone in the dark, a rush of nerves and feeling, a rush of euphoria when she opened her mouth and kissed me back. She asked me where I lived, and I told her I was from Martin. She told me she lived close by and asked if I wanted to walk her home, and of course I agreed because we both knew the steps to the dance we were dancing. At her front door I kissed her again, then she asked me inside and I followed her into the hallway, holding her hand, walking on tiptoe so as not to wake her parents. It was as easy as that. I had found the meaning of my life in the course of an evening. A pair of amber eyes, a sweep of auburn hair, a blue scarf glimpsed across a room. I never wanted to go out looking for another girl again.

None of this, of course, is what the policeman sitting opposite me wants to hear. So I don't tell him any of it. I give him the colder facts instead.

MH: I see. I'm very sorry for your loss, Mr Street. Was her death sudden?

GS: No, no. She died quite peacefully really, after a long illness. It was all calm; it was all very much expected.

MH: You must have been very distressed.

GS: What do you mean?

MH: Only that it must have been a very distressing day for you.

GS: Of course it was. By God. Of course it was. How else do you think I might feel?

MH: I'm sorry, but I'm only trying to ascertain your state of mind this evening when you got into your vehicle.

GS: My state of mind? What do you mean, state of mind? What the hell does that mean?

*

'Long illness' indeed, who am I pretending to be, the obits writer of *The Times*? I should have the courage to give the thing a name and call it cancer, to tell him what happened, to say it out loud. Anything else is just shirking the fight, and God, how I want to fight now, when I think of what happened to Valerie.

The sickening impact of metal on metal, the crunch and the rending. I barely had time to apply the brakes before I hit her, then swerved violently away and into the building, the whole sky closing over me as the dark of the brickwork blocked out the light and I thought that everything was ending. And I fancy now, though I can't be sure, that even as I shattered the window, as it flew over me, I heard the body of the woman on the moped hit the ground. What was it that killed her precisely? A broken back? A broken neck?

GS: I was upset, of course I was upset. I felt very angry. I felt much more than upset. I don't know the word for how I was feeling. There isn't a word for something like that.
MH: Mr Street, what time of day did your wife pass away?

Painful to reduce it to such a cold fact as the time of death. Where would you place that, would you say? The minute she stopped breathing? The day of the diagnosis, one year earlier? The first bout five years before that, the first course of chemotherapy and the subsequent remission? Surely this had been a relapse of all that, a return to the dark old days, the thing coming to claim her a second time round? Or if you were feeling bleak enough, and I am of course feeling bleak enough today, perhaps you would point to the moment of our marriage, when her fate was sealed and the life she was going to live was all mapped out for her, or even the moment of birth as where Valerie started to die?

GS: It was early this afternoon. So a long time before the accident. And I wasn't crying and I wasn't shaking and I felt very empty but I felt under control when I got behind the wheel, which I think is what you're asking.

I had known the previous evening what was going to happen, but they hadn't let me stay at the hospital. She was too tired, they said; it was best if she were given time to herself, if I went home. All the same, I think she and I both knew what was coming when I kissed her good night and headed for the car park.

When she first went into the hospital it seemed ridiculous to me that I might ever leave her side at all, but atrocities such as that quickly become habitual. Because of course you can't stay there and let everything else fall away, not if you've a farm to run. Not if your wife is telling you she wants her peace in the evenings sometimes as well. You must reconcile yourself to the fact she needs her sleep, that work must be done, and learn how to walk away from her day after day and get into the car and drive home. And sleep alone in the big bed, thinking of her. And try to be hopeful in the mornings. And try to survive the nights.

When the milking was done I headed for the hospital like always, shirking half my work and leaving it to the young men who have taken the place of the young men I grew up with, the boys who have done the lion's share of my work since Valerie fell ill. And I suppose will be doing all of it very soon, if the place doesn't have to be sold. I won't be much use for much longer. As always, I stopped at the Nisa on the road to the hospital to buy her some bananas and a bottle of water and a copy of the *Telegraph*. While I queued to pay I was overcome by the most awful certainty that today what I was doing was hopeless – that the bananas I had just put into my basket were never going to be eaten. She had been unwell yesterday, worse even than the day before, which had been a deterioration in itself. The state of things hung unspoken in the air. Neither of us could ever have talked about something like that. It was never our way to come at such things head-on. Nonetheless, it was there in the looks that passed between us, and that was why I had asked the nurse for the first time in weeks about staying the night last night.

When I got to the front of the queue I didn't know whether I could bear to buy the things I had in my basket. I felt sure she would never need any of them, that everything I was about to pay for would end up unused. I didn't mind paying for it, of course I didn't. What I couldn't bear was the thought of having to throw them all away, later that day or that evening, as if I was throwing her out with the last of the light. I had never even liked bananas, and I doubted I could have made any use of something meant for her on the day she had died anyway, it would all have to go in the bin, and I thought there must be a very real chance that having to do that could actually break my heart. I might end up dying of grief on the same day that she died of cancer.

Then I imagined the scene where I arrived to see her without my usual offerings, my pathetic day's provisions in their Nisa bag, and she realised I hadn't brought them because I didn't think there was any point any more, and that was far more horrible to contemplate. The idea of her face in the moment she knew I had written her off. I paid in a hurry when I thought of that, because I wanted, just for one last time, to take her hand in mine and hold it as tight as I dared, and try to persuade her just once more that it was all right, that things were going to be all right.

Then I saw what she looked like on her last morning as the light from the window fell over her face. Her breathing was laboured, and by that time the nurses knew as well as we had done the previous evening that her story was ending. It was clear in the way they were gathering around her, like the egrets who fly over Martin Down. Someone took me aside when I had sat with her for about an hour, to tell me how very ill she had become in the night, because she was slipping in and out of consciousness and they wanted me to understand that it was almost over now, it couldn't be long. I hardly listened at all, just nodded my way through everything that needed to be said so I could get back to her as quickly as possible. I wanted her to see my face for all the time she had left awake now, so she knew she was safe. Just in case it stopped her feeling frightened. That was all the influence over things that was left to me by lunchtime. Mankind can build cities, split atoms, create life. We are all but helpless in the face of death. I felt like a baby, and it was all so unfair, because of course what I really needed just then was her. Her strength and wisdom and understanding. She, perhaps, would have known what to do, if only she hadn't been dying.

When the nurse had said all he wanted to say I went back to Valerie and sat down next to her again and took her hand, and she woke and smiled and stayed awake for a little while. I told her, I'm here, my love. It's all right. She told me she loved me, and I told her I loved her as well, and then we sat there holding hands like lovers till she fell asleep again.

I can't imagine any life feels like a real life that isn't lived entwined like ivy with someone else's. That's how your days can matter and take on a weight, if you can make another person laugh, feel something, if your life can become part of a richer pattern. That seems to me to be the one truly beautiful thing there is in the world.

GS: She fell asleep for the last time around one, and it was quite quick after that. She just stopped breathing in the end, you see. And have you known that feeling, those five minutes?

The policeman took a breath and nodded, and I made a mental note that I must find a way to thank him, from whatever cell I ended up in after tonight, for engaging with me like that in that moment. I'm sure that's not how you're supposed to treat murderers, if that is indeed what I am. It's certainly what I think I must be, because didn't she die when I ploughed the car into her? Like a rabbit going into the blades of a combine, wasn't she scattered out of existence? I would have to write him a letter to express my gratitude for his consideration from my prison cell. I doubted that I would be able to express any feeling properly now.

*

MH: Yes, I have.

GS: Well then, you know what it was like. And the time straight after that.

It had been as if I had gone deaf. I didn't let go of her hand for a long time, not until I was asked to, probably not the first time I was asked to either, because for a long time I really couldn't hear anything. I think my body was going into shock, because that is one symptom of fainting, isn't it? You grow pale, your senses fail, you can't hear or see anything, then you collapse. So perhaps I sat there with her when she died and went white as the sheet she lay on. I didn't want to let go of her hand until I absolutely had to, because as long as we were still together like that, while we still shared that much, I felt I had not yet left the clearing in the woods where we had walked together. I knew letting go of her hand would be going on into the dark.

Another siren has sounded.

GS: What's that noise?

MH: I'm very sorry, Mr Street. That siren means I need to leave for a couple of minutes. Will you be all right here?'

GS: On my own?

MH: Just for a minute. The siren means another officer needs some help.

GS: Then of course you must go. I'll be all right here.

MH: I'll be right back.

And I am alone again, and the memories well up now there is no one to distract me from the prison of myself. I can hear the sound of the car hitting the motorbike. I can hear the sound of the cardiac monitor, going on forever on the same single note. I think when she flew from the bike I heard the crunch as she hit the ground and her body wrapped impossibly, contortedly round the bollard. I can't have done, over the sound of the car, but it is here in the room with me now, that sound; it is taunting me with what I have done, it is trying to drown me in the horror of this evening.

I had walked up that same road earlier in the afternoon, as if I had been planning the crime, it appears to me now, though of course that wasn't what I was doing. I was simply trying to get away from myself, and what had happened, and to control my breathing, and get a grip on my grief and stop myself crying. I knew Winchester Street was quiet, and no one would see me if I started to cry down there. I thought perhaps if I walked that way I would be able to distract myself for a moment. There were memories here that could lead me away from her. The cobbler I always used was on Winchester Street, a dowdy little shop I liked because it had no pretension, it made no attempt to look beautiful for its customers. It sold new shoes and mended old ones, and the proprietor seemed to trust that was enough to keep him ticking over. So the little shelf racks on which his shoes and polishes were displayed had been hammered together out of old ply and not replaced in the twenty years I had been going there. The shop had a pleasant smell of machine oil, which made me feel I was in my workshop at home. I liked the owner. I had never known his name, but he seemed to know me when I came in to have things mended, from the way he greeted me, and that made me feel like the shop was a place I belonged. That, I suppose, is a trick a shopkeeper learns, to make his customers feel like the owners of the place, as if they could be at their ease and take their time, so they spend their money and feel good about it and keep him in business. He was a quiet man, the cobbler, and I used to fancy sometimes he had lived through some great trauma that made him seem so distant from the day around him, as though there was another skin between him and the rest of the world, as though he was under water. I walked past the shop that afternoon and was surprised to find it was closed. There were boards across the windows. I wondered idly where I would get my shoes mended now and what had happened. Perhaps he had gone bust. Perhaps he had simply had enough.

But there were memories on that street that led me back to her as well, so I found no peace in its quiet. On this street as well was the Anchor & Hope, a good pub where I had taken Valerie and her parents once for a drink, a young man nervously trying to show he was an adult by buying a round. God knows where we had been in the day, perhaps we had all gone shopping together or been to see a play, because when she was young Valerie had liked going to the theatre. I had always liked her parents. They were as visibly contented as any two people I had known, and I had felt encouraged by that, remembering the story that women tend to turn into their mothers. I hoped that a happiness like theirs would be catching, and, indeed, perhaps I can say now that it was.

The first time I took Valerie to meet my parents I remember she said when I arrived to collect her she was so nervous she wanted to be sick. I had passed my driving test by then and borrowed Ned's car for the occasion. I drove her back out to

Martin and couldn't help smiling at the anxiety that showed in her every movement, the way she brushed her hair behind her ears, the way she held her hands so tightly in her lap and kept checking her make-up in the mirror. She got annoyed with me for laughing at her, and I couldn't make her understand how very little there was for her to worry about, that my parents would think she was wonderful. People are very slow to accept how wonderful they are. I have noticed that with everyone I have ever been close to, and valued, and tried to praise.

She said she liked our home very much when we arrived and parked in front of it, and seemed impressed because she asked whether I was really going to inherit it one day. I told her yes, as the only son, this would be mine in turn to look after, and I remember she said then what a strange responsibility that must be. I asked her why, and she said in her own lifetime she had lived in three different houses in Salisbury; moving house felt to her like an ordinary part of the rhythm of things. The idea of a building that was passed down the generations seemed extraordinary to her. Imagine all the memories whirling round in there, she said, and I replied, oh yes, it's swimming in that, believe me.

Dad came out to greet us, and Mum was standing behind him in the doorway. I could see in the way they spoke to her they liked Valerie as much as I had known they would. They thought she was beautiful and charming and intelligent and perfect for me, far better, really, than a boy as uncomplicated as I was could really have hoped to catch. That was what Dad teased me with later, anyway.

I do not remember what we all talked about, the four of us,

over that first breathlessly nervous meal. I remember us laughing, and the feeling it was all going better than I could have hoped, and pride in my parents, who were on their best behaviour, and in Valerie, who enchanted us all. After lunch she and I went for a walk over the nearest few fields and talked about how beautiful it was there, and how surprisingly close to Salisbury and what she called civilisation, laughing as she did so that I knew she was joking. Then she told me she felt tired. We agreed we should cut short our walk and go back to the house and have a glass of water, and then I should drive her home. At that time she didn't yet know she was pregnant, so we put her tiredness and her sickness down to nerves about meeting my parents.

MH: My apologies for the interruption.
GS: That's quite all right.
MH: Are you ready to continue?
GS: Yes, I suppose I am. What do you want to know?
MH: Well, we need to pin down your movements during the
      afternoon.

I had stayed in the hospital for hours after she died, stayed with the body and then filled out forms and spoken with a lot of people I didn't listen to, and then when they told me I ought to go home I had driven into town and walked, aimlessly, hopelessly, thinking of Valerie. I had thought of the child then, the child who had never been born. I had wished there was a child today for me to talk to.

It would be fair to say that the discovery of Valerie's pregnancy did accelerate our plans for marriage, but that is not to suggest that such plans did not already exist. I knew with frightening certainty on that first morning I woke in her bed that it was what I wanted to happen to us, and I believe from all we have said about that time ever since that she felt much the same. Though I think she was always a little more rational than I was and waited a little longer till she knew me better before she admitted those desires to herself.

Once we knew there was going to be a child, things changed quickly, and a wedding was planned for that summer. I couldn't believe my luck. Our families met for dinner in a restaurant a week after I proposed. We all ate and drank and celebrated together, and it seemed that her parents got on with my parents. I invited Ned along in case they didn't and we needed someone to do the talking, and he got drunk and insisted on giving a speech about how perfect Valerie and I were for each other. It is one of the great duties of a friend to play the fool enough to make you yourself look like a catch by comparison, and poor Ned was always good for that when required. After the meal he and I went home with my parents, and Valerie went home with hers. It was still dark when she called me to tell me she had miscarried in the night.

Her mother knew, but she never told her father, and I never told my parents, so we didn't allow it to change our plans for the wedding. I didn't know how to reach her in her sadness, but we told each other it was something we would grow stronger from, that there was a long future ahead of us, that there would be other children. We were married in June in St Martin's church, where she had been christened, and she moved in with us and became the wife of a farmer. She and Mum always got on, so it was a very happy home then, the light of speech always dancing from mouth to mouth in the kitchen. She had a wonderful singing voice and would sing for us all some evenings, accompanying herself on our rickety old upright, and of course we still went out to dances and drank with our friends, with Ned and his girlfriends and with the other boys on the farm. But she never conceived again, and after five years a quiet kind of acceptance that was like defeat settled on her because, despite her youth, I think she had decided it was not meant to be.

GS: There was a lot to do at the hospital, of course, and I did all that, all they asked of me. I couldn't tell you exactly what I did; it's not clear to me now. I can't remember it all bit by bit, only all together in a rush. I hope that doesn't matter?

MH: No, that doesn't matter. I understand.

GS: I was at the hospital until perhaps five, half past five.

MH: Did you go to get something to eat after that?

GS: Of course not. How could I have eaten?

MH: Did you have anything to drink?

GS: Ah. I see. No, I didn't have a drink.

That was when the thinning of the tribe began, after Valerie had decided we weren't going to add to it. Ned died one day, and she lost her mother and then her father in the three years that followed. Then my father died, and for the rest of our youth it was just me and her and Mum in the house all together. Those were long sad years, because Valerie wanted very much to be a mother, and the time slipped hopelessly by, and nothing changed for us – there was no new life. We told ourselves we were happy. But it was only after my mother had died, when the time had passed when we could have had children, that I believed Valerie to be really content again. Once the possibility of family was well and truly gone, it seemed she was able to give up on those ideas, release herself a little from her own expectations. Though I don't think she ever stopped remembering the child that died. On her fiftieth birthday she told me it still moved her to tears sometimes, not ever to hear younger voices in the house, and that she had always felt in a way like she had let us down. I spent the rest of her life trying to show her that had never been the case, that we had been happy, that we had known love.

GS: I didn't feel hungry at all, you see. I just had a glass of water. I caught a bus away from the hospital. It's beautiful out at Odstock, have you been there?

MH: I have.

GS: There's a church that's nestled in the hillside beyond the hospital. No houses around it, as far as I can see, just the spire of a little church that rises up among the trees. And I have wondered from time to time over the years what church that was and wanted to visit it, but in the end I thought perhaps I should never go, because there are some things you're only meant to glimpse from a distance, aren't there, and never get to.

MH: I think you mean St Mary's at Alderbury.

GS: Yes, I looked at a map once and thought that was probably it. But I decided some time back I never wanted to go and know for certain. I wanted a mystery about it. I wanted it to stay secret.

*

It was then she felt able to tell me her last little secret. I had long ago forgotten, by that time, the fact that both of us had had a life before we knew each other, a youth. I had told her all my stories – the adventures, the plans I had nurtured for myself and let slide as I came into a fuller understanding that my life was going to be the farm, and of course the other girls I had known before her. One doesn't go into very much detail, naturally, but I had told her about them all, and she had teased me, laughing, because of course we both knew what that life had been like, having ourselves both met at a dance.

It transpired, though, that she had not told me absolutely all her own stories in return. She told me haltingly, almost tearfully, one evening while we sat by the fire in the house both reading our way through the hour after dinner, that there was one she had always been afraid of. So she had hidden it for years and years. I don't know why she decided to tell me that evening. Perhaps she was thinking of him. She told me the first boy she had ever been with had been Ned, my friend who had died, with whom I had walked into so many dances feeling like we could do anything. Valerie had fallen for him on a night perhaps a year before we met, swept up in his charm and his looks and his confidence. She told me they hadn't met again after the night they spent together, until to her horror and terror he had appeared at that first meeting between her parents and my parents, that dinner I had brought him to as ballast. They both recognised each other, and she said she could have wept in gratitude when it became clear he was going to pretend they hadn't met before. At the end of the dinner they parted like friends

165

new-made and said nothing dangerous to each other.

Weeks passed before they found an opportunity to speak, and when they did, Ned was all reassurance, she told me, and put her at her ease. He told her he knew the first time I talked about the girl I had met at the dance that I had fallen in love with her, and that he had never seen a better matched couple and could want nothing less than for a shared night of their youths to get in the way of me and her getting together. So they agreed to let the matter lie and get to know each other on a different footing, and nothing more was ever said about the matter.

And, indeed, Ned ended up taking the story to his grave.

Her story amazed me, of course. I felt a new love for my friend, that he had kept that silence I suppose in the name of protecting me and Valerie for all those years. I thought of the day of our wedding, when he was best man, and how he had calmed me and told me I had never got anything more right in my life. I thought of how Valerie must have felt for him to give the rings away that day, and that seemed very strange to me now, that scene with hindsight, but all the same all I could feel was love for those two people who had done so much to protect me, who must have loved me so much to want to keep me so safe from their little secret. Love, and perhaps just the slightest concern that they might think it would matter so much to me, that they might not realise I would understand. But who knows whether they might not have been right. Perhaps it would have broken the peace between us.

Valerie said to me then that when Ned had died she had felt a new guilt about the old affair, which by that time had all but passed out of her mind after so long having Ned for a friend. It had pained her to think of that hidden past between them on the morning when I found his body, the tractor's wheels still turning in mid-air and Ned beneath it. She hated the idea that because of her there had been a secret between me and my friend that had lasted the rest of our lives. And she had wanted to tell me all about it there and then, but found she couldn't, for fear I would leave her on her own.

I stopped her talking then, crossed the room and held her and told her everything was all right, because I couldn't bear to think she had ever been so afraid of me. I found her story extraordinary, but that was all. It changed nothing between me and her, altered nothing of any memory I had of Ned. Except that it made me think with some amazement that perhaps us young men of Martin had been right after all. Perhaps we had indeed been beautiful.

The idea that I would ever have left Valerie alone in the world is physically painful to me. I always thought neither of us would ever be able to cope without the other, would barely be able to go on at all. And yet, of course, that is what has happened to me now, and it appears, for the moment at least, that it is a separation I can survive. It has hardly been a smooth progress – a woman has died today, after all – but I am still speeding away from the place where I left my wife. Are we really on our own in the world and only sometimes sharing the way with other people?

MH: So you drove into Salisbury and you walked around?
GS: Yes, that's right.
MH: Did you not have anyone you wanted to be with?

GS: No. We never had any children.

MH: No other friends or family?

GS: When you get to my age most of your friends and your
      family tend to have gone on.

We were never very good at keeping friends. Dinner parties
weren't our way of life. We knew everyone in Martin; we knew
our world and did not venture beyond it. All the new relationships that came into our lives after the death of my mother, in
fact, took far more curious routes than the traditional method
of meeting and befriending and entertaining that other
people seem to use to keep up the interest in their lives. After
the time had passed when we could have had children, Valerie
took up mothering every waif and stray that crossed our path,
and that was the only way we really seemed to meet new
people. This started with the boy who cut himself on the
combine harvester. I was out in the fields when the first
chapter of this story took place, so she told it to me later,
when the moment of crisis had passed.

   The story as Valerie told it was that a town boy, out on a
long bike ride, had stopped to eat his lunch on our farm and
for some unfathomable reason decided to clamber around
on the combine harvester. I can't imagine what possessed
him, looking back. I suppose there is the impulse in everyone
to get up as high as you can and see what the view may be
from the highest branch that will hold you. Anyway, this boy,
we learned later that his name was Luke or Liam or something like that, when he had finished his ham sandwiches or
bread and cheese or whatever it was he had to eat, had
clambered up to sit on top of the cab of the combine, and

from there had proceeded, by a slip or otherwise by his own idiocy, to fall into the blades. He cut his right hand a little and his right leg very badly at the ankle, so that he could see right down to the bone, and when he extracted himself found he was losing blood very quickly. The boy – I am sure it was Luke – was therefore presented with a dilemma. If he cycled for help he would lose blood faster, but if he waited where he was for someone to find him he might die sitting around. He made the wise decision to get on his bike and seek help, and the first place he came to was our house, where Valerie met him, led him into the kitchen, bound his leg and called an ambulance. The leg was all right and after a spell in hospital and a blood transfusion the boy was all right as well. I am wrong – his name was definitely Liam.

Valerie received a letter of thanks from him a week later, and another from his parents, and must have replied with an invitation because the next week I came in from the fields to find this boy sitting talking with her in the kitchen. These visits continued for a little while. Valerie would cook a meal and ask Liam while we ate all together about his life, and he would tell her about his school, and what he did with his weekends. After six months he stopped coming to visit us, but while it lasted I know she loved it very much. We never spoke about him again once he stopped visiting. We knew that boys grow up and tire of things, and let it remain undisturbed as one of her happy memories.

Then there was the story of Rita, a woman who turned up in tears at our front door one afternoon and told us she had nowhere to stay in the world. Most people would perhaps be suspicious of such an introduction. Valerie did the Christian thing and put her up in the spare room. Then when Rita asked to camp on our land for a little while, Valerie agreed to it and lent her the tent we used to take on holiday to Lulworth in the rare years we found the time to get away. She had been through a lot; it was clear from the way she looked at the world she had seen a lot of trouble. She needed a helping hand to make her way back into the swing of everything, Valerie told me, and the least we could do was give her what she asked when it cost us so very little. Valerie tried to do more than that; in fact, told her she could keep on living in the spare room for as long as she liked, the room where we would have put our children if we had ever had them. Rita had shown by then that she wasn't there to steal the silver, and we would have both been happy for her to stay in the house. She refused, smiling, and told us she would rather live outside for a little while, as long as it didn't start snowing. And try to find her bearings. And live as close to the stars as possible without a roof to hide them from her.

We watched Rita as she calmed down, as she seemed to become more sure of herself. After a few months she came and told us she'd got a job. It wasn't long after that before she brought us the news that she had found a flat in town, and that was when she left us. We were very proud to see her go. We felt we had made a little contribution to someone's life, to see her walk away from the house the last time she left us, making her way down the drive as if it was all just starting for her, as if everything lay before her to enjoy.

It is so strange to think that now I am the only person in the world who knows about everything Valerie and I ever did together, all those lovely evenings when the night drew in, all those afternoons when the shadows lengthened over the long lawn till they touched the house, while we listened to the larks, the sound of the river in the distance. Did all those days happen any less, are they less real now I am the only one who knows about them? Perhaps it doesn't matter. Perhaps everything is unimportant and eventually forgotten, and all that matters and all of the meaning we'll find is the taking of pleasure in the life that flows through us and round us and finally over us, so we are submerged once more, returned to the heart of the river.

I have always been so fascinated by the life in other people. I wish I had spent my life among people and not in the fields. I wish I had taken up my interests and done something with them – done what I wanted with my life and not just what was in front of me.

GS: I ended up under the cathedral. And I looked up at it, and I don't have the words for how I was feeling. I looked up at it, and it didn't seem to care about me at all, does that make sense to you? Like the whole world was oblivious to what was happening to me. I was only on the surface of it, I never mattered to it, I never got under its skin. But I looked up at the sky and I thought of her and I sat for a long time on a bench there, in the close. And I started to feel calmer once I was still. I've never really known whether or not I was religious, but I started to feel calm there. Like perhaps it didn't matter that no one knew what had happened to me. Perhaps that was just the way things were. But it felt very soothing just to stare at that building, and not have to think any thoughts,

171

but just get lost for a little while in staring. And then I knew I ought to go home, but of course it's only me in the house now, and I used to have a whole family, and I used to have her, and now there's no one else in the world who minds about me, and I feel like I must have got something very wrong for things to end up this way. Because no one should be on their own, I don't think. And that was when it happened. I drove through the Market Square towards the Brown Street junction. The moped drove out as I was about to go round the corner, and I couldn't stop for it. I hit the woman on the moped, and the car went, you know, I lost control of it, and I went into the building. My air bag went off, and I sat there till the paramedic got me out. And I knew what I'd done, but I couldn't even get out to see if she was all right.

MH: Thank you, Mr Street. That's all we'll be needing for the time being.

GS: Are you going to charge me?

MH: With what?

GS: With killing that woman, of course.

MH: She isn't dead, Mr Street.

GS: Not dead?

MH: She has been taken to hospital, where she is in a critical condition. She isn't dead. If she doesn't pull through, we'll review the statement you've given us, but honestly, Mr Street, in the interests of setting your mind at rest, I think I can say from what you've said and from corroborating statements that you have done nothing wrong in this case.

GS: What?

MH: You are not responsible for the accident that occurred, Mr Street. You were an unwitting and innocent party in a road traffic accident – that's all as far as I can see.

GS: I thought I'd committed a murder.

MH: No.

GS: So I can go home then?

MH: Yes. I can arrange a lift for you back to your farm, since your car is damaged, if that would be helpful?

GS: I thought you were going to arrest me. I don't know whether I want to go home.

MH: I see.

GS: Once I get back there I'll be on my own for ever. I don't want to go home. She'd had it all done up in the last year; it doesn't even look like it used to when we were first together. So how can I remember her there? She had them change all the central heating. She put in a stairlift. She got a new fridge.

MH: Perhaps you should consider the possibility that these things were your wife's gift to you once she knew she was dying, so she was able to die knowing you would be all right in the house?

GS: Do you think? Do you think it was her gift to me?

Deep in the Middle
of Nowhere

Saturday, 11ᵗʰ May

I saw an accident in town tonight and it made me so scared because I was sure it meant you had died. I was walking past McDonald's. I'd just crossed the road by the Cross Keys in front of this car that frightened me because I didn't think it was going to slow. It let me pass then sped right on down the road into the corner, you know that corner where you think you should give way but you don't actually have to? And just as the car got to the turn, a moped came out of the side road in front of it, and the car hit the bike, and veered, and went into the front of a second-hand shop. I stood and watched it all happen; I couldn't move. All I could think was that it must mean someone had shot you. Your jeep had crashed. An IED had blown off your leg and the ripples had made it all the way back to Salisbury. I was sure I had just seen your life end, as if I was standing on the shoreline and you were miles out and drowning.

A police car and two ambulances turned up while I was standing there in the light of the McDonald's window, frozen and thinking of James and what I would tell him if the news ever came of your death, feeling my heart in my chest because I thought yours must have stopped and now I was living for both of us. I thought I could feel the strain of it like a plumb

line pulling heavy through me. It looked plain enough to me
that the woman on the moped must have died. I had no
context for comparison. I have not had much experience of
violence or death; I suppose you have had enough for us
both, but something about the way they stood around her
made me think there was nothing to be done. There was a
boy about James's age watching who hurried away; I thought
he was going to throw up from the look of him. The driver
who had hit her was an old man. They put him in the back of
a police car and took him away, while a second and third
police car turned up and a little flock of officers spilled out
from them and cordoned off traffic. It must have snarled up
all the roads round Salisbury for miles, to close that corner,
because there's no other way round the one-way system. I
wonder what diversion they put in place. The old man stood
on the pavement and had a light shone into his eyes before
they swept him off, a killer now, though he looked like he
wouldn't have hurt a fly. I suppose they were checking for
concussion. Even if you have killed someone you might still
be concussed, you might still want help. He looked childlike.
You know the moment after a child has fallen on its hands
and can't yet decide whether it has hurt itself enough to cry or
whether it would rather get on with playing? That was what I
saw while they were checking him on the kerb, the child
buried deep under the surface of that old man's face, hopelessly out of his depth, hopelessly uncertain. Because we never
really grow up, do we?

It looked just like losing your balance, the way he waited
on the pavement with the paramedic, head bowed down. The
weight of the world seemed to be on him, and I wondered

how he could stand up. He must have been too old for driving. Eventually the statement-takers started doing the rounds, and a woman came over to talk to me, and that was when I fainted, and that was how I woke up in the Odstock hospital.

My first thought when I woke was that I might be able to find out whether the woman on the moped really was dead. She would be here, perhaps, if they were treating her. I thought there was no doubt at the time, but when I came back to consciousness I found myself filled with the hope she might somehow have lived. She might not have broken her neck, perhaps only her back, perhaps she would only be paralysed. Would that be better, to be paralysed rather than dead? I have sometimes asked myself that, would I stay with you if you lost all movement, or all memory, or speech? I think I would. Would I be right to? I don't know the answer to that; that's a harder question. Would you stay with me? That's harder to answer again.

What does it mean when a back breaks? Have the vertebrae unslotted or are they themselves cracked or shattered or powdered up? It's probably not what happens to the bones, it's how it shoves the spinal cord around that does for you. Someone said to me once all our emotional thinking is done not in the brain but in the brain stem and the spinal cord. A teacher, maybe. I can't believe that's quite true, but it has made me careful of this root running through me.

My second thought was for you, when I had finished imagining the state of that poor woman's spine, and then I was terrified again. I got out of my bed, pulled the tube from my arm and started to walk out of A&E. I could hear a child screaming. All of the little booths were filled with too many people. You're only supposed to have two visitors at any one time, I remember that from the time James broke his leg, but everyone here had three or four people with them. Everyone except me, that is. There were only two chairs in each booth, so people were standing around or sitting on the floor, like this was a big airport and a plane had been delayed, and I thought about offering them my chairs since no one was waiting for me in them, but then a policeman put his hand on my shoulder and took me back to my bed. You're not allowed to wander round, it seems, if there's a chance you might be ill.

They already knew there was nothing wrong with me. They had taken blood samples to make sure. A nurse came, and I told her I had been afraid, that was all, and I was very sorry to have wasted their time. She told me not to worry, but she didn't seem to have much sympathy. Why would she? I had wasted her time, and the hospital bed, and the waiting chairs. I suppose a lot of people waste nurses' time. I suppose I wasn't even the first that evening. She discharged me, and I walked out into the night, caught the bus back to BHS car park, got into my car and drove home to Tidworth. I texted James to see whether he was alive, and he texted straight back, which was good of him and not very like him, and I'm not ashamed to say I read the text while I was driving, because I knew it would make me a better driver to be certain he was alive. If a lorry had ploughed into the wrong lane while I read that text, I wouldn't have been able to do a thing about it, of course, and normally I hate people who check their phones while they drive, but sometimes things are more important than the rules.

I still didn't know whether you were alive. I went to the

computer and started Skype up and I saw you were online, so I thought it must be all right. But then I started wondering, would you go offline if you died? Probably you wouldn't. Your laptop was at the base; if you died, you'd probably die on patrol and no one would shut down your laptop for you. So I called, and you picked up, and I couldn't tell you what was wrong, because it seemed so silly once I thought about it, and that was why I was so quiet tonight. You told me such horrible things, now I think back over them. About a new recruit who had been tied up in a sleeping bag and dragged round by his mates from the back of a Landy. About two boys of sixteen under your command who had blinded themselves in a competition to see which of them could stare longest at the sun. That's what happens to you, that's the world you have to live through. And I hardly had the strength to say a thing. I barely managed a sympathetic sound. I suppose I am far too wrapped up in myself. I suppose I live in too small a world, where even something as ordinary as a car crash, two used-up lives colliding with each other, looks to me like the end of the world. I couldn't shake myself out of the fear that was in me.

And now I am doing what I always do when I can't find the strength to tell you what I'm actually feeling. I am telling you everything here instead. I am unburdening myself where no one else can see the shame of my struggle to do a thing as ordinary as cope. I am hiding in a diary.

Sunday, 12th May

A good morning. I had shopping and chores to keep me busy; I didn't have to think. I was tired, of course. It had been a late night. I couldn't sleep for hours even after I had finished writing. Normally I can sleep once I have emptied myself here and the ink is drying, normally that way things are out of my head. Isn't that the point of a book like this?

Not last night. I lay there listening for you for hours, and you didn't come.

On an average day very little you might constitute as real actually happens to me. I don't think I experience very much of actual life. Perhaps that is everyone's feeling – that they are just sitting around and life is happening in the next valley, I don't know. So last night was inevitably a shock to the system, a human being shattered in front of my eyes. That is a far cry from Lucy across the street and what she thinks of the new road markings, or whatever it was I wrote about last week. I can't read it back. It would look too small and cheap in the light of day, and none of us want to think about how small our lives are.

After lunch I didn't do so well. I kept imagining I was her – the woman on the moped, I mean. I tried to do something, keep myself occupied, read a book, but I felt faint and even had to put my head between my knees. I went upstairs and lay on the bed for an hour without undressing. You would not have been proud of me. I couldn't stop thinking of my back closing up like a concertina. Fear, again and again. I wished that today was a day for rehearsals, but there was nothing at all in the calendar till tomorrow.

When did this start happening, this fear? It creeps up on us so gently. I don't remember when I lost my head for heights, or when I first became uncomfortable with running down hills, but now I think of snapping my leg and the break never

quite healing, or falling on my neck and never moving again.
There – I am thinking of the woman who died once more.
Now I think of the fragile body of our son, though he thinks
he is so strong, his body that he hurls around the rugby field
or through the woods when he rides his bike without thinking
of the consequences. It gives me a rush of blood to my heart
when I see him racing around the way he does – a rush of joy
and fear and anxiety for this boy we have created between us,
who is so free and unafraid. I wonder how I could ever teach
him how precious a thing his strength is, and I know he'll
have to lose so much before he realises.

Forgive me, but I did what nervous housewives have always
done and hit the gin about three o'clock. It doesn't feel any
better, but I will be asleep by nine, and we must count our
blessings where we can find them. I have been sitting with a
glass till then, trying to learn my lines. I used to be good at
line learning, but these days I find the bastards won't go in. I
don't know whether I've lost the habit or whether my head's
filled up.

Thursday, 16th May

Awful sickness in my stomach that will not go away. I read in
the paper that the woman in the accident was the woman
who used to run the flower stall in the market square. I was
speaking to her just last week.

Her name was Rita, and she always seemed very free,
because she never cared what anyone thought of her. I
suppose I shouldn't speak of her in the past tense – that's
terrible, that's tempting fate. The last time I saw her she had
been convinced she was going to prison. I don't know whether

it was true, or what anyone would send her to prison for, but I wasn't completely surprised, because there was undoubtedly something sharp at the edges about her, and I worried afterwards that she might have seen that in me. I have always struggled to suppress the assumption that people who work on market stalls or work outdoors in any capacity come largely from less fortunate worlds than my own, and all have their crosses to bear, and perhaps lash out against it all from time to time. I don't know a very great deal about country people, not really; even living round here I feel I'm only visiting country people, and I wish I could get deeper in amongst them.

'Thing is, Alison,' she said to me, and I liked that, the fact she remembered my name, that was always one of the best things that happened in my week, 'I almost don't care, you see, cos no one else gives a toss, so why should I?'

I'm not sure why I'm writing down this whole conversation here. In person I would never think for a moment that you would be interested in this story. I must be careful not to idealise you so much in written form that the real you becomes a disappointment. It would be unfair of me to expect you to be interested in every last person I speak to when you get home.

'I'm sure people do give a toss,' I told her, trying not to sound silly swearing in my posh voice. I suppose I must have sounded posh to her, anyway. It's all relative, isn't it? In Kensington I sound like a country woman. 'I give a toss.'

'Yeah, but you don't really, do you? It's just a story for you to feel bad about. You're not actually gonna do anything about it, are you?'

'What can I do for you, Rita?'

'Well, nothing really. If I done the crime, I do the time.'

This is how she talked. A sad, depreciated sort of language really, with a very free approach to the matter of tense. Everyone in the south of England speaks Estuary these days. I read about it in a magazine article. After the war a lot of Londoners were rehomed across the counties in new housing built more cheaply than it could have been in the capital, and I think that movement has levelled out the accents. I don't know what else it has done to us – imagine a whole community, a whole city, where nobody's grandparents are buried in the same county everyone lives in. What kind of displacement is that? What does it lead to, to be distant from your history, from the roots of you?

Rita went on, blowing her nose loudly into a handkerchief she took from her sleeve. 'The people who don't care I'm talkin' about are my people, my family. And that almost makes me feel better really, cos if I'm not hurtin' anyone I don't care where I lay my head, even if it's a nick bunk bed. I just don't want to hurt anyone, that's all.'

'I don't think you could hurt anyone, Rita, especially your own family. I think you have a good heart.' I was surprised at myself for saying that, it felt a little over the top, a little unguarded, but Rita looked at me very intensely, as if the thought mattered to her very much.

'Well, I always liked to think I did, but I've had all these doubts, do you see?'

'No, you mustn't. You must believe this much in yourself – that you're a good person. And obviously good people, the best people, make mistakes all the time. I'm sure Gandhi made mistakes; I bet there are whole chapters in the Bible where Jesus makes mistakes – I don't know, it's been years since I read it.'

'You should read it. It's good, the Bible.'

'Is it?'

'Yeah, it's parables, isn't it? It's a How To guide. I've read all the books of all the different religions. I go back to them a lot, for advice, for comfort, to make me feel better. I've got almost all of them. The big ones, I mean. I'm not reading the book of fucking Mormon. Or the one whose god is called The Bob, have you heard of them?'

'I don't think I have.'

'They done an interview on Radio Four. A woman who said she worshipped The Bob. I thought, fuck off, to be honest. If you go in for all that shit you've gotta dress it up in a bit of dignity, haven't you?'

'That seems like the thing to do, yes.'

'But I'm pleased you say I've got a good heart, Alison. I am. Thank you. I think I have. I just sometimes wonder.'

That, now I come to think of it, is the last thing she said to me, really. I bought some chrysanthemums and thanked her and wished her luck with the court case and went about my day, and I suppose she was right. I didn't think about her again until I read in the *Journal* that she is in a coma in Odstock hospital. It doesn't say whether they expect her to regain consciousness. I should go and visit. But if she can't hear the world, what would be the point of it? I would only upset myself and waste more of the nurses' time showing me in and out. I suppose I must just think of her and hope she wakes up and that when she does she is still able to live her life.

186

I didn't feel at all well thinking that it was Rita who had been on that moped, but when the light started to go out of the day I pulled myself together and got in the car and got to my ushering shift at the Playhouse. I couldn't stop thinking of my ribs caving in on themselves, of my bones crushed to dust. On the drive over I felt very dazzled by the lights of all the cars that were travelling in the other direction. It seems to me always that it would be so easy, so terribly easy, to lose control of the steering wheel and veer like a moth right into the bottomless endlessness and pain and agony and shrieking and screeching of metal through limbs of those lights one evening. Apparently moths don't actually aim for the flames of candles – that's a misunderstanding. They navigate by the sun, or the moon – I don't remember – by keeping it always on their right. Or their left. Electric light confuses them; they mistake it for the moon, or the sun, and circle it, thinking if they only keep the light on their right, or their left, they'll get to where they're going eventually. Then sometimes their circles decrease in circumference as they continue to circle, and that's when they tumble into the flames. It's a terrible thing to see a moth burn itself, I think. People swat them sometimes, like you might swat a fly, but I couldn't bear it. If you look closely at a moth after someone has crushed it, you'll see its wings powder up into silver. They scatter apart into grey dust, like solid smoke, like the lead from a pencil. They are made of different stuff from us; I think perhaps they are spirits. The thing to do when you drive at night, of course, is not to look at the lights that are coming towards you, because we tend to direct ourselves towards where we are looking. If you look at the lights it's hard not to turn the wheel a little as well.

I think I'm going to have to ask the doctor for some sleeping pills.

Monday, 20th May

Rehearsals this evening. It is a little bit nerve-wracking, watching the first night creep closer and still knowing you aren't any good, no good at all. Sometimes I wake in the middle of the night feeling cold about it, all the people who will be watching me, all the lines I will forget. I have a real part, you see, a big lead role with a lot to say, a lot of stage time. What I never know is what to do with my hands.

Tuesday, 21st May

Rose at work's husband has died. It happened last week, but the news was announced to us this morning. He had cancer in the lungs and lymph nodes; people say once it's in the lymphs there is very little hope left and you must prepare yourself. All us girls on the reception desk at work have been looking after her while he's been ill; it is very sad now the story has come to its ending.

She was told straight off it was going to kill him. All that was possible was slowing the progress of things, so of course they went for chemotherapy. He wanted to last as long as he could. I think anyone would, although I must admit I wondered at the time what the point of all that pain could be when there was so little left to fight against. But that was because it wasn't happening to me, that was a failure of sympathy. I only had to think of you or James falling ill and then I knew what I would do to keep you both from pain, to make anything better. Which is that I would die for you and

James, gladly; I would do anything I could, anything that was asked of me.

Rose cried and cried and couldn't answer the phones or deal with the boys when they came to us sick or asking for anything. We're the catch-all team you find in every school or big organisation – secretaries and receptionists and amateur nurses who look after all the lost property and deal with angry parents and confiscate mobile phones from the boys. We sweep up whatever isn't covered by an actual job description, that is our role. 'The front desk' is how we're summarised, and I don't think it's ever so different from your life on the front line, in a smaller way of course. Whatever goes wrong, it's our job to fix it.

The headmaster had to give Rose time off, and we all worked round the space she left behind her. They told him he had six months. And it was awful of me, but I thought of myself when she told us that, because six months is such a long, long time to say goodbye to something, I was almost jealous. If you were to die I would most likely have no warning. No explanation or reason, no sickness I could use to rationalise what happened. I would have only violent death and loose ends; everything would be interrupted and unfinished. I would have to go to my son and explain to him, and he would have seen nothing coming, and I don't know if I would be strong enough to carry him through that. I don't know whether James would even be able to take it in if you died. The young spend too much time on computer games to take the thought of death as finally as they need to. I grew up in a society that said there was a second life, a life after death, but even us Christians never had to deal with the psychological effects of being able to replay a level in a computer game if you couldn't get through to the end without getting shot. We never thought you got more than one shot at life. I wonder how easy it is for James and his generation to understand that.

I felt so bad, so vain and self-centred thinking of anything but Rose and her situation when I first heard how long her husband had to live, but I thought as well how strange it was that time can mean different things and stretch or contract depending on the situation. Because we will have been more than half a year apart next time I see you, and that for me is an ocean, a lifetime. I can hardly bear it every time it happens. But of course for Rose and her husband, and I think they have a son as well, that is the shortest sentence they will ever have read.

She cried and cried and cried.

I have pains in my hands sometimes. Very strange. I don't know where they come from. I take a few paracetamol and they go, but of course there's caffeine in paracetamol, it's not good for me, and too much of the stuff and you get addicted and it stops working anyway. I wonder whether I have carpal tunnel syndrome? I don't really know what it is; I remember it makes your wrists hurt, though. Am I driving enough to give myself RSI? Whatever it is, it keeps me up nights. I buy a new packet of aspirin or ibuprofen or whatever comes to hand every other day at the moment, it seems. Just so I know I'll have something nearby if my hands are aching. If I can't be sure there's anything for me to take I get so uneasy.

Rose is strange, really. Every other woman on the reception desk where I spend my days is there because she can't start any more of a career than working in a school. When your husband's in the army you are tied to his life and must surrender that part of your own. But Rose's husband runs a shop. Or I suppose I should say he ran a shop. I don't know why she has stopped at this and not built up anything more for herself. Perhaps there is nothing more she could do, but I don't believe that. It's probably not true, but I like to think we're all as talented as each other. It's just that some of us find what we're good at and some don't. Perhaps Rose is a good mother and that is her talent. I always think she worried too much to be really good at anything, though. She is too con-vinced of her limitations to ever really be calm in what she does, and wonder whether more might be possible, and try to find out.

Apart from Rose we're a group time forgot, a ragbag of unemancipated women, and that makes me hate working at the school. A gaggle of army wives, wives of academics, married to the medical profession, whatever life our partners chose. We can't put down roots, or climb any ladders, or build anything; whatever metaphor you want to offer will be use-less to us. We do this simple, unskilled, unrewarding work and pack the house up when we're told and tell ourselves these are our lives. But it's like we've been missed off a list; it's like our real lives are passing us by.

I don't know how I allowed this to happen to me. There was a time in my twenties when my work didn't matter to me at all – it was just a way of bringing in money, a sideshow to the main event of you and me and James and our evenings together. But some time in my thirties, things started getting away from under my feet. James turned ten, and from then on it felt like I never did quite reach him again, because there was never another day when I really believed he would rather have been with me than on his own in his room with his music or his radio or his toys or his thinking. And I think somehow I got it into my head that when we really got started on life together, you and I, the house moves would slow down and we would find more of a rhythm, or, rather, more of a rhythm that suited me. Which of course was never going to be the case for as long as you were in the army. But I think as the years went by and our lifestyles didn't change, I began to feel lost about the way we were living, as if I had no control over things, as if I didn't know where we were going. And once you have started to feel you're adrift, everything gets worse, doesn't it, because the whole trick of a good life as far as I can tell seems to me to be not to admit that life is drifting. To forge as much of a path through the swell and ebb of everything. Somewhere between being thirty and happy and feeling things had a purpose, and turning forty, I lost my enthusiasm for things. Because you didn't leave the army, and a time didn't come when I got to make the choices, and even now we still haven't reached it.

What makes me feel so bad is that I don't know what world I might have succeeded in, and I think now it's not very likely I'll ever discover what my talent was. It seems awful to me that a woman my age should think in the past tense the way I do. Or in the future tense, speaking of you. But never in the present. Perhaps if I had been an actor then things would have been different. The job of an actor is verbs. They get to do things, and live.

After Rose's husband fell ill someone at work suggested we

might do something for Cancer Research. It's so difficult to show support and solidarity when the case is already terminal, because what you do must of necessity always seem a bit apologetic, I think, but we thought entering a race or something like that could show Rose we were with her as much as we could be. So we entered a Cancer Research race on the rugby field up by Old Sarum and started to train in the evenings, thudding through the streets in ones or twos. I joined the gym at the Five Rivers Leisure Centre because I didn't want people to have to put up with the sight of me sweating round Tidworth with my earphones in. I felt I'd be glad of the excuse to stay at the leisure centre in the evenings too. I've never been a fat woman, but I lost a lot of weight at that time. It was very liberating. I didn't have to go home till nine, evenings I went to the gym. I didn't like the running, but I enjoyed not being in the house. I found I could fit back into clothes I hadn't worn in years, had more energy. So a month ago we all ran the Cancer Research race together, all wearing pink, and raised a few thousand pounds. I know I told you this at the time, I just like to remember it, and I almost felt guilty because I enjoyed it so much. I didn't feel like I'd done it for Rose or to raise money. I felt I had got so much that was good from running that race, I couldn't believe I'd done anything worthy. Rose didn't come to watch us either, and that just fed the feeling. We had no one to look to on the sidelines when we got to the finish, no one to remind us of what we had been doing, so all of us who had run together hugged each other, and I wondered how many of us thought about Rose. I stopped going to the gym after that. I couldn't pretend I was doing it for Rose or her husband after the race.

The one time I did go back reminded me I hadn't really done it for them in the first place, how selfish I am.

Sunday, 26ᵗʰ May

Going through the attic yesterday evening I came across a shoebox of old photographs of us. I can't tell you quite why I was shuffling round the attic. I was hunched up under the roof, and now my back aches, my calves are aching, I can feel how old I am, how mortal. At first I was looking for my CDs, because I wanted to listen to Joni Mitchell, so I went up in search of *For The Roses*. But once I was in amongst our things I just forgot myself. Silly, really. I was poking through all the boxes, all the records, remembering the days when we had a record player, which was so pretentious of us really, but I loved it. And this shoebox was in amongst your old papers and some old school books of James's. From the time before we were married, so we look very young and slim and full of the future. It's quite a shock to see what you used to look like when you're not expecting it. I can't help always feeling that I never really change, but there it is in the shoebox, plain as day, I very clearly have, I have got much older, as we all do, as no one can help doing.

So much has changed since you and I first met that if I ever had the chance to meet my younger self now, I don't think I'd recognise her. When we first met I was so sure I was going to be an actress, and you were just a bit of squaddie rough to flirt with over the summer. Even if you were at Sandhurst, that was my fantasy of you. It was quite dirty, some of what I imagined of who you were. What did you do that forced me to revise that first crude stereotype I had, to start looking at you differently, like a human being, and respect you a little? I suppose you were always well turned out. Always well spoken. There was always a reserve about you, and when you don't know what people are thinking they become more interesting, don't they?

I think I fell for you over that week when you drove me to my drama school auditions. It feels like it happened to a different woman. We got lost in the suburbs of Bristol looking for the Old Vic Theatre School, having got the wrong end of the stick and gone to the Old Vic Theatre first, which is ages away in a different part of the city, and I started to panic because I wasn't going to have time to do my warm-ups, so you made me practise my singing in the car and laughed along with all my scales. I always used to think when I made you laugh that you were laughing at me. I could never understand until I loved you how I might make you so happy. In the audition they thought my singing was much better than my acting, I could tell, and perhaps I have you to thank for that, for making me do my warm-ups. I didn't get a call-back in the end.

Then you drove me out to Oxford, to that field in the middle of nowhere where they had set up the Oxford School of Drama. I would have loved to have gone there. It was so isolated and alone; for three years you could do nothing but think and look at the fields and sky and learn how to live in your body. I don't know where you went while I was in the workshops and the audition; I think you had a Thermos flask, so perhaps you parked the car somewhere with a view and put your feet up and read a book. I remember you were reading Hardy at the time, because you read me a passage after Bristol where he described a dawn as being like a still-born child and we agreed he had the bleakest mind ever. I was quite good with my audition pieces in Oxford, I thought, but I could tell I fluffed the movement session. I just felt so silly waving my hands around as slowly as I could to their music. At lunchtime they took me into a room with a dozen other hopefuls and told us we wouldn't be needed for the afternoon. So you and I went into Oxford and got drunk instead, as if we were students there. I hope the students of Oxford are drunk all the time, because their pubs are lovely. And perhaps that was when I loved you, when you shook me out of feeling sorry for myself that day and held my hair back when I threw up later that evening, and when we made love in the back of your car at the end of the night and lay together afterwards, you telling me all you knew about the red kites who flew in pairs in the skies above Oxford.

My dream of being an actor died two weeks later on the Talgarth Road in London, at LAMDA. I knew they didn't want me the minute I walked in the door. I was terribly sad, because I knew before I started doing my pieces that it was the last time I'd perform them. So I did my Margaret like I was saying goodbye to her, then walked out and no one felt the need to say very much to me. And I looked around me on my way back out the doors and almost persuaded myself I wasn't in love with it.

That's how a lot of people find their lives, I think. They try on different social groups till they find one that fits them, or one where they feel at least a little bit at home, then do the work that's needed to belong to it. But I seem to have stopped after I realised I couldn't belong to the theatre. I never did find that group of people just like me. But I found you, and that has felt like home ever since that summer, and then we had James, and he became part of that home I carry with me too.

I have kept the shoebox out. I didn't go through all of it. I found I was becoming suddenly quite upset, looking over everything and remembering that time, so that I had to come down out of the attic. I saw my hands were shaking and I didn't feel well; I felt weak inside, as if I hadn't eaten. There was a bottle of white wine open in the fridge, and I took it out and poured a glass and drank it, just to distract myself, just to have something to do. And it's so easy, isn't it? That first glass, when you feel it rush through you, and all of your body relaxes. It's so easy to feel better that way. I know I shouldn't. It's a road to ruin if ever there was one. But nothing works so fast, and at the bottom of the glass I found I was calmer. I sat down, turned the radio on. I listened to bad music and thought of nothing, and for as long as the wine worked through me I didn't feel upset. I didn't find my Joni Mitchell. I don't know whether I will have the courage to go through the photos with you.

What do people do with their lives? I mean seriously, literally, hour for hour, what does everyone do? When I was at school I felt perfectly ordinary, just like anyone else, but now it is as if I have forgotten how. I have to do impersonations of a real human being to fit in anywhere or even get served in the supermarket. I have lost my instinct and my taste for life, and my days feel like eating with a cold now, knowing you need soup, swallowing, not being able to taste it.

Friday, 31ˢᵗ May

You have been away for four months today. I'm getting to like the area. Salisbury's a nice city. I go in as much as I can just to potter round and look in the shops. I can spend the morning going in and out of them or looking round the library or going for coffee and reading the papers in the cafes and watching the people. It's not too far from James, and I like knowing that if he needed me, or if I wanted to go and see him, I could get there without too much trouble. I haven't gone, of course. It would embarrass James, so I must be disciplined and wait for the holidays. That is the awful truth of a boarding school: they teach their students not to need anyone, and I suppose they teach the parents not to need their children as well, in the end, though for me it is hard to learn. It is a graceful softening of the process of separation that I imagine falls on us all more completely when our child enters university or starts their career. We aren't there yet, James and I, which is a relief to me for now. I have all those separations still to go through. I don't really know what I'm talking about there just yet, except for remembering my own parents and the way it felt. I never spoke to them properly again after I left school. Isn't that strange? The way you get to the end of school and suddenly you are required to enter your life, as if it were a river you were plunging into, as if you had been sunning yourself on the banks all this time? And suddenly you must make choices and get on with it, with all the structures you have been educated into removed, or at least made invisible, because I suppose we live within the confines of our schools from the neck up for the rest of our lives. But isn't it strange that a starting pistol is fired and all of a sudden we must get on our feet and begin to run? I don't know what I will do when that happens for James, when he is really running away from me. If he stops speaking to me like I did with my parents I won't have anyone to speak to at all.

Rehearsals for *Hamlet* are still going well, and I will run through my lines once, all the way through without the book, before I sleep. We will have rehearsed the thing for three months by the time it opens, but I still feel the terrible pressure of time. It has been so long since I did anything so exposing. I feel sure I won't be able to get it right, and everyone will see, and everyone will feel sorry for me. I think that, above all else, is my greatest fear in life. The pity of others. That's what makes my neck tight and my shoulders seize, makes my back curl up like paper in a fire. And the worst of all is that you can't do anything about that feeling while you're at a rehearsal, you can't stop for a sit down or a drink to steady yourself. Everyone would see you couldn't cope; to look for help would only make everything worse.

There is more pressure because I am having to play Ophelia. It's because there are never enough people in these amateur dramatic societies. They are always looking for women who can pass themselves off as younger than they are. Women under sixty, really. The older you get, the more easily you find people who want to participate in amateur opera or theatre, in voluntary activity, in society, in life. Perhaps because we are all aware it is ending for us, ever so gradually.

You would like Studio Theatre, I think. I fell in love with it the first time I went to visit the building they were based in. They had been going on for years and years, maybe thirty years, and in all that time they had been saving for a building. Around the millennium they finally raised enough, and in between Waitrose and the Five Rivers Leisure Centre, looking out over an empty stretch of grass by the fire station, they built a theatre. It wasn't a beautiful thing. The car park wasn't tarmacked and the building was all breezeblocks with a sort of gridiron roof, but looking at it and knowing people had saved so long to make it, that couples who had spent a long time working on it had got married in there, that under its rough surface was a whole world of love and ambition and dreaming, made it seem very beautiful to me. This was the real theatre in Salisbury. This was where the city spoke up. And it seemed like the sort of place that might welcome someone who hadn't been welcome in LAMDA or the Old Vic or anywhere else. So I went and auditioned for *Hamlet*, and they asked me to play Ophelia, and I'd never felt so happy because I'd thought I would be auditioning for Gertrude, and it's always nice to be told you're too young for something, even if it is only because everyone else in the play is far too old for their parts and even more badly cast than I am.

In fact, I didn't think I would be good enough for a part at all, even Gertrude. I thought it would be a chance to do a bit more ushering. But they've let me get involved, and so I'm getting as stuck in as I can. I help with the upkeep and cleaning of the building, doing the loos and the sinks every week. I buy a bottle of bleach and get through all of it dousing the toilets and the urinals. I always wonder why there isn't a security check if you buy a bottle of bleach in a supermarket. If you drank it down, it would kill you in an instant, and in some places they'll stop you before they let you anywhere near paracetamol, let alone alcohol, but bleach is easy. I wonder how often people kill themselves like that these days? I associate it with poor housewives after the war. There are less terrible methods now – the swallowing of sleeping pills and painkillers. I wonder what criteria go through your mind on the day you decide to kill yourself. You probably go for what's nearest, what's most easily accessible. Surely no one in their right mind kills themselves, after all, so I doubt the thinking is ever sophisticated. So perhaps there are still lots of people who kill themselves with bleach. They say you always have to close the coffin for people who do that, because you end up with terrible burns down the side of the mouth.

For all the pressure they put on me, I do love the rehearsals. It is wonderful to be sitting in a room with a group of people talking about a play and trying the lines out; I haven't done it in so long. It has been so exciting to get out our scripts and fill our mugs with tea and wrestle with that play, the biggest play, the greatest play in the world. Bits of it are so frustrating to me, because it's all about men, and the first thing you realise when you look at old plays is that people in the past hardly thought of women as people at all, the way they were used in the plots of stories. Ophelia and Gertrude sort of come on so the men can express new aspects of themselves; they're shunted through the story without ever really getting to affect it at all, poor things, and it kills them both in the end of course. You feel like a bit of an eavesdropper playing a woman in *Hamlet*, because it's a story about a boy deciding whether he loves himself or his father more, when you get right down to it. You can tell Shakespeare wasn't a woman, whoever he was.

It's still a wonderful play to be part of. I love the mad bit, singing and throwing lavender around. I get to change into a torn dress and trail on like seaweed caught in a tide. My favourite part, though, is the nunnery scene. Shakespeare hardly writes her like a person at all. Or if she's a person she's like a very battered wife, because Hamlet turns round and shouts at her for a whole speech and she just takes it. Doesn't say a thing back. She just stands there in this huge silence and looks at him. It's so sad, because she really loves him and he throws it all back in her face. She can't bear it; she can't even speak. In that moment I feel like Shakespeare did understand Ophelia, even if he didn't write her that much of a part. That is the bit that shakes me most in the acting. I stand there looking at Stuart, the man playing Hamlet, and think of you. Imagine you tearing me apart like that. I imagine the violence you face every day, and then I picture you turning it all on to me so that it is like a TV set screaming static right into me. And I shake and shake, and Bridget, the lovely old lady directing the play, always says it is the best thing I do.

I'm not sure whether it's very good or very bad for me. Most of the time I block out the life you must have in Afghanistan. I can't stand the thought of the heat and the boredom and the bullets and the danger – all of that happening to my man, I can't bear it. Sometimes I get home and cry after rehearsals, but even while I am crying like that I get a feeling it might be doing me good. Missing you is like a pressure that builds in me, and I think in the play and in the crying after rehearsals I am able to release some of it. Even to find a use for it. Perhaps I could have been an actor after all, if I had just had a bit more to worry about when I went to those auditions. That may be what they mean when they tell you that before you become an actor you must first get experience of life.

Tonight on my shift at the Playhouse one of the actors rehearsing the next play came and spoke to me! A very nice man who I think was being kind because he knows all of us ushers get terribly star-struck by actors and wanted to make himself feel famous, but nevertheless it seemed nice of him. He's never been to Salisbury before and asked me where was a good place to get away from the rest of his company because he'd had a hard day in the rehearsal room and they always went for a drink together and today he wanted to be on his own. I told him I wasn't the best person to ask but gave him all the tips I could think of all the same.

Sometimes I think social contact like this, however small it may be, is what's keeping me sane. I have my work at the school, but I dread the bell at half three that means the day is ending. The night is such a long stretch of time when there's no one to share it with. Phone calls with you and James sometimes, but never any real sharing; a voice on the end of a line isn't being with anyone, is it? Tidworth is not somewhere you would choose to spend your life. It's a place to get out of as much as you can. We all hold ourselves apart round here. It's so strange how so many women all in the same boat pretend they have the life raft to themselves. I watch them in Tesco, sailing through the aisles, the same distracted look on all their faces. We are all trying our best to forget this is the only chance we get at life; we are all trying not to admit this is what we have ended up doing with it. Of all the things that could be possible for us in the world, we're doing this. Tesco. I want to talk to them, but I'm too afraid. They must be lonely too.

They must be frightened. They must fear the end of the day, and going back into their houses, and bad television. I want to ask them how they cope, but I'm too afraid to say anything.

Even without the conversations I sometimes get out of it, I love ushering, which surprises me and might perhaps surprise you, because I worried it would be too passive, too like sitting on the bench. But I love the way watching the same show several times makes you appreciate it differently. You stop listening to the stories and start to look at how it is all being done, what is technically happening in front of your eyes. Some nights I can watch the play as if it were music, structures and patterns repeating and varying; some nights it is like a lesson in geometry, the arrangement of bodies in space, varying in relation to each other, the traces of a director's instructions in front of your eyes as the actors find subtle excuses to move round the rooms they're in, refill their glasses, stoke the fire, keep the bodies moving and the patterns changing across the stage. I have started to get to know the audiences, and when the show changes I like meeting some of the regulars again and finding out who remembers me, who is friendly, who thinks they own the place. And I have come to appreciate in a way I had never known before that the permanent thing, the lasting thing about a theatre is the audience who visit. I have watched the actors go from rehearsals and on to the stage and realised that already, only a few months after arriving here, and without earning a penny from it, I own the theatre more than they do, belong there more than they do, will outlast their mayfly stays.

This imaginary world. It will always be a beautifully dangerous place to visit. All these people, all so bright and talented, who could have been anything, done anything, been lawyers or teachers with pensions to look forward to or made millions in the City, willingly and knowingly surrendering all thought of career security or career progression, or comfort in old age, or lavishness in the way they live, in order to take part in this ramshackle project. It is almost a political act when you live in the theatre, because you turn your back on what people are supposed to value, on profit and loss, in order to participate. And I'm no great one for political acts, but I enjoy the courage of people who go in for them. That is something I have always loved about you, because your life is a kind of politics as well, to be out there fighting on behalf of other people. But my own political statement of choice, had I only got through one of those auditions, would have been to be part of the theatre. To use my life as a way of arguing that people should tell stories to each other, share their lives and care about each other. That would have been my kind of politics.

It is very late. I do not know why I have been writing for so long. I don't want to put down the pen and be on my own in the house again. Perhaps I will take a pill again tonight. A sleeping pill robs the night from you, but at least you get through it faster. The computer button I wish I could install into my life would be Edit Undo, that's the function I dream of, a way to go back; all that medicine has invented so far is the sleeping pill, a way to fast forward. Still, anything that breaks up the passing of time is an improvement on what I have stretching before me in the mornings, behind me in the evenings.

Saturday, 8th June

I am frightened by how many packets of sleeping pills and painkiller pills and pointless drugs are filling the cabinet in the bathroom. I look in the mirror each morning and see my face and can't stand the woman in front of me. I am so low, so beaten down by life, and yet there is nothing really wrong with me, is there? I am just a silly woman, worrying about nothing, imagining all the world into opposition with itself. When really I am so lucky. I must seem so ungrateful to everyone who meets me, to live in this world, in this country, to have security and family and even hobbies I enjoy, and still not be able to smile in the mirror in the morning. What has ever been denied me in my life? What have I ever wanted for?

Then I open the mirrored cabinet and see that behind my face there are pills and pills, all waiting to be swallowed. And that's when I really hate myself. I have such a good life, an easy life. Why do I need to dope my way through it like that? And why can't I get through a day without something, a way to take the edge off? What is it I find so difficult about being alive? But still I keep buying the little pills just as fast as I consume them. Faster. I should get rid of all of them, but I don't. Every morning I stare at my face and I hate my privilege and my ingratitude, and then I see all those pills piled up, and I wonder.

Thursday, 13th June

How long do you have to spend on hunger strike before you become actually, dangerously ill? Roaming idly through the Internet in a quiet hour this afternoon, I came across some statistics for the weight loss of people who refuse to eat, and of course I know it's very bad for them, but really it seems to be a very effective way of losing weight. Pounds a day just falling away. Might starvation ever be an advisable way of getting into shape? It's so difficult to find out, because of course no doctor can ever really recommend it. I suppose it might all be the kind of weight that you put straight back on when you start eating again. And I think if you don't eat at all you do damage to your liver or your kidneys, I don't remember which. All the same, I don't know why no shock doctor hasn't recommended it as a course of action for the overweight. It seems to be very effective, to make the body eat itself.

Someone said at work today that whenever they see me they always think I look sad. It took me by surprise, hearing that, as you can imagine. I suppose I am a reflective person, and people who keep themselves to themselves must look strange to those who prefer to be talking with someone else. I suppose it's a product of my upbringing – lots of books, lots of outdoors, lots of solitude. But I didn't recognise that reading of myself. I didn't think I was a particularly sad person in comparison with everyone else. I mean, I know I get sad, sometimes I'm very lonely for the longest time, especially when James starts a new term and I have so long to wait to spend time with either of you again, and that gnaws at me as it would anyone, but that happens to everyone, doesn't it? Surely everyone longs for more than what they are allotted in just the same way I do?

I just smiled, just laughed it off. I think I said I was very happy, thank you. I think I gave off the impression that my heart was my own business and no one else's. But I feel unhappy now, thinking that that is how other people might see me. Now I am home and alone again I am wondering whether I have the look of someone who is caged too deep within themselves. Someone who is hard for other people to reach. Is that what sadness is? I don't know how you could put a feeling like that into words, really.

I am going to use the keeping of this journal to make myself so much stronger. I will force myself to read it back each morning to see what I wrote the previous day, and where I find it miserable I'll buck my ideas up, and where it is self-pitying I'll take a good long hard look at myself.

The first buck-up is a house plant. I am going to buy some-thing to look after. It is so strange being in this place with nothing else living with me. Rattling alone, far more solitary than any prison should ever be, surely. Because there is no sound of other people's voices anywhere near. Then there will be my play, my Ophelia, to look forward to. And after that, James will be coming home for the holidays, and I will come up with things for us to do, and talk to him as much as I can, find out what he is looking forward to and what he is hoping and what he is happy about.

When I was a girl I wanted to know about everything. I used to read everything. I used to ask questions. Ever since I realised I'm not that woman any more I have been wondering who it is I have become instead.

Tuesday, 18th June

Rehearsals are almost at an end. I feel sick with the thought of it. We are about to begin. Would you remember what a tech is, I wonder? I don't know whether you ever really listened when I used to talk about acting; I'm sure it was just some-thing we used to do before sex, because I know you liked me when I got passionate, and I always got passionate thinking about the theatre. Techs are rehearsals where you work out what will actually happen, the way everything will get on and off stage and which lights to turn on when, that sort of thing. In Studio Theatre they give a whole week to this activity. I am missing some of my ushering shifts for a little bit to go in every other evening and rehearse and help, go through the scenes but also stand under lights when needed to, to make sure they're bright enough I suppose, and hold things and lift things and mend things if it is needed. So forgive me if I don't write very much in the next few days – my days are busy, thank God, for what feels like the first time in years!

Friday, 21st June

In between work and rehearsals and sleep there seems time for very little else. It has eased the loneliness, as I knew it would. Missing you is less physically painful when there are other things in my life. I haven't spoken to James all week and must be sure to make time for him at the weekend if he has time to Skype me. I suppose he plays a lot of sport, though, at the weekends, so I won't hold my breath. We spoke tonight, and you told me about the stillness all around you in the night, when you go to the edge of the compound and listen to what's beyond it, the sense of isolation you live with all the time. I thought of the solitude of this army base. Its one curry house, its laundrette. I feel very small next to what you go through every day. Because of course it's hard here, of course I'm lonely, but it's only really half an hour from a cafe and a cinema and somewhere to relax. When I think of the loneliness that must follow you every day I can hardly imagine how you bear it. In the good times like this, when my days are full, when I have something to look forward to, I can see beyond myself and recognise that my troubles are all of my own imagining, and that the troubles of others, above all yours, are far greater and more pressing than anything I have experienced. I must remember that, and be sympathetic, and talk to you, and ask you questions, and be a place where you can go in your head and feel calm and feel at home. Too often I think I make you look after me, and it ought to be the other way round. It's just that I find it so hard to see beyond the high walls of my own life if there isn't something special to lift me up out of it.

Saturday, 22nd June

Getting on well with the actor I wrote about the other week. He is a good listener, he asks questions in a way actors never remember to, and has winkled all of my acting life out of me in two or three little chats in the foyer. He has suggested we go for a drink. I was a bit hesitant about it, but no one else ever takes me out for a drink, so I thought what was the harm in saying yes? He doesn't like seeing the other actors in the evening, he says; he finds it all consuming. So I suppose I'm a bit of light relief. His name is Owen. He's not Welsh, though I suppose you'd assume he would be with a name like that. There is a trace of a Yorkshire accent under his vowels.

Tidworth looked like the moon when I parked the car. You know how the light of streetlamps makes everything unreal? Not quite orange, just uncertain in its colours and all washed in the same palette. It's strange the sun doesn't do that, but allows us the variety of all the colours of the world. Unless perhaps under other lights it would be possible to see completely different colours, and sunlight is just as biasing as lamplight in its own way. I made myself a cup of tea and didn't drink it. I had the radio on so I didn't feel alone. Honestly, everyone else here can't be as pathetic as I am, can they? All the women of this town waiting for their men can't be this lonely? It would amount to systematic violence by the army if that were the case, if this was inflicted on all of us. There would need to be a judicial inquiry.

Unless the truth is even more desperate, and this feeling doesn't stop with the army wives. Perhaps this is only one of millions of evenings that everyone is having that are just like this.

Monday, 24ᵗʰ June

Production week begins. I feel so afraid that everyone's going to hate me, it's almost debilitating enough to call in sick to work. I won't, of course. Almost everyone else in the world has worse to deal with, after all, than first night nerves.

Wednesday, 26ᵗʰ June

Tired today. My legs feel heavy and my back hurt all the time I was walking round in my uncomfortable shoes; every minute I spent out of the house was uncomfortable to me. On the days when my back hurts I think of Rita and the car crash I saw, the horror of being in an accident. I wonder what a person thinks in the moment their back is snapped. Then it takes all the strength I have to blot that darkness out.

When I see a young person now, unbowed and untired by life, I feel I can never have been one of them, ever, and it makes me laugh to think everyone old has had that thought, I suppose. We all become strangers to our histories. I loved our beautiful years. Back then it was an adventure even to be near you, and everything we did seemed extraordinary. The postings, of course, that's how the memories organise themselves above all else, one place after another. Our marriage and then Bovington, Fort George, Colchester, Aldershot, Germany. I thought of that, back then, as seeing the world. I hadn't yet noticed how similar everything was wherever you went with the army. The way the same kettles are plugged into the same sockets in the kitchens every time. The way you always know where the cutlery is kept whichever army house you walk into, because everyone lives their life along the same tram lines. I didn't realise the limits of what I was doing back then. I had a baby and brought up a son and marvelled at the different views from the window as years rolled round and we moved from one place to another. I never wanted you to request a stay in the same place back then. I wanted us to keep moving. I wanted to keep seeing the world.

Thursday, 27th June

First performance. I am in a daze, in a dream. I don't think anyone hated it at all. I had two glasses of wine and then drove home. What would you say if you knew I'd done that? I can't help thinking it is quite exciting of me. I never do anything scandalous. So perhaps I can think of drink-driving as my little indulgence on first night, because there was no one there to give me flowers. As daredevil, Oliver-Reed-hell-raiser as I get. Now I must try to sleep it off before work. Not the drink, the exhilaration.

Saturday, 6th July

And it is over. I wish I had written more when it was happening, but there seemed to be so little time. I thought I would be tired, but I wasn't tired, I was simply so busy, and everything was so exciting, I couldn't sit down to write. It was a wonderful thing. We got a review in the *Salisbury Journal*, and I thought I was going to burst when I read they had praised my performance. 'Subtle and moving,' they said, and you will see that cutting when you come home, because I'm afraid it's framed now on our kitchen wall and will not come down from whatever kitchen wall we call our own for as long as I'm breathing. The only proper review I've ever had. Proof I exist. And by someone who thought I was good. I look at it when I drink my tea, and it makes me happy every time.

Saturday, 13th July

It is a week since the play ended, and the way I feel today I almost wish it had never happened at all. Isn't it always so anticlimactic, so draining, when something you love has come to an end? Theatre is the worst, and I had forgotten this aspect of plays. Because you all make yourselves so very vulnerable, doing something as silly as pretending to be someone else in front of each other, it makes you feel during the rehearsals that you are getting very close to each other. And then it is doubly painful when the play ends and you realise that in your ordinary lives, you and the rest of the actors are never likely to meet at all.

There has been the usual drifting apart I remember from other adventures long ago. There was a half-hearted party where the richest cast member got to show off their house and their drinks cabinet, and promises were made to keep in touch that no one seemed to mean to keep, and the very next day I was back to having nothing but my ushering in the evenings, as if nothing had happened. And you and James hadn't even seen the show. No one who has any part in my daily life, my real life, knows much about it having happened. It was just an interlude in between silences, a jaunt I went on, not a real thing. I told you about it on Skype, but because you hadn't been there I started to feel as if it hadn't really happened at all. It has made me lethargic. I can't get out of bed in the mornings. Then when the night falls I'm angry that I lost my day, so I stay up late writing all this down, and then the cycle continues – I can't get up the next morning again. I wonder, does everything we don't like about our lives start with us?

I think we all live our lives a bit through other people. Nothing's funny that wouldn't be a good story to tell to your husband. Nothing's important if I don't want to tell someone else about it. But I wonder more and more whether I haven't got the balance wrong, if I'm not living through you too much. Sometimes I feel as though the life I don't share with you, the days you aren't here, aren't really lived, don't really happen, as if my life is a project I have embarked on with you that has to go on hold when you are away.

Look at this writing, even. Looking back over all this ink I can see plain enough that I spend too much time on my own. I have time to write this all down, for one thing. Is it good for a person to be so wrapped up and echoing round the inside of themselves, bouncing around in their own head?

It is easy to feel incubated in a place like this. These barracks homes, white and faceless like a street where everyone has turned their backs, with their fire escapes out of the back bedrooms making them feel so provisional, like hotels, like film sets. All the hollow eyes of these places, and Sky TV and the digibox for company, and some nights I want to scream because I can't read a proper book, I never have the mental energy to read, and some nights I can almost hear myself screaming just under the surface of myself. If we stay here next year, if they don't change your posting, I will buy flower-pots and plant things in the garden. There is no point now. I couldn't bear it if we moved in the autumn and the plants I bought died in the moving van, the terrible waste of it. But I can't look out of the kitchen window much longer at that bare square of grass looking false as a carpet because it has no weeds or reality woven into it. I would grow mint and thyme and things we could put into proper salads. When you come home I'll never cook us ready meals again, because there is almost nothing in my life that seems real to me, but at least while I'm kneading dough it feels like something is happening.

Sunday, 21st July

Oh my love, tonight I am feeling so frightened, and the feeling's so deep in my stomach it makes me almost sick. It is almost physical, the way emotions get when they turn rotten inside you. I don't want to be writing this at all, because it means now I can never show you this journal, and somewhere in the back of my brain I imagined one day you would get to see this diary, but I have to write this out or I think I will go mad.

I know I must have done something wrong and brought this on myself, because whenever you point a finger at someone else you're pointing three in the other direction, but I am telling you, I am being completely honest with you, I had no idea what was going to happen.

You mustn't think I've ever in my life been tempted even for a moment to stray from you. I wouldn't be able to live if you thought that. Marriage to me is commitment enough, but that's nothing next to James. As far as I've ever seen things, once you have a child together that's a commitment between two people for the rest of their lives. For better or worse, that's the undertaking of being a parent. Because they never stop needing you, do they? I still need my mother long after she's gone. Her strength and her wisdom and her way of taking the importance out of things so that when you thought the world was going to end you could suddenly look again and find it all rather amusing.

I don't know whether you've ever cheated on me. God knows we've both had the opportunity, and the need, the years of our marriage we've spent apart. It feels almost disloyal even to phrase the question, because I don't think that's who you are. It has never till this moment really occurred to me to wonder whether you have always been faithful. And that is the strength of us. That is how happy I am because you exist. So this is not a confession; there is nothing to confess. It is a story about a time when I stayed constant to you.

I am talking about Owen, of course. You would have seen

it coming a mile off. I don't know why I didn't. I don't know what I thought was going to happen. I wrote here before that we agreed to meet for a drink. We met in the Chough on the market square, had a glass of wine and told each other a little of our lives, careful like birds with breadcrumbs. It was all fine at first. I was a woman interested in the theatre enjoying asking an actor about his work. Then when we walked out of the pub to get something to eat he touched my arm, his hand against my elbow, and I knew something terrible was about to happen. I realised I was doing the wrong thing; it was too much like romance and I hadn't seen it coming, I had walked straight into it. I couldn't believe myself. I felt so angry. I hadn't even told you I was going out, let alone who I was spending the evening with, and once I knew what the man I was walking with thought this evening might be about I wondered why I hadn't said anything to you yesterday evening when we spoke. It made me feel terribly afraid.

I couldn't just walk away, of course. I had to get through the evening. We went to Pizza Express, and I couldn't make proper conversation because I was convinced I'd been trying to start an affair and hadn't realised what I was doing till the moment we walked out of the pub. I couldn't have wanted to be anywhere less than sitting in that restaurant with that man. I found I couldn't look him in the eye. Conversation dried up; at the very least I know conversation was stilted. He must have known something had happened, but he ploughed on, trying his best to be carefree, amusing, debonair, and now it was so obvious to me what was going on. Some of the women on the base have flings, but most of them are mothers and don't have the time. I was a mother who did have the time, but I didn't want to be the sort of woman who had secrets from her husband, even though I know you must have your secrets from me, even though I suppose every little empty moment I don't share with you becomes a secret in its own way. We finished dinner, and in the market square by the statue of Henry Fawcett he tried to kiss me. I wondered for a moment whether I had come out that evening because I wanted to kiss him, whether I had stayed quiet and not mentioned this to you because I wanted a secret of my own worth keeping. He looked me in the eyes, and he had beautiful eyes. I suppose he was a beautiful man, and I knew that I wanted him, in the way one animal might want another, at the level below thought. I wondered what it would feel like to kiss someone I didn't know, someone who wasn't you. I wondered whether it would make me feel alive. But I felt more fear than longing. He leaned forward to kiss me and I told him no, that I was sorry, that I was married and it wasn't what I wanted. And I thought as long as no one could see into my soul, where I am far less certain of anything I have ever wanted or done than I have ever admitted aloud, I was absolved in the eyes of the world by saying that to him.

People have cheated on me. Long ago, when I was at school. You feel all sorts of things when you find out it's been happening. Stupid, embarrassed, ugly and rejected and low, angry and spiteful. You dream of revenge. You feel uncertain and lost and sad, like the ground's falling away from under you. I could not believe that in some way, however small a way, I had risked exposing you to that.

I drove home barely able to see the road through the tears I found myself crying, and I had to turn up the radio so as not to have to listen to myself and the way I snivelled all the way home, feeling stupid and fooled, feeling duplicitous towards you. And it is so hard lying here now wanting only to call you but knowing I can't, for the thousand usual reasons – because you won't be free, because we have our schedules, and also because I will cry again when I see your face and think what an idiot I've been, and you will ask me what's the matter, and then I'll either have to lie or tell you the truth, and which of those could possibly make me feel better? Or do any possible good to you?

What would happen to me if I took the bottle of bleach from the toilet, or snapped the razor blade by the bath out of its plastic casing, and swallowed one of them down? Would it all be easier not to be alive any more, not to have to think about all this? And wouldn't I deserve it, whatever happened to me?

It is dark in the room; only the reading light throws a pool of light over this paper. I want to sleep, but I know I won't for hours. All I can do is lie here or go for a walk and weigh my head heavy in my hands. The pills are tempting, but I have been taking too many of them and it scares me. I have to stop. I have to get clear of them. I cannot go through my life half drugged; I want to do more than half experience everything. I can't stop wondering what it would be like to have sex with someone new after so many years only knowing one man's body. This is my life, it is my one and only life, and I am spending it alone with the thought of you, and the whole world seems to be getting away from me, and I wish I had the bravery or ingenuity to grasp all life and drink it in.

Wednesday, 24th July

A brief entry. I am tired. I have to sleep. Only to say that work was very hard today. I could not keep my smile on.

At lunchtime a young man came into reception and loitered by the trophy cabinet, looking at the names. I asked him whether I could help him, and he told me no, he was just passing, and he used to go to school here, he was sorry, he didn't know why, he had just wanted to look in. I asked him when he had been here, and he said it was ten years ago now. Before my time, I said, and he said, yes, I don't remember you. I introduced myself and he said his name was Liam. He asked me the names of a couple of teachers, whether they were still knocking around, and I had to tell him I hadn't heard of either of them. He left. Ten years from now, I don't want James to look like that. Lost and drifting, already overcome with an old person's romantic vision of their history. Just like me, I suppose.

It has been days now since I remember writing here that I was going to buy a house plant, and I still haven't got round to it. But there is no need to now – James is coming home for the holidays tomorrow. James is coming home, and I won't be on my own any more.

Monday, 29th July

James came back three days ago, and since I heard the doorbell and found him waiting on the front step looking as though he felt nothing to come into this house, I have tried to spend time with my son. I have tried to live in the same world as he does and not go off into little stares or dazes and live too much in my own mind, or let him go off to his room and live too much in anticipation of going away again when the school year rolls back round. Because I can see us both starting to do that, it's what we have to guard against. I have tried to get to know the new person he has become this holiday, because of course he has changed again. Every time he comes home from another stretch at school I see he has become someone else. His ideas, his points of reference, his ambitions, his imagination. His stories, his friends, his jokes, his fears, his dreams.

I know why we sent our boy to boarding school, why it had to happen. But I do feel like we lost the best part of him to other worlds on the day he first left us with your old luggage and that blazer we'd bought for him to grow into flapping round his fingertips and knees. People change so fast in those teenage years while they're becoming themselves. Every time he comes home it is like I meet another person, and every time that person is a little harder to get close to. And he and I are forced to share the same failure to get to know one another, again and again.

He came quite quietly into the house this time, announcing himself with the taxi's crunch on our gravel, and we had a polite, strained cup of tea together. It was as if he felt for the first time that he had become a guest when coming home to me, that the protocols of visiting needed to be observed here and he couldn't just head straight to the room we had called his bedroom this time and turn his music on and shut the door. He had never come into the kitchen and asked for tea before. I would almost rather he had disappeared off with his music, even though I was desperate to talk to him. Talking to him hasn't been entirely easy since he went away to school, of course – he developed a difficult, teenage manner of communication some years ago. A strange detachment, a way of speaking that is not accompanied by eye contact, as if I weren't his mother but a family pet he never quite learned to love, who is nonetheless part of the furniture, something he neither appreciates nor questions.

But I had thought I heard a change in him when we spoke on the phone this term, felt very distinctly a reserve towards me and everything around him I had never noticed before. And now at the kitchen table I saw it more clearly. It was as if the child had gone out of him, like air from a balloon, and he had become suddenly conscious of the size and strangeness of the world.

This is how we talk to each other now.

'So how was your term?'

'Good, yeah. Have you been all right?'

'Yes. Always busy, you know. And Dad's all right.'

'Yeah.'

'And he's in touch with you, isn't he?'

'Yes.'

I had no idea at the time, when I was a teenager myself, that my mother must have been coping with me every day, tiptoeing round my truculence, but now I know James as he is these days I feel sure my mother must have had as much of a fight keeping the smile on her face while I moped around. When James had finished his tea he went upstairs to change and unpack his things, and I loaded our mugs into the dishwasher and wondered what we two perfect strangers were going to do together in the long stretch of time before you came home.

The number of obvious days out it is possible to go on diminishes as your child gets older. Until he was ten, of course, just taking James anywhere that was out of the house was good enough. We could stroll to the park or the nature reserve, and I could pass an afternoon watching him tire himself out chasing beetles or climbing trees. Then when he got a bit older, when he was ten or so, that was a wonderful time, because we started to go further afield to keep James interested. Trips to the seaside or the woods, nature trails and adventure playgrounds, trips to castles and stately homes and other towns. Sometimes if it was a special day, when you had just come home and he was home as well, it would be Alton Towers or Legoland, and I used to love those times because he would talk about them for weeks afterwards, months sometimes, and it meant something to know he had enjoyed days with me so much. It is a wonderful thing to build memories with your child. But in the last few years it has become more difficult for me to keep him entertained, and seeing the latest change in him I have started to despair of finding anything we could enjoy doing together. You can't take a fourteen year old or fifteen year old for a walk or a day at Paultons Park. The sea still works, but he'd rather go with someone other than me. It's difficult not to feel hurt, that first summer when you realise what he'd really like to do is not spend time with you but go into town with friends or with a girl if he could meet one, and go round the shops and do nothing at all as ostentatiously as possible. It's the natural shape of things, of course, but I still can't help feeling rejected. I hate the fact that mothering isn't just one thing you can get good at and keep improving, but a thousand different relationships you have one day after another as your child goes through the shapeshifting process of becoming himself.

I had once been in the habit of listing the things we would do together in anticipation of his coming home. This time he was in the house and up in his room already, and I still hadn't thought of anything we could do, except maybe taking him to the Playhouse and letting him get his hands on my tape collection and teaching him about Joni Mitchell and Janis Joplin and Joan Armatrading, because last holiday he had seemed to be getting into music, and I might not be very up to date but I think I know a thing or two about music of a certain type, and I thought he might be interested in that.

I cooked macaroni cheese for us in the evening, which I hoped was still his favourite food – he didn't let on either way – and once we had started eating he warmed up into speech. He has developed, I fear, that curious, somehow third-person self-interest teenagers grow into, as if they begin to see their lives as a story being told, begin to watch themselves from above. He was interested in detailing his experience of the world, recording its sensations, outlining its future trajectory. I think it is something in education now that makes teenagers believe as they grow up that they are important, leads them to think in terms of destiny. Perhaps that's all very well if the opportunity exists for you to truly excel at something that will make your name, or to marry a millionaire. But that doesn't describe very many of us.

There ought to be conferences on the kind of fairy tales that can be told to the mass of children who are statistically unlikely ever to earn over £26,000 a year. They ought to be given dreams they can realistically aim at. But it would so quickly become political. Lots of stories about learning to accept your lot and performing your role within the social order efficiently, 'The Diligent Warehouseman', at war with tales of men and women who went on quests to search out other ways of valuing a life, other models of living that might equalise the whole thing and make it all irrelevant. 'The Passionate Jobseeker'. 'The Happy Hobbyist'.

During termtime James has started going into London at the weekends with his friends. I'm not particularly happy about it but I was assured they always had to be back at the school by a certain hour, and I supposed I used to go into town at the weekends and it must have terrified my mother as well, so what she had been able to tolerate I ought to tolerate in turn. He wanted to tell me about his experience of that city, the new stage on which he saw his future playing out, and I listened happily enough, because I haven't spent time in London for years now, not properly, and it was interesting to overlay my old map of the place with another version, and I thought perhaps I would learn something about this stranger who was my son.

'You don't hang out in the centre. That's rubbish – it's just tourists and overpriced pizza. Soho is the most awful consumerist, capitalist slum. Lots of people on middling incomes limping round looking to blow the little bit extra they get each month on an overpriced shirt.'

I found it sad to listen to the way he spoke. How can a boy sound so bitter and weary with everything? I suppose it's the Internet. There's so much cynicism to be memorised for free on the comment pages of the Internet, I'm sure every child can mimic a political position reasonably deftly without having actually read the books or been to the meetings these days. I thought about telling him almost everyone in England lives on a middling income, and a lot of them enjoy shopping, and why would he want to sneer at that? But I don't think learning off the Internet equips you for counterargument, so apart from making him angry I didn't see the point of answering back.

'Honestly, Mum, if you spent an hour in central London you'd think we were all slaves. Bad shops, bad fast food, bad bars, bad clubs, and loads of people wandering round for something to do, trying not to think about how awful their lives are.'

I wondered whether I liked the person James was pretending to be this time. It is easy for young people to pose as cynical, because they do not know the emotional cost of anything. I never know what right I have to say anything about the poses he has tried on over the last few years of his growing up. I'm always terrified that if I draw attention to the face he's making, the wind might change and leave him stuck with it.

'We've been to all the places people think of as hang-outs. They're all rubbish. In Camden these kids dress up as punks and charge you a quid to have your photo taken with them. It's awful. In Shoreditch everyone wears these, like, self-consciously bad jumpers. And drinks chai lattes. It does have a kind of personality, though. The shops haven't all been dictated by the same three or four American companies or whatever, and there's this type of Shoreditch haircut where people shave one half of their head, like they fell asleep and a lawnmower ran them over. But it's sort of sad, because these people are trying to be individuals, but they wear more of a uniform than anyone else in London. I've been to Brixton too. Electric Avenue. That's got a life of its own, actually, people I don't really see anywhere else in London, but the shops are horrible and there are all these expensive bars that want to be in Shoreditch and look like they're trying too hard because they're next door to a kebab shop or whatever. And it's so strange, because you realise walking around there that you can't have, like, nice things, expensive things, without taking money away from somewhere else. That's what I think walking past the Ritzy in Brixton, then past a pound shop five seconds later. And in east London, you can have a coffee in the nicest cafe in the world in Stoke Newington, but if you walk along the road to Stamford Hill or Dalston you see these places where the council's not spent any money in years, and it feels like there's, like, an imbalance. So I actually get quite sad.'

I had lived on Stamford Hill for a little while. You know that, but I suppose he doesn't. It's strange to think of the things your son doesn't know about you, things you might think were perfectly obvious or at the core of your personality. And yet he has an understanding of you that omits those essential facts but is still enough with which to operate a relationship, a friendship, a love. We are not our deeds, are we, or what we know.

When I was a Londoner I used to catch the bus into work down the Seven Sisters Road. I loved it. I thought it was a bit like the Bronx you see in old Robert De Niro films, everyone playing dice in the street, half the shops not paying any tax, everyone greeting each other as they passed, landlords in fur coats eating in the greasy spoons and threatening anyone who didn't pay their rent on time. Except on Seven Sisters everyone was North African instead of Italian, so you added to the mix the beautiful clothes of Egypt or Morocco, and the beautiful sounds, the dense crowds of the call to prayer. I thought it seemed so alive and beautiful because it was so separate to everything around it, nothing to do with the chain shops and anonymous bars that tried to take those people's money back from them as soon as it ran through their hands. Sort of what James was saying, really. But I had a feeling he wasn't talking in order to tempt me into talking back, he was talking to hear himself talk, so I kept my mouth closed and kept listening, and tried not to smile at how certain he seemed.

'What we like to do is go to out-of-the-way places. Real London, the places people don't think about visiting. Brent Cross, walking on those grey flyovers past these sad houses where people are living whole lives. All Polish, or on benefits anyway. Peckham in the evening, when it feels like a film set because everything's closed and you don't recognise the name of a single shop, and they're all in these, like, Portakabin buildings that look so temporary. I saw a load of kittens shivering by some bins in Peckham one night, tiny little new-born kittens. I suppose rats and foxes got them all. Putney's brilliant. We walk round these beautiful quiet houses, or up the river to Hammersmith past Craven Cottage, and when the sun sets it reflects off the river and lights up the undersides of all the bridges.'

Apparently he has a new group of friends he was doing all this exploring with, three boys whose names I couldn't remember hearing before, that he spoke of as if they had been around for ever. I thought to myself, I am missing this, I am missing out on him, a whole world is passing me by because he's not here with me in the evenings. But then I tried to remember the names of his friends this time last year, the boys he had told me about when his interest had been comics, and I wondered whether I was really missing anything at all. Or perhaps trying to keep up with him is just a losing battle. His life changes so fast. Minutes after he's devoted himself to one cause I find myself unable to get him to acknowledge it had ever been something that concerned him at all. What is that, I wonder? The trying on of young lives preparing to live a real one? Or do we start out moving through life as if it's water, experiencing whole new worlds each different day, and only when we're older end up wading through treacle, stuck in the life we were in when the strength went out of our legs or we lost the will to change, and plough onwards?

After we had finished eating I washed up and he dried up, and a silence fell between us as he ran his wet dishcloth over the pans, spreading the water around them.

'I suppose we'll have to think of things for both of us to do till Dad gets home,' he said.

I could have sat down and wept to hear it stated so baldly.

'Aren't we happy just spending time together?'

'Yeah. Obviously. But we should come up with plans, shouldn't we?'

How has it come to this? I had a child because I thought it would be wonderful to have a best friend for life, to be so close to someone that you're part of each other, to have someone in the world who needed me. And he just doesn't need me at all.

I am an irrelevance to everyone. I simply exist, and there are a handful of people who have undertaken to deal with me for as long as I do.

'I suppose so. What do you want to do with this summer then?'

'I don't know, really. Me and Tim and Raj are starting a punk band next year, so I have to work on that.'

'A punk band?'

'We sort of want to shake the whole country awake.'

'Oh yes?'

'School and everything. Have you seen the film *If* by Lindsay Anderson? We want to be in a punk band called *If*. So we have to practise, and we have to come up with songs, and look out for places we might get gigs once we're ready, and sort of – I don't know. Be on the look-out for a movement to be part of.'

'Well, we could go to political meetings and research anarchism in Salisbury library.'

'That might be good.'

I could tell there was nothing he wanted to do less than research anarchism with his mum in Salisbury library in order to write better punk music. Sometimes it's fun embarrassing your children.

'I want to write a novel as well.'

'Oh yes. What about?'

'The last days of Woolworths. I want to call it, *The Last Days of Woolworths.*'

'Oh yes?'

'It's about the recession, obviously. I think the first time all that sort of stuff really hit home to me, to everyone in my class, you know, was when Woolworths closed. Cos that was where we got our pick'n'mix. Then suddenly it was gone. So I might write about that. Because there was this amazing 'everything must go' sale in the final week, it was like the end of days. And then my friend told me in the Woolworths in Salisbury, after it closed, the sprinkler system broke, and for days it was raining inside the building and no one did anything about it because it wasn't anyone's job. That was before we moved here, obviously. I thought it was a coincidence, and my English teacher said the whole point of novels is to write about coincidence, so I thought it might be a good start.'

'Yes.'

'And an amazing metaphor too. For us. The sprinklers raining down and no one doing anything about it.'

'What does that say about us?'

'That everything's gone wrong and no one's doing anything about it.'

I wondered what exactly he thought was wrong with the country he lived in, whether he meant anything in particular or was just expressing the Sodom and Gomorrah moral reflex teenagers often have against the world. Teenagers can be the most conservative people.

'I think that's a good story. What will the plot be?'

He became suddenly hostile at being questioned, and said he didn't know that, and went back to drying up, and I wished I hadn't asked, because he seemed to have taken the question badly, as if he had been challenged.

'There's a good story to how Woolworths started,' I told him.

He looked up at me, interested in spite of himself.

'Yeah?'

'Have you ever noticed how all the Woolworths in every town were in really ugly buildings?'

'I suppose so.'

'Those were the Army and Navy stores. They were put up in a hurry in the war, which is why they look like that. Built as quickly and cheaply as possible. And when the stores closed after the end of conscription, Woolworths bought them up as a job lot. They just sort of flooded into the space that was left.'

'Was that while you were growing up?' he asked.

I laughed. 'No, I'm not that old! Your Mum just knows a few things.'

Wednesday, 31ˢᵗ July

James asked me today what I had wanted to do with my life when I was his age, and I tried to remember what my dreams had been, whether the theatre had interested me at that time or come later. And it dawned on me as I tried to remember that all his talk, all his filling the air, might not be a new confidence but rather a new insecurity. Perhaps he is growing up just like we did, unsure and wanting to test out his place in the world. I decided I hadn't known at his age what I wanted to be. If I ever did have a firm idea at all. My idea about acting is long abandoned, and I suppose that probably proves that in the end it can't have been a thought worth having. Because if it's really going to be what you do with your life you keep going, don't you? You don't just give up when someone says no. So acting was probably just a phantom, one of those ghosts you see when the dew rises up from the grass in the mornings and into thin air, never a thought with any weight or gravity to it.

I think that's why I fell so in love with you. In you I could find a purpose. I was always so aware, when those chats with the careers adviser came round in school, or when I came into the last year of my degree and people asked me what I was going to do next, that I didn't actually know why I was doing any of what I was doing. The careers advisers never thought acting was a real career, even that was something I was made to feel guilty about. Meeting you that summer, at that party on Liverpool Street, our first kiss at the Spaniard's Inn, that was the first real thing that happened to me. I was always clingy with you when we were first together, even after we were married, and I think it was because I was very afraid I was wasting my life before I met you. And it's creeping up on me that I feel the same way now, as if I am wasting all of my time. We grow into our little neuroses, don't we, the little unhappinesses at the heart of us, and have to live with them all our lives, they are never solved, and mine has always been this restlessness, this sense there must be more that comes either of doing too little or wanting too much or just looking the wrong way through the binoculars and seeing with the wrong perspective. You eased me for a little while, but that fear I have that I will never mean anything has always been there under the surface, waiting. It was very bad back then, at the end of my teenage years. It's not much better now, and I can feel myself sliding further into it. But for a time you eased things.

I didn't tell James all this, of course. I told him when I was his age I wasn't sure what I wanted to do, except I knew I wanted to go to university and continue my education, which seemed like the right hint to drop. He gave me a look. There was disappointment in his eyes but pity too. I could feel my face getting hot. He can hear as well as me when I'm dropping hints instead of being honest. It frightens me to think how much he must know about me that neither of us discusses. How low I feel, what a lie I am living whenever I smile, whenever I imitate happiness. I hope, very much, that he doesn't suspect about the pills. That is the horror of having a family. They see right through the act, the lie you construct; they know everything.

Friday, 2nd August

James said yesterday that he would like to visit Stonehenge, as it was only down the road now and he'd never seen it for real before. I said we ought really to go tomorrow, as my work meant I couldn't easily go with him in the weeks. So tomorrow I have official permission to turf him out of his bed at a reasonable hour, put a mug of tea in his hands and force him to have a shower. Then we will drive to Stonehenge, to see the new visitor centre being built, and the site itself. It's supposed to be a bit of a rip-off, the Stonehenge Visitor Experience, because you're not allowed within twenty feet of the thing – too many hands run over the surface of the stone would wear it away. But I'm looking forward to it all the same. It will be so good to do something with James. It felt like such a relief to hear him volunteer something he might like us to do together, that he might like us to do something, anything together.

Perhaps that made me overly optimistic though, because this evening I made him go to a concert with me, and I don't think he was very grateful for that. The local choral society were doing the Mozart *Requiem* in that big church on the roundabout by the Andover road, and I've always loved that piece of music, so I wanted to go. I asked James if he wanted to come, because I thought it couldn't hurt him to get out of the house. He didn't feel brave enough to say outright that he didn't want to, and when I saw the look on his face I couldn't think of a way of taking back the suggestion without it turning into an argument, so we had an early dinner and got in the car and headed into Salisbury. He was sulking and wouldn't talk to me while we waited for the show to start. I didn't really mind at first. Even if he's annoyed, it's nice to go out and do something with him. We sat near the back, and James played on his phone till the music started, and I read the programme and looked at the people around.

We sang Mozart in my school choir. I suppose perhaps it is a ritual half the children in England are put through while they're growing up. It would be good if that were true, I think; if that music was part of the inheritance we shared with one another. The performance we were treated to that night was a mixed bag, the women much better than the men, and the soloists not all as good as each other, but it's still an absorbing experience, listening to a thing like that. Because you don't know the plot, it's not one thing after another like a normal story, it's more complex than that, and you can't think your way to the end of what you're listening to, not really. You just have to suspend yourself in the ritual for a little while and listen. The bit of your brain that wants to solve things has to lose the argument while the choir is singing, while all the poems play themselves out.

James said it had been all right when we got in the car to go home. He didn't feel moved to say anything more than that, but I was glad to have got that much from him. If it had been really bad he might have wanted to start an argument.

'Are you in a choir at school?'

'No. We have to sing in assemblies.'

'Don't you like singing?'

'It's all right. I like proper singing, like the band. I like good music. I'm not into choirs or whatever.'

'What do you do instead then?'

James turned away from me to look out of the window and into the night.

'I don't know. Whatever.'

We drove in silence for a little while, and he didn't turn back to look out in front or to look at me again.

'Up early tomorrow,' I said.

'Yeah. Thanks for taking me.'

'That's all right. Thanks for coming to this tonight.'

'Yeah.'

We got back to the house and James went up to his room, saying he would go to bed. I said good night as he went. Of course he wouldn't go to bed for hours yet; he stays up late; he sits on his computer; he watches TV. I wondered what the point of trying to be friends with him really was, if he was always going to prefer to go upstairs and be alone in his room. What would be the point of Stonehenge, or any other place, or any other time I might get him to spend with me, if it was all just waiting for something more exciting to come along. It seemed so pathetic to me then, the little rations of experience we eke out and called our lives. A trip into town to hear a mediocre rendition of something that someone else had invented just to fill the silence of their lives, years and years ago. And they had died anyway. In the end, what difference had it made to them, what real difference? And we call that an evening. We call that a life. It is all just a shroud for something, I felt certain, a way of filling in the emptiness of ourselves. How could I ignore how pointless my life was when another evening of it was past, was gone, and James still just went back up to his room? Couldn't he see that both of us were very slowly dying, that time was running forever down through the gaps between the lino and the skirting boards, that we were the only people in this house? Couldn't he see I was alone? Did he mean to be cruel? Did I even deserve it, perhaps?

I stayed in the sitting room and couldn't think of what to do. I stared at the blank black screen of the television and I couldn't think of anything in the world that I would ever want to watch. I got up and went to the foot of the stairs, and I couldn't hear anything. It felt as if someone else was in my body and moving me through the house. James must have had his headphones in. Otherwise I would hear music coming from his room. I went into the kitchen and poured myself a drink, a glass of brandy. I don't know why I have brandy in the house; I suppose it's left over from Christmas. I drank it back. It was difficult, the burn in the throat, in the pit of the stomach. I'm not used to drinks that strong. I wanted to retch. I poured myself another glass and drank.

What I could feel all around me was the terror of death.

You must live with it all the time, I know you must; it is so much more real and immediate for you. I have had it on and off since my early twenties. I don't remember being afraid before then. I think I was twenty-one when I discovered what it meant, being mortal, the fact that I was going to die. Sometimes I can go for months without thinking about it, but then there are days where, for no particular reason, the knowledge that I am going to die one day quite soon is almost overwhelming to me. I stared into the brandy in the glass and wondered, if death was so inevitable, why anyone ever put it off, why people didn't just get on with it now. I drank the rest of my glass and poured another. Even as I stood there, I could imagine how ridiculous I would look if James were to come downstairs now to get himself a drink. A woman standing alone in a kitchen, drinking a bottle of brandy as fast as she could, who had seemed perfectly happy when she was driving him home just half an hour earlier. But there's no logic to the things in our heads. One thing simply connects to another, and there are no maps between neurons, only leaps in the dark, only darknesses.

I could not understand, staring into that glass, gripping the kitchen table so the whites of my knuckles showed, the light of my bones, my head bowed, with the light of the kitchen striplight on the back of my neck, why any of us have ever been alive at all. If all that is going to really happen to us is that we are going to waste our time then stop being alive again. I couldn't understand the grief of it, the loss after loss of being alive – what was the value of that? To anyone at all? And the brief interludes of happiness, what did they mean to anyone if everyone you ever met was going to die one day, and all the memories anyone ever collected would one day be lost, almost as soon as they were gathered? Thinking about how close it was now for me – because I am getting older all the time, by the law of averages I feel bound to say I am more than halfway through – I could not understand how anyone ever got through the day. What do other people do to deal with the fear of it? How do other people live?

I went upstairs to the bathroom and found all the paracetamol and ibuprofen and sleeping pills in the bathroom cupboard, my shameful hoard, and I popped them out of their blister packs and took the little chalky things downstairs. A handful. Perhaps I had about forty pills of different shapes and sizes. I sat at the kitchen table with the pills and the brandy and I thought of Owen, and I wondered what the point was of not kissing him if you and I were both going to die practically any day now, any year now anyway. Or twenty or thirty years, but what was the difference, really? And how could people bear to take the gamble that their lives would last that long, and keep going to work doing jobs they didn't love, and all that just to pay rent to live in places they couldn't love – how did people live with that compromise and that hazard all the time? I wondered why I hadn't slept with every man who had ever looked twice at me, if life was going to be so cruelly short.

You know what? The truth is that I wish I had gone to bed with Owen. Even if it had ended up being the worst thing I ever did, even if it had proved to be the end of us. There is a part of all of us that doesn't feel safe around open windows, isn't there? Something in everyone that wants to jump from the bridge. And at least it would have been an action.

Something deliberate, something that proved I was alive. My whole life has been a catalogue of fears that stopped me from acting on any impulse that ever passed through me. One plan after another that I never saw through because I worried about the consequences, because I didn't have the courage to commit to anything. I have dreamed again and again of escapes I might make into different lives. I have never made any of the necessary leaps. All the time I am held back by timidity. I have asked myself each time a dream took hold, what would I lose if I went for this, what would I risk, what would I miss out on? And as a result, all my life it seems I have been standing still.

If I were to die tomorrow, I wouldn't have done anything I was glad of, not really. Except you. Except James. But neither of you were there with me then. And I'm not sure any more that either of you are glad of me. I tried dissolving a pill in brandy, but it didn't seem to work. So I took a pill and washed it down with the brandy instead. I took another pill and washed it down with the brandy. I kept taking the different pills, swallowing becoming harder and harder as I went along, because of course if you swallow several times in a short space of time it always does become harder. I came upstairs and lay on the bed and waited. I am still waiting. I don't know what for.

It is late. It is dark and silent in the house; all I can hear is my own breathing. After that last furious entry I threw the book away, off the bed. It was no more use to me. I had failed at it like everything else. But then suddenly I didn't want to die. I wanted to be better than I was. I wanted to keep existing. I went to the toilet and threw it all up. All the drink, all the pills. I could count the pills in the bowl. I stared down into them for a long time, and they started to stare back into me. I left the lights on downstairs and got into bed and hid from the world. I curled into a ball and looked at the wall of my bedroom, and it was so sad to me, that I have lived a whole life, I have felt so much, but all I have to mark out the parameters of my living are these anonymous rooms I rattle round, this cheap furniture, these small ambitions, this diary full of pointless ramblings. I tried to write it all down here, but before long my eyes hurt and my hand cramped, and I knew I wouldn't get everything I was feeling into writing. How is it that I have never found a way to express the scale of the feelings inside me? How have I never managed anything more than to be ordinary?

Saturday, 3rd August

We got up at a relatively reasonable hour, had breakfast and went to Stonehenge, and trooped dutifully round the cordoned path that circled the site, which never allowed you closer than twenty feet from the stones. It was extraordinary to me in the grey light of a new day that I could see this thing for real, that this miracle was on my doorstep in this quietest part of the world, but James felt cheated because he couldn't walk among them.

'It's only at the solstice you can go right in,' I said. 'The rest of the year they keep people out to preserve it all.'

'I won't be here at the solstice.'

'We could go next year, get it in the diary early.'

He laughed as if I had told a joke.

'I don't think you'd like the solstice, Mum.'

'I'm only forty. I'm not collecting my pension yet. I can still have fun.'

'We could break in one night and have a better look; it's quite low fences,' he said, and it was my turn to laugh. 'What's so funny? That might work.'

'If I'm too old to take a bottle of cider to the solstice, I'm definitely too old to break into English Heritage sites.'

'It might be cool. We could try and watch the sunrise.'

'You can see the sunrise from our house, you know. You can see it anywhere. It comes up wherever you are.'

'Yeah, I know. I just thought it might look good from here.'

We finished our circuit of the stones and got in the car and drove home.

Tuesday, 6th August

I spent a minute or more today deciding whether to keep or throw away the order of service from Rose's husband's funeral. It is awful to put something like that in the bin, but without looking at the service sheet I couldn't even remember the man's name, so is there really any reason for someone so distant from me to clutter up our drawers? It is not a day I want to remember. The funeral was the most awful thing, without hope, without meaning, just filled with sadness for everyone there. His death was quicker than had been expected, and he was too young to be dying, as well, so there was of course a sadness lying heavy over the whole thing. We all felt the injustice of it. We all went to the funeral, all us girls from the front desk, and it was very sad to see Rose and her son up at the front of the church, the boy clinging on to his girl-friend, Rose standing alone, both crying but standing apart, not looking after each other. I would have gone and spoken to them both and told them no son talks to his mother enough, you should at least try to talk as much as you pos-sibly can, then perhaps you'll get somewhere. But a funeral's not the place to give advice.

I didn't go to the grave after the funeral. I didn't know the family well enough for that. I walked through another part of the graveyard instead, looking at the headstones, reading the inscriptions, enjoying the peace you find in graveyards. After a minute I turned back to look at the entrance to the church and saw Rose's son standing there, head bowed, all on his own and not with the rest of the burial party. I walked over to him. He looked up and saw me as I approached, but didn't walk away.

'I'm so sorry for your loss,' I said.

'Thank you. I don't think I know you.'

'My name's Alison. I work with your mum.'

'Oh. I'm Sam.'

'Hello, Sam.' I hesitated, wondering whether I should tell him what was on my mind, then decided I must, no matter what he was feeling. 'Listen, I don't want to intrude, but don't you think you should go with the others to the burial?'

He looked at me warily. I imagined quite absurdly that he might spit at me or hit me for interfering.

'I didn't want to be there.'

'I see.'

'I don't want to look in the grave.'

I took a deep breath.

'Do you mind my saying that I think you'll regret it if you don't go and catch up with them now? You don't have to look. But I think you'll regret it if you don't go there.'

'I'm too scared,' he said, and seemed impossibly young and afraid as he tried not to cry.

'But you should go for your dad. And you should go for your mum as well. You can't imagine how much she needs you, Sam.'

He seemed to think about this.

'Does she?'

'Of course she does. You're the person she loves most in the world. She needs you very much.'

He nodded. I thought he would speak again, but he didn't. Instead he moved away from the wall quite quickly and hurried in the direction of the funeral party. I watched him crossing the graveyard. When he had almost caught them up I turned and started walking back to my car, and left Rose and Sam to their grief and their privacy.

Looking at it in my hands now, I am seized with a sudden clarity, and I know I must keep the order of service. It is provocative to look at the coldness of words on paper and think how completely it would break me if we were ever parted as Rose and her husband have been parted. I have always known I would not be able to live without you. But now I wonder, thinking back to that funeral, that boy standing around on his own, in need of his mother, whether the same is true for you and for James. Perhaps you need me as well, and I shouldn't think of myself only as hanging on to you both, to keep some hold in the real world and have something to love. Perhaps you need me just as much as that boy needed his mother. There is a thought to stop me in my tracks. It doesn't ever occur to me that I might be important. To you or James or anyone. It didn't occur to me when I was swallowing down pills that I might be throwing away anything except a few more days and months and years of my own experiences. But what if I'm wrong?

Friday, 9th August

Two weeks have passed since James came home, and he and I have eaten our meals together, and gone to the Odeon on the Wednesday evening to see a disappointing thriller, and now he has left for Norfolk for a week to visit a school friend, with his bag seeming almost as full as it was when he arrived here. He gave me a kiss when he left. It was awkward. Neither of us felt comfortable with physical contact any more; that kind of love was too naked for us both now. I went back inside and watched him walking to the bus stop from the kitchen window. I had offered him a lift, but he said he liked catching the bus. He said you got to really see a place when you got a bus through it, got a feel for its landscape and its architecture and its history and its character as well. He said he liked buses best of all methods of transport he had ever tried and planned to use them in order to annoy the ghost of Margaret Thatcher. Not that he has the slightest clue what she was all about. I was all for her at the time, God save me, though I see that as regrettable now. Much of what she did was necessary, when you get right down to it. She just did it all too fast, too thoughtlessly.

That's something I've never been guilty of. My life is so small and unenlightened. I am just another Tory woman who thinks she has a story to tell about how unbearably genteel her life is. If I were in a story, I'd run away to Africa and have a child with someone I would have to struggle not to refer to as a native, and name it Rainbow or Hero or Pomegranate. I would wear saris, precisely because they were wildly inappropriate to the continent I was on, in an attempt to appear liberated and non-conformist. I would drink too much and sleep around and tell myself I was liberated. A young Meryl Streep would play me in the movie. I would learn an instrument and several languages. I would die of a beautiful and romantic disease.

It actually sounds rather wonderful, thinking about it. All my life I've thought about performing one real action, really leaving the country or somehow breaking the cycle of things. That year round Italy we used to talk about. The pilgrimage to Santiago. Not on foot, God no, life's too short, but the route at least, or a bit of it. Or I would like to see where tea comes from, as that has been the longest love affair of my life. I would like to visit Darjeeling, take in the mountains of Nepal on the way back. But somehow all that life I dreamed of or read about in books never quite happened. Somehow I never quite get round to it. I suppose none of us do, really. Somehow you keep on singing in the same key for ever, and every plan you half concoct never turns into more than an idea for you to mull over while you drink your tea in the same old kitchen, in the light of the same endless mid morning of your life. Or, in my case, a different kitchen every year that just looks the same as the last one, filled with the same silence as I wait for you.

It's embarrassing to admit, but that night with the pills and brandy has forced me to realise that I have, over the months without you, had what you might call a bit of a breakdown. I have sleepwalked through my daily life and sometimes merely slept. I have been tearful and afraid for no reason. I have spent a lot of time staring at the review of *Hamlet* on the wall. I have hated myself.

I'm going to Skype you. I'm going to talk to you. I need to talk about this. I have to do something. I have to get back into my life. It's two years now till you leave the army. I'm going to tell you it's time we started thinking about buying a home and deciding where to put down proper roots. I must do something; I must have something; I must work at something. And if it cannot be a job or a career or running away to Africa or a talent for watercolour painting, which I have accepted I am terrible at and will always be terrible at, I will find satisfaction in a different kind of life, in different values, in a different way of being. Millions of people across this country do it. Instead of pitching headlong at wealth or importance, at success or growth or consumption, they define themselves and value themselves by the corner of the world they have made for themselves, by place and history and rootedness. I'm going to Skype you and tell you I need a purpose, I need to take back some control.

Tuesday, 13th August

An utterly different day today. I am shining. I feel as if I have just come out of the dark and into new light, fresh oxygen. The whole of me is singing. I called you and told you I wanted to be one of those people who kept house and had a house worth keeping, because I have never found any calling but you and me, and because we had our baby too young and he is not ours now, he has moved away from us, even though we are still his, and even though there will be days when he still needs us, they will only be days here and there, not enough to build our life around. I insisted that as there are only two years till you leave the army now, we ought to be thinking about the future. Work can come second for once. We can buy a house, perhaps let it out till you leave service if the money would help, then settle at last once you're able, and then finally grow up and come out the other side of this itinerance, which seems to have kept me in a delayed state of almost teenage indecision all these years. We will have pets, and they will die, and we will bury them there, and the place will take on a meaning that will be part of us, and our lives will become bigger as a consequence.

I have just gone up to the bathroom. I took all the pills and packets that were left from the cupboard over the sink and put them all in a carrier bag. And I've come back downstairs and put the bag in the outside bin. I have to put all of it behind me. I'm going to put all of that far away from me.

It was strange when you asked me where I wanted to live to try and explain what it was about Salisbury that makes me want to stay here. We have lived in so many different parts of the country, we could go back and settle almost anywhere and feel some familiarity with the area. Our families are nowhere near this place. But in all honesty I never much cared for visiting either of our families, so that feels like a blessing, if you'll forgive me for saying so. A bit of distance between us and them will keep a healthy limit on the number of hours I have to spend making small talk with your sister.

Salisbury's a nice city, of course, and the countryside around is beautiful. But I think it's something more than that. I could satisfy my curiosity anywhere, I could probably live almost anywhere if I could only be with you. What seems exciting to me now about this place is that it was here that I decided we were going to change – it was during this tour of yours and my lonely days in Salisbury that I decided to take some control over what was going to happen to both of us. I hadn't even thought about it till you asked me why I wanted to be here, but I realise now that is the reason. It was here that I felt alive for the first time in a long time. That is something to be celebrated, something to hold on to. That is a memory I want to live near.

You told me a number you thought we could work to, and yesterday I went to Myddleton & Major and asked about places on sale for something like the figure you gave me, and I saw a house in a brochure which seemed to perfectly express the way I want us to live when you come home, a farmhouse hidden deep in the middle of nowhere, and today I went to view it and fell in love with the windows like hazel eyes looking soulfully over the land like a ship that is looking out over the sea, and the low beam of the main room, and the knotholes in the floorboards that showed you the secret worlds of the rooms below when you walked through the bedrooms. You said that if I was certain then I should arrange a conversation with a mortgage provider, and once I knew the money would be available I should put in an offer, and we would go forwards with it when you got home.

Friday, 16ᵗʰ August

Things move so fast in those rare moments when you know what you're for. I have found a house, and put in an offer, and learned that the seller is an elderly widower who had lived there forever, and I feel very bad that I should be buying his whole life like it was a commodity, but at the same time I am happy because I knew when I heard about him that it would be right for us. This is a house with weight, with meaning. This is an idea big enough to be the centre of the world, the centre of a life.

I went to visit the house on a bright morning, and I suppose that always makes a difference. Driving out along the Coombe Road was difficult because of the steam fair, which must be held at Blandford or somewhere like that. Dozens of old steam trains were being freighted down on big lorries, and there was a train actually driving along the road, which held everything up. I don't know how that is possible, but I have seen that it works, against all probability, because I overtook it coming over the hill as I left Harnham. Then I drove on as far as the turning for Martin and found my way to the farm. The man waiting for me there to show me round had driven the same way as I did, and I asked him about the train travelling on the road, but he said he hadn't seen it. We stood and looked up at the house and the yard around, bright in the sun with honeysuckle climbing the walls as if we had walked into a story. It was a simple place, and unadorned, and the view across the down was very lovely. I asked the estate agent how much of the land around belonged to the farmer, and he said it had been most of it till now, a few hundred acres, a rare small farm persevering with the old way of doing things in this part of the country where farming has become so industrial and big organisations farm thousands of acres. But now most of it was being sold off separately to the big farms around, except the field in front of the house itself. I told him I might like to turn that into grass, a little nature reserve of our own, and he said it would be ours to do what we liked with if we wanted to buy the house. Then we went from room to room, peeking in on a very simple life that had been lived here. The estate agent told me that the farmer was having to move into sheltered housing due to ill health, and that his wife had died a few months ago. But it didn't seem like a sad house. I felt it had been very loved, that two people had loved each other very much while they were living here. I suppose that's just my fancy, but I couldn't help it.

As I drove back past the convoy of steam trains, I was on fire with the place. I was in the bank talking about money before the end of that day.

I know I have been mad and impetuous and impractical, and that when you come home you'll either be very angry or laugh at my silliness, but the thing is that I need to do this, I really do. So I will always be grateful to you for letting me make these mad and extraordinary commitments to the estate agent and the HSBC mortgage assessor man, because since I found the house I've felt like I've woken up.

I think that is why I love you so much. I think you know me, and what I need, and who I am, and so you have let me commit you to a thing like this because you see that for me it is necessary. To be rooted like a laurel in one place. To plunge down deep into this idea we have of 'home' and try to drink some meaning from it.

I can hardly believe I've found the place to put down those roots. But this part of Wiltshire's a nice neck of the woods. We could do worse than here. And perhaps there comes a time when you must make a stand and believe in something and lend some meaning to this endless, beautiful everything, so I will ask you to make our lives happen in this place, and take on all their meanings against the backdrop of this landscape.

I took a walk round the cathedral before I went to the bank. Not the inside of it – it costs about twelve quid to get in I think. I walked round the close looking up at the building. How often do we really look at buildings? Wonder why they are like they are? The cathedral close is a comforting place. It makes me feel like no human life really matters very much at all. You can feel easier in yourself when you know you are part of a society that did something like that, and lose yourself in marvelling at what is possible if people only think and act a little consciously.

On the drive home I thought about Rita. I must confess I hadn't thought of her in weeks and weeks. It's shaming to think that I had forgotten her, and she had been so ill. But then perhaps I have had an illness of my own all this time, perhaps I have been living somewhere very dark and deep. I wonder what has happened to her now; I wonder whether she is out of the hospital, whether she is living her life again like it's new, the way I am? Perhaps I should have visited her after all, while she was there. I just didn't think I knew her that well, and if I was her, and a stranger came to see me, I'd be embarrassed; I wouldn't want the attention. If I had religion I would pray for her tonight. What can we do instead, now we don't believe in anything?

Monday, 19th August

We are almost all back together now. James came back from Norfolk to find me much changed, a woman with something to work towards, a woman with a purpose. I feel so much more capable, life is coming so much easier now I am doing something with it and I don't have to ask what to do with our evenings or how he feels. I know it all. I can tell what is needed. We are planning for your return. We are planning our futures. I don't think he could believe that I had more or less bought a house while he was away. I think he thinks I'm mad. It's nice to make your son feel you're mad now and then.

'When will you move in?' he asked.

'I don't know. We might own it and not live in it for a bit, if that's what Dad's work needs, if he has to take up one more posting before he comes out of the army. We could rent it out for a year. Or you could use it for house parties and drinking and impressing girls.'

He blushed, in spite of himself.

'I don't drink, Mum.'

It was the youngest I had heard him sound since he came home, and I smiled at his obvious fib.

'Sure you don't.'

He looked at the ground.

'I don't mind if you have a drink now and then, James. It's a normal thing to do. I just don't want you to get smashed and throw up everywhere.'

He smiled, in spite of himself.

'There are boys at school who do that. I just think people who get properly drunk are really boring.'

'Wait till you meet people who take cocaine. That's what boring really looks like.'

He stared at me in amazement.

'Have you met people who've taken cocaine?'

'Of course I have. I haven't always just sat in this kitchen, you know.'

'I know, but I didn't think you'd know that sort of people.'

'Cool people?'

'No, I suppose – dangerous people.'

'Oh, I've been dangerous in my time.'

We were silent then for a moment, smiling, taking in the light through the window as it fell on our hands, our faces.

'I've enjoyed this summer, Mum,' James said. I was careful to say nothing, in case I broke the spell. 'It's been nice hanging out with you.'

'I've enjoyed hanging out with you as well.'

'Stonehenge was cool, wasn't it?'

'Did you think so? I'm so glad. I wish they let you get closer to it.'

'Yeah. But it was still cool. Thanks for taking me.'

It was the closest I had heard him come in years to a declaration of love.

'I love you very much, James. I hope you know that.'

He rolled his eyes and smiled.

'I love you too, Mum. You're all right, really.'

'When did anyone say I wasn't all right?'

'Never. You just sometimes stare out the window for ages, you know?'

'Oh. OK.'

'Oh, Mum, by the way, is there any Lemsip? I feel like I'm getting a sore throat.'

'Oh, no. Sorry. I threw it all away.'

'Why?'

'It was out of date.'

That night when I was brushing my teeth before bed I looked in the mirror and said through my toothpaste, Alison, you are not lonely. You are alive.

I feel much better for having written all this down. I could never really tell you how much I love you because I could never put it all into words, what you mean to me, no matter how hard I try. I don't mind that, though. I have the rest of my life to try to show you what I mean to say.

The Burning Arrow
of the Spire

S TORIES WEAVE INTO one another. Lives intertwine. And the result of tracing these patterns through the air is that you begin to know the air they are moving through a little better.

About a year ago I was in McDonald's having dinner before my shift when I witnessed an accident. From my window I saw a car being driven by an old man plough into a woman on a moped. I saw a young boy watching from one side of the road and a woman watching from the other. It seemed no more real to me than a piece of theatre. An event, a real event like that, always seems to take on a dreamlike quality when it happens to you, as if it had some greater meaning you didn't understand. You think to yourself, this is the kind of thing that only happens in stories. Why is it happening to me? What is it trying to say? Surely there's some meaning waiting for me here, under the surface?

In my work I have a lot of long evenings I spend on my own. And these four faces I had seen while I ate in McDonald's started coming into my mind while I drifted through the nights. They sank deep into my imagination and rooted there, lives I knew nothing about, which I had seen coalescing for a moment around that street corner, that accident. I found it extraordinary to think that five strangers – five if you included

me, the observing eye who saw it all and so cohered the picture – could have been brought so close together like that, for
that fleeting moment.

Perhaps it was something to do with togetherness that
meant I couldn't stop thinking about them. When I came
back here to Salisbury I'd broken up with a girl I thought I
was happy with. I hadn't seen the end of our story coming,
and when she left I didn't know how to cope, I felt unmoored.
Perhaps I was feeling susceptible to the neatness of coincidence
when I saw that crash, because even if it was awful, it still
fascinated me. It felt like something to belong to. I started to
wonder what I might learn if I could only find out more about
the lives I had glimpsed for that moment, if I could only get
to the heart of them.

The five rivers that meet in the middle of this floodplain
never come together in the same place at the same time. The
Nadder and the Ebble and the Wylye and the Bourne flow
into the Avon at different points, intersecting piecemeal with
these other bodies of water, gathering in halting increments
into the single voice of the Avon, so that, while five rivers
flow into this city and this story, only one sings on out of it,
and all the other voices are lost in the chorus, all their stories
never end, but disappear instead back into the greater body
of water they came from, and make their way out to the sea.
There is never a clean chord where these five rivers are all
singing in the same moment, and yet they are the rhythm and
the pulse of this landscape; if you map out the passages of
these rivers and their songs, you will have mapped out the
whole of the city.

I thought to myself, what if the same might be true of the

lives brought together that evening on the corner of Brown Street? What if there is a map of the world waiting to be excavated beneath the surface of that moment?

I was born here and grew up here and moved away to be a student, like so many people who come from Salisbury. When I had finished with those years I gave no thought, really, to how I wanted to live my life. I did what everyone else was doing, and moved to London, and found myself a bedsit, and got a job on a paper in digital media. I never thought I'd want to come back to the city where I had grown up. There's nothing for anyone here, really. Not for the young. And my parents had separated while I was at university, and it felt strange to go back to the place where they had been happy together and know they weren't together any more. I didn't like to wonder too much about whether they had been happy at all, all the time we had lived under the same roof, or whether they had just kept up a pretence for me. What a terrible waste of a life that lie would be. But people do it, I know, never thinking that the guilt for the child when they work out what happened might be worse than the legacy of the absent father, the visits at weekends, the second Christmases, the extra presents. Both Mum and Dad moved out of Wiltshire after the divorce, so I put Wiltshire behind me as well. I didn't want to belong to a place where no one knew me. In the course of a life you will build up plenty of debts to other people, but we never owe anything to the stages where we play out our days. They are pure circumstance, after all; we could have been born somewhere else just as easily. And you can be sure the land you walk on will forget you when you're gone, so why tie yourself to any part of it, when that tie can only ever be imaginary? The world is other people, not the places you visit. That was what I told myself, anyway.

In London I lived off the Holloway Road, caught a bus to King's Cross in the mornings, and tried to be ambitious, and tried to enjoy what I was doing, and struggled to fit in. If you grow up where I did, you experience London as a whole different way of life, a whole new philosophy flowering around you. And that's neither a good thing nor a bad thing, it's just difference and change, but if you're going to cope with it, with the pursuit of growth as an absolute good, with the fetishisation of novelty over continuity, then you're going to have to make an adjustment. Because it's a different way of seeing the world, to live in the city or live in the country. The country I come from, anyway. So I tried to adjust, and stay out late, and enjoy the conversation of strangers, because that always seemed like the ultimate goal for everyone around me, to lose a night discovering someone they had never met before. What it seemed we were all supposed to be chasing was delicious anonymity.

I met Chrissy at a gig in Kings Place. I hadn't been in London for long, and I was going to gigs or plays whenever anyone in my office invited me, to make sure I got out of the flat. June Tabor was playing, and the person I'd gone with knew the person Chrissy had gone with, and the four of us were decades younger than everyone else in the audience, so we ended up talking to each other afterwards. I asked her out, and we met for drinks on Upper Street a week later, and then she came home with me, and before either of us had really discussed what was happening three months had passed, and we had seen each other every weekend, and it seemed like something was beginning between us. We started to meet each other's friends. After half a year we even met each other's families. We never discussed living together or anything as serious as that. We just liked seeing each other. For eighteen months we spent the weekends together, and sometimes we'd stop and look in the windows of estate agents, or Chrissy would talk about how much she wanted us to have a dog, but I thought both of us were happy with the way things were. We were both young, our lives were just starting; we didn't quite want to be fixing anything. That was the way of things as I understood it, anyway. Then one Saturday Chrissy told me she thought we should stop seeing each other, that she didn't know whether our relationship was going anywhere and couldn't honestly say whether she wanted it to, either. Then she collected all her things from my flat and told me to come round and get mine from hers. I never did. I was too afraid of what it would feel like. I had never been so frightened of anything in my life as I was of how I felt about her when she left me.

I went into retreat, I suppose, into hiding. I hadn't known I loved her, not really. I'd said the words, but I hadn't known what they meant. Then I couldn't tell her any more, and I understood. So I slept around to try to forget, trying to drown myself in other feelings, other highs, other breakups, other silences, other one-night stands. Her friends, who had briefly been my friends too, thought I was a dick, I knew. I let them – it was better than them knowing the truth. It felt very empty.

That was more or less when Mum remarried. I liked the bloke she'd met, and I was happy for her, but all the same, it was disquieting. I became a visitor in her house, and an infrequent one at that. We would sit in the living room with our tea and our biscuits, and talk about the view out the window, and struggle for things to talk about, because we had stopped belonging to each other. We were strangers with history in common – that seemed to be all there was between us. I never stayed the night there because I wouldn't have known how to behave in the mornings, whether I would feel the need to get dressed before I went downstairs, whether I would feel like I was allowed to make my own breakfast or whether I ought to have waited for them. I felt as if my parents were moving on from me. And all of a sudden I found myself lost in the middle of the project of my life without any purpose, with nothing to cling to, with no roots anywhere among anything I loved. Of course I still loved my parents, but they had started new chapters, and I couldn't help feeling I had held them back all the years they had looked after me.

It was very sad, in a way, to watch what they were doing. Dad got an allotment and spent all his time there, and even though I could see him beginning to walk with a bent back, as if the digging was caving him in, as if he was doing an impression of an old man, I wondered whether he might not always have preferred to have been on his own, with his broad beans and his wind-up radio and the sky above him and nothing to do all day. Maybe the whole life of our family had been some kind of accident.

Both Mum and Dad talked about starting again, but they were both over fifty and planning out lives like they were still twenty-five. There was no talk about the pensions they were going to need before very long; they only spoke of new things.

It seemed to me like they'd somehow got something the wrong way round. Moving somewhere new, meeting new people, planning new adventures. Perhaps that was beautiful, but it frightened me. I was frightened of seeing them fail, of seeing them realise my lack of faith in their new beginnings, that I suspected them of being too old. And I was frightened of them rubbing out the years we'd spent all together, the little things that had made those years, my life, matter to me. Because the places where our lives happen are purely coincidental, yes, and I could have been born anywhere, of course, but the thing is that I wasn't. I was born in Salisbury, and that was the stage on which my life and the lives of my parents had been played out, and arbitrary as that might be, it is still inarguable, and all my memories are still tied to the same landscape. To change that halfway through felt like an act of near panic to me. An abandonment of the life that had been lived there. As if both my parents were trying to ward off their endings. I couldn't believe it was completely healthy.

I started to wonder, what do you need in order to be able to say with a semblance of conviction that you had got your life right? What are the necessary components of that successful fiction? I looked at my own life, and it struck me that now was the time to make choices if you wanted to be happy when you came to the end. Now was the time to build the foundations of your life, and find a purpose, and imagine a trajectory into being that could guide you through the vastness of your days. To think your life was still ahead of you was only a way of delaying and robbing yourself of years when you might have been able to live deliberately, to build something. To let life happen to you was the way to bad marriages, and missed opportunity, and needing to take things back. I didn't want to live a life that started again when I was in my fifties. Because no matter how happy my mum was with her new husband, I could only imagine that if they loved each other, really loved each other, then whenever they thought of the years they hadn't known each other, when they hadn't been together and might have been, their hearts must have broken. To love someone is surely to want to breathe all of them in. I never wanted to love someone whose first fifty years of life I could only learn about from stories, anecdotes, photographs. I wanted to make my choices and build a life. The trouble was that I looked around me for something to live for, and nowhere could I find anything I loved, except perhaps Chrissy, who had left me, and what was behind me, my youth, the days when I had lived in the future tense.

I started to think about home. About what it meant, and whether such a thing existed. The feeling came over me as I sat in my office day after day that I was floating through my life, that I was not really living. I felt like nothing I saw was really happening to me. And the real reason for that may have been that I just didn't like the flat I was living in, or my boss, I don't know, but for want of any firmer foothold, I found myself performing the age-old human reflex in stormy and uncertain waters, and turning back to the port I had come from. And I'd never been totally happy in Salisbury either, of course, no one is ever totally happy for more than a few moments at any one time. But I had nothing better. So I let the idea of my city grow in my imagination, and I started to see its attractions. I started coming back to Salisbury at week-ends, walking the streets and wondering why it was that the more dissatisfied I felt in my work, my life, my bedsit, the more interested I became in this place, which I had thought I might have left behind me. Was that just a variation of the child's knee-jerk need for its mother when it falls over? Or could it be there was something here that I had lost or walked away from?

After six months of visits at weekends, I saw an advert on the English Heritage website one afternoon for a security guard who was needed to work nights watching over Old Sarum. Must have own car and be comfortable working with dogs, they said. I clicked on the link. In a sort of dream I made an application. I didn't know whether I was really going to do it. It wasn't the kind of work you do with my degree, and I knew in a way I was being stupid, I was being irresponsible even to consider giving up what I had in order to become a security guard on a hill in the middle of nowhere. Because I was one of the lucky ones. I'd been to a good school and a good university, and found a route into the kind of work most people would think might be enough to fill their whole lives. But the thing was that I wasn't happy. And in the end that changes everything, doesn't it? Everything becomes possible or impossible because of that. So when English Heritage interviewed me and subsequently offered me the job I could think of no earthly reason to stay where I was. Living in London, I never stopped feeling that if I died one morning, no one would notice. It would be as if I had never existed. And I had imagined into being this world in Wiltshire where people knew each other, people smiled at each other, where lives had weight. I logged on to Facebook and went to Chrissy's profile and looked at photos of us for a little while. I thought about calling her. I dreamed a scene where she changed her mind, where I told her I was thinking of leaving the city and the thought of my disappearance made her realise she wanted me after all. But I knew it was never going to happen. It had all been so clear. I knew that if I called her and told her I was thinking of leaving, she wouldn't really care. So I didn't tell her, or any of my friends. I left them to figure out I was gone, let them think I didn't care about any of the life I had been trying to build. I handed in my notice and moved back to Salisbury, was assigned an Alsatian and began spending my nights up on Old Sarum listening to all-night talk radio, patrolling the perimeter with the dog and watching the city. At night I would look down on the cathedral and listen to the roar of the trains that passed through the station and tell myself stories about the people living far below me, the way that living in the shadow of that cathedral changed them, the way their lives revolved around it. I started to imagine that the cathedral, which seemed so vast and solid across the distance from which I viewed it, was really no more than an idea, a reflection as if in water of a feeling in the city that had been there long before the spire was ever dreamed of, a longing that animated the place where I lived. I started to think it was something in the water. I started to think it was something to do with this being a place where five rivers met. I thought to myself, this city has a life that is far more vivid and turbulent and beautiful than the view of the spire from this hillside alone can express. No map has ever caught the looks in the eyes of these people, or what this place means to me, and perhaps that's not important – mine is only an ordinary life, after all, there's no reason what matters to me should matter to anyone else. But it's important to me. It's my life. It's the most important thing in the world to me.

When I watched those people from the window of McDonald's, I wanted more than anything else to know what happened to all of them. To drink in their lives. Then later that evening I was sitting in my car on the hill with the dog and the radio when the boy I'd seen watching the crash broke into the compound. The dog went mad in the cage behind me, and I nearly pissed myself. It had never actually happened to me before, someone breaking in. When I saw who it was that was standing in the light of the Portakabin, I felt like someone was trying to tell me something. It was as if someone had reached right into my life. The boy's name was Sam. I let him out through the front gate and didn't report him. I went back to my car and watched the night.

The truth was that I was lonely. It was very simple, really. I was halfway through my life, and there was no one with me on the journey. I stared at the orange of the streetlights in the distance and saw as clear as day that I had done the wrong thing, coming back to Salisbury. I had confused one thing for another. I should have been looking for someone I could speak to, not a place I could watch. I had isolated myself. Now I was alone at the top of a hill, and the apparition of that boy appearing at the edge of the Portakabin light seemed to taunt me, remind me that life was going on elsewhere, that people were dreaming and drinking too much and climbing hills, and I had taken the wrong line trying to become part of it. I was out here on my own in the darkness, and I didn't know what I could do about it. I imagined Sam walking away from me and back into town, perhaps stopping for a pint in the Harvester on the way, and I felt lonelier than I had ever been. I texted Chrissy. I said I was thinking about a trip to London, asked her whether she'd be up for going for a drink with some of the friends we used to share, said I fancied getting properly wasted. Of course, she didn't reply, and I wished I hadn't done it, wished I had thought of something smarter to disguise the fact that what I really wanted was just the two of us together. I looked at her photos on Facebook and wondered what she was doing now, who she was sleeping with, what she was planning for the summer.

I read in the paper the week after the crash that the woman on the moped was in Odstock in a coma. I had a shock when I saw her full name; it turned out I had known her. She had been my dealer when I was in school. There had been a time when I had her number saved as a favourite in my phone. I checked to see if it was still there, but of course I'd changed my phone too many times since then, and somewhere along the line I hadn't transferred her across into the new address book. I had thought I was going to move on. Now I sat with the paper and felt closer to her than anyone else whose number I did have. I had liked her, when Salisbury still belonged to me; she had been a florist in the daytimes. She was a good storyteller.

I walked past her old pitch in the market square that afternoon, where she had sold her flowers, I suppose until very recently, until the accident, but there was nothing there. I watched the people passing the spot and wondered how many of them knew there had once been a woman who sold flowers from that street corner. Even if a few of them did for now, they would forget quickly if she didn't come back and make the spot hers again. In ten years' time, I thought, no one would remember that flowers had once been sold here. The thought upset me, and I went into Tesco and bought some carnations and went up to the hospital. I didn't want to see her, didn't want to gawp or to upset myself. I was willing her to realise that there was still a place for her in the world, that she should come back for it and live for it, although I knew there was no way a bunch of carnations from a boy she hardly knew could achieve that. But I asked at the reception whether I could leave some flowers for someone, whether they would be passed on, and the woman there said she'd do her best to make sure they were. So I gave her Rita's name and headed for the exit. And I felt a little better to know that whether she woke up or not, I, at least, would remember for as long as I was on this planet that she had sold me weed and teased me about the girls I liked, and I had seen the moment her life was changed in the violence of that accident, and I had bought her flowers, because once she had sold flowers in the market square. A woman passed me at the door, in her seventies or eighties maybe, hobbling as if in pain like old women do, a worn-out blue cardigan with holes in the sleeves hanging off her. As I shut the door behind me, I saw the receptionist hand the flowers to her, and she turned to look in my direction. I hurried away. I didn't want to intrude on her life, that family. I hadn't meant for anyone to see.

Three months passed, and someone else started selling flowers from Rita's old pitch, and I knew what must have happened. Rita had died. She had never regained consciousness, the paper said, when I read it later in my car on the hill. I felt helpless, reading it. Now the process of forgetting would begin; one by one the people who had known her would disappear, in the years to come, the decades to follow, until no one living had ever known her, until she might as well never have existed. Now she couldn't tell her story any longer it would start to disappear.

I went along that Saturday to see her buried – the details of the funeral had been in the newspaper. I felt involved; I couldn't help it. I had seen her life end, and now it was ending all over again because her story was being finished, a line drawn under it. I turned up ten minutes early and sat at the back. No one questioned me, and I didn't introduce myself to anyone. I just wanted to sit and remember her. There were quite a few people who came to remember, or say goodbye, or whatever it is people think they're doing at a funeral, I don't know. That's the mystery of rituals, they have so many meanings, you never quite get to the heart of them. Her family were at the front – a man who might have been her husband, a man and a woman sitting next to him, one of whom might have been her child perhaps. There was no way of knowing, really. They had a little blonde girl squashed between them. The room was full of people you could never imagine meeting anywhere else: hippies, druggies, drinkers, farmers, well-heeled women who must have been her customers at the flower stall. I thought I saw the old woman with the blue cardigan from the hospital off to one side, sitting huddled by herself in a coat that was too big for her, but I couldn't be sure it was the same person. It is amazing how many walks of life a single life can touch. I hoped Rita had known while she was alive how many people cared enough for her to come to her funeral. The people who did the readings spoke of her with love in their voices. She must have known. You couldn't share the world with so much feeling and not know it. It was horrible to think of how she had died, but as I sat there I felt better knowing she must have lived a happy life.

Sitting with me at the back of the room was an old man who cried all through the service. I thought I recognised him but could hardly believe it. At the end, when everyone started to filter out, I went over to speak to him.

'Are you all right?'

He looked up, and he seemed afraid.

'Oh, yes. I'm all right.'

'I think I know you.'

'Do you?'

'I think I used to visit your house. You live on a farm outside the city, don't you? I cut my leg one day, and your wife bandaged me up, do you remember?'

He blinked, as if he must be imagining me, as if he was trying to blink me away. When he opened his eyes and I was still there, he spoke.

'You're Liam?'

'Yes. You remember.'

'Of course. How are you?'

'I'm all right. Did you know her?'

The old man – I am ashamed to say I had forgotten his name – turned to stare out the church door, in the direction the coffin had gone.

'I did, in fact, yes. A long time ago, she used to live in a tent in my garden.'

'Really?'

'A lifetime ago.'

He didn't speak again, and I supposed he was remembering things that had happened to him years earlier.

'And how is your wife?'

'She died very recently, I'm afraid.'

'Oh God, I'm so sorry.'

'I buried her a few months ago.'

'I'm so sorry. I didn't know.'

'She passed away on the same day as Rita, really. I was coming from the hospital when I drove into her.'

I thought I must have misheard him.

'Sorry, what?'

'I killed Rita. I hit her moped, and she never woke up, she was never really alive after that. Even though they let me believe that she might be. I am the reason she died.'

'Oh God.' I sat down next to him. 'I saw it. I didn't know it was you.'

'You were there?'

'It wasn't your fault. She just drove out in front of you.'

'The police have said that. The family have been kind too. I called, of course, to ask whether I could come to the funeral. They were understanding. They were happy to let me pay my respects. Once I knew her name, knew I had known her before, I was so filled with – I don't know. When we took her in I really thought we were saving her life, because she was a very unhappy woman. Now I have killed her.'

'There was nothing that you could have done.'

'The worst of it all is that it doesn't even seem to matter to me. Not really. Not after the loss of my wife.'

'I understand.'

He smiled and turned to me.

'Do you?'

And I bowed my head, because of course I knew I didn't.

'I'm sorry, that was an unfair thing to say. I should go. Would you help me up?'

'Of course.'

I stood, and helped the old man to his feet, and walked with him as far as the door of the church.

'I'll be all right from here.'

'Are you sure?'

'Oh, yes. I'll walk down to my wife's grave before I go.'

'She's buried here?'

'Just at the end there.' He pointed into the distance. 'Goodbye then.'

'Goodbye. I hope you'll be all right.'

'Thank you.'

He walked stiffly away, and I stayed by the door, watching him till he was in among the graves. All those stones he passed through had been whole lives once, and now they were bodies in the ground, they were just markers of something that was gone, though they had felt as deeply as I did and lived so keenly it had hurt and amazed every one of them. The lives of others are all too complex and extraordinary for us to really understand them. We spend little enough time looking at how we live our own. Surely it would be impossible, from the muddles of ourselves, ever to see into the heart of how someone else lived? I was still standing by the entrance to the church when the old man walked back past me, on the way to his car. He stopped and smiled when he saw me.

'You know it's so strange. I was standing there by Valerie's grave, speaking with her, and I could have sworn as I did that she was standing beside me, just for a moment. I could swear I saw her for a second out of the corner of my eye, the colour of her hair in the sun.'

'Really?'

'Well, no, not really,' he said, with an embarrassed little cough. 'But all the same. Well, goodbye.'

He walked on, and I didn't say anything else but watched him leave through the gates of the churchyard.

A little while after he disappeared from sight, a woman came out of the church arm in arm with a broad-shouldered man with grey hair, and I saw as she did that it was the woman who had been in the road when the accident happened, the woman who had fainted. I had watched as the paramedic revived her. She had been taken away in another ambulance, up to the hospital, out of sight. She must have known Rita as well, or otherwise wanted to follow her story all the way to its ending. I thought about stopping her, speaking to her, telling her we had both been there. It was so strange to think the world we inhabit could be so small and we might gather here like this. But I stayed still, and said nothing, and she and the man walked briskly away and out of the churchyard and out of sight as if there was somewhere they were hurrying to be. It wouldn't have meant anything in the end, that we had both gone to the service. She wouldn't have known what to say. We would both have been uncomfortable. It wouldn't have mattered.

I walked out into the churchyard myself once the woman was out of sight, and took out my phone, and called Chrissy.

I didn't know whether she was going to pick up. I was terrified when she did. I hadn't quite decided what I was going to say.

'Hello?'

'Hi.' She sounded like she was outside. I supposed she wouldn't want to talk to me in public. 'You OK?'

'Yeah, I'm fine. Look, I just wanted to ask you.'

'What?'

'What was wrong with me?'

'What do you mean?'

'Why didn't you want me any more?'

She didn't speak for a moment. I suppose I sounded pathetic. But suddenly I wasn't afraid of that any more. It seemed so important to know. All I could think was that I wanted, more than anything else, to be that old man when I was his age. To have lost something worth losing. The colour of a girl's hair in the sunshine, a shoulder to lean on, a house full of happy memories that didn't disappear because the people in it left. I wanted to learn that. I wanted to know why I hadn't been able to before.

'It's not as simple as that.'

'I just want to know. It's OK, you can be honest.'

'No, Liam, you don't get it. Maybe that's your answer. You don't get it. It's not as simple as that. I have to go.'

'I just—'

'I'm sorry. I'm late for something. I have to go.'

She rang off, and I stared at her number in my phone for a moment. Then I turned around and saw that the people who had followed the coffin to the grave were coming back towards me. The people I had thought must be Rita's family walked at the front of the group. They smiled at me as they approached, and I smiled back at them.

'I'm sorry for your loss,' I said.

'Thank you.'

The older man I had guessed must be Rita's husband replied, nodding his head as he spoke. He was holding the little blonde girl by the hand, and she leaned into his side shyly when I looked at her. And again, I wished I was him. I wished I could have something worth losing. I stood at the side of the path till the group had passed. Then I put my phone away and walked out of the churchyard, and I knew at last what it was I should be looking for. I knew more clearly than I had ever done that the world is other people.

I should leave this place now. Perhaps it was a mistake even to come here. I solved nothing, changed nothing, only succeeded in carrying my problems with me into a new landscape and isolating myself yet further. I've known that for a little while now, but I haven't quite been able to act on the knowledge. Not yet, not quite. Soon I'll make a change. I am going to leave this job, this hill, this relic, from where I have watched life going on in the city where I grew up and felt so distant from it. I'm going to re-enter life, and spend my time with the living, and not among these memories, these imaginings, these ghosts. It's not a way to spend a life. What I have to find is something to long for, something to actually love. I thought I might try and find work in a florist's, or a garden centre, or somehow doing something outside, gardening or farming or something as yet unimagined. I think of Rita sometimes, and what it might be like to spend your life among flowers, among life, and I wonder whether I could find a job like that.

The good life. I'm sure it would be as awful as any other life once you got stuck into it, but all the same, perhaps it's what I'll go and look for. And perhaps the search for it will be where the pleasure hides. In a week, a month, a couple of months, I'll hand in my notice, and I'll go searching. But I haven't done it yet. Because I think when I do, it might well be that I have to leave this city. I might have to be ready to go as far as to cross the world. If I really want to look for a life worth living, I'll have to be ready to go anywhere for it, I think. So I have been waiting up here on the hill, saying my goodbyes. I wanted to stay here just a little longer and hear the song of this city where my life took shape played out to its ending, in case I don't have the chance to hear it again.

In the mornings when my shifts have finished and I have returned the dog to kennel I walk round the haunts of my childhood while the sun comes up. I can never really revisit them now, never inhabit these places as I once did and belong there completely, because I am no longer the child I was, and what I try to revisit when I walk round this city thinking of the past is my own history, not any place in the real world. I glimpse myself like a ghost sitting on certain steps, climbing trees, drinking on benches. In those hours when the world is coldest just before the dawn, I can admit I took on a dead-end job here because I was trying to live in hiding from the exile of my future, the exile that is the fate of everyone who ever watched childhood and youth streaming away from them, behind them, receding into the blue of the distance. I don't know how everyone has the strength to face it, the way that life burns up into memory, until there is no life left except what you keep in your head, until even that snuffs out; it is extraordinary to really look at how strong people are. In those hours I can admit I ran away to this place because it was where I remembered feeling safe, because I had got old enough that being alive had started to feel perilous, to feel like a miracle, and I had started to feel afraid of it. And I can see now that's unhealthy. I can see what I was doing was looking back over my shoulder at a world I can't revisit, when what I should have been doing was finding a way to go on, because that's what people do every day, that's human, that's heroic. And I'm almost ready to leave, move on, find a new world, and take hold of my life, and really begin. But then I walk through Lizzy Gardens as the sky begins to open like a flower, as the world around turns blue in the half-light of morning, passing through curtains of dew falling from the high, loving arms of trees that have held the water close all night and now set it down with the arrival of morning. And I remember nights on shrooms in this park, vodka burning in my throat on these benches, kisses so beautiful I could never have dreamed of stealing them behind these hedges, songs played on out-of-tune guitars that felt electric in the moments when they broke the peace of this place. And I hear the song of birds around me lacing their music together through the air. And I think, not yet. I won't set off quite yet. I feel as I walk that there is a grace to cupping your hands and catching your life as it pours past you, holding it close for just a few moments before it's gone for ever and new water, new time, flows over, and loving your life as it passes. The world is ending all around us every moment we're living. Every bar in the score of ourselves is receding already into memory, into imagination, even as we play it out. We might as well listen.

Acknowledgements

I would like to thank everyone who has supported me over the years of this writing. In particular, this book is the result of a collaboration with my agent, Laura Williams, which has been as rewarding as any creative relationship I have been privileged to enjoy in my life, and I would like to acknowledge my gratitude to her and all the family at Peters, Fraser and Dunlop. The other family whose adoption of my cause has made this book possible is the extraordinary team at Transworld, whose enthusiasm for this work has been completely humbling. I would like to thank Suzanne Bridson, my editor, and Sophie Christopher, my publicist, for shaping the work, and changing my life, and teaching me to be proud of what we've made together.

Finally, I would like to thank Charlie Young. I will never know whether I would have had the courage, back in 2013, to walk away from my job and commit my life to writing if she hadn't been there to tell me I might as well try; I'll never need to know, because she was there for me, and that has made everything possible. As rivers end at their beginning, I would like to conclude by dedicating this song to her.

Barney Norris was born in Sussex in 1987, and grew up in Salisbury. Upon leaving university he founded the theatre company Up In Arms with the director Alice Hamilton. His plays include *Eventide* and *Visitors*, for which he won the Critics' Circle and Offwestend Awards for Most Promising Playwright. His short plays are collected as *What You Wish For in Youth*, and he is also the author of a book on theatre, *To Bodies Gone: The Theatre of Peter Gill*. In 2015 he was named one of the 1000 Most Influential Londoners by the *Evening Standard*. He is the Martin Esslin Playwright in Residence at Keble College, Oxford. This is his first novel. Follow him on Twitter @barnontherun.